Galenorn, Yasmine, 1961-
Bewitching bedlam /

2017.
33305243690322
gi 07/13/18

INE

NEW YORK TIME OR

GALE N

BEWITCHING BEDLAM

A BEWITCHING BEDLAM NOVEL

BOOK 1

A Nightqueen Enterprises LLC Publication

Published by Yasmine Galenorn
PO Box 2037, Kirkland WA 98083-2037
BEWITCHING BEDLAM
A Bewitching Bedlam Novel
Copyright © 2017 by Yasmine Galenorn
First Electronic Printing: 2017 Nightqueen Enterprises LLC
First Print Edition: 2017 Nightqueen Enterprises, LLC
Cover Art & Design: Earthly Charms
Editor: Elizabeth Flynn

ALL RIGHTS RESERVED No part of this book may be reproduced or distributed in any format, be it print or electronic or audio, without permission. Please prevent piracy by purchasing only authorized versions of this book.

This is a work of fiction. Any resemblance to actual persons, living or dead, businesses, or places is entirely coincidental and not to be construed as representative or an endorsement of any living/existing group, person, place, or business.

A Nightqueen Enterprises LLC Publication
Published in the United States of America

Acknowledgments

I want to thank Mandy Roth, for inviting me into the anthology where Blood Music—the prequel to this story—first saw print—Maudlin and her crew were first conceived when I was trying to write a more "serious" vampire story. But Maddy Gallowglass insisted on climbing out of the woodwork that is my bizarre sense of humor and I instantly fell for her and her world.

Thanks to my beloved husband, Samwise, who is more supportive than any husband out there. (Hey, I'm biased!) He believes in me, even at times when I'm having trouble believing in myself. Thank you to my wonderful assistants—Andria Holley and Jennifer Arnold. And to my friends—namely Carol, Jo, Vicki, Shawntelle, and the whole UF Group gang I'm in. They've held my hand more than once this past year as I've made the jump from traditional to indie publishing. It's been a scary, exciting, fast-track ride.

Love and scritches to my four furbles—Caly, Brighid (the cat, not the goddess), Morgana, and l'il boy Apple, who make every day a delight. And reverence, honor, and love to my spiritual guardians—Mielikki, Tapio, Ukko, Rauni, and Brighid (the goddess, not the cat).

And to you, readers—thank you so much for sticking with me. I hope you enjoy this book. If you want to know more about me and my work, check out my bibliography in the back of the book, be sure to sign up for my newsletter, and you can find me on the web at Galenorn.com.

Brightest Blessings,
~The Painted Panther~
~Yasmine Galenorn~

Welcome to Bewitching Bedlam

As Maudlin and Aegis prepare to open the Bewitching Bedlam B&B to guests, they immediately find themselves embroiled in a battle for customers. Ralph Greyhoof, the owner of the Heart's Desire Inn, doesn't like to share. The conflict heats up when Maddy finds a local witch dead in the rose garden. The woman looks a lot like Maudlin and suspicion falls on Ralph. But Maddy knows that as competitive as Ralph is, he wouldn't resort to murder. Maudlin and Aegis set out to find the killer, even as their own relationship is put to the test. Aegis's old flame has returned, determined to win him back, no matter what it takes.

Chapter 1

"BUT WHY WON'T you paint it pink?"

Franny was standing in the middle of the kitchen. She also happened to be standing in the middle of the *kitchen island*, which gave the effect that she was cut off at the waist. Disconcerting to say the least, but I had quickly learned to keep my complaints about her displacement to myself. She took criticism hard, and I wasn't up to the fallout, which included full-scale whining and moaning à la Jacob Marley. There's nothing like waking up in the middle of the night to see a weeping ghost by your bed, staring at you with puppy-dog eyes, which was why I had banned her from my bedroom.

"We've been over this at least a half-dozen times. I *hate* pink, unless it's fuchsia or magenta. I am *not* painting the kitchen pink just because you like it." Hands on my hips, I stared at my uninvited roommate. I might have to live with her, but I didn't have to let her call the shots. *I* had paid for the mansion. She just happened to be an added bonus, although I used the word "bonus" loosely.

"How do you think *I* feel? I can't leave this house. You changed my favorite parlor into a media room and put that horrible monster you call a television in there. You chased me out of your bedroom. And you're letting that...that...*vampire* live here." She spat out the word so vehemently that I was grateful that she wasn't corporeal, or I would have been hit with a mouthful of spit.

"That *vampire* is my boyfriend, who also happens to be one of the sweetest men around. You know perfectly well that Aegis doesn't harm his..."

I stopped. Technically, "victim" really *would* be the appropriate choice of words, but I felt like a traitor using it. Aegis didn't *hurt* anybody he drank from. Not unless they tried to stake him. And he never chose anybody who was anemic or diabetic. Vampires had the ability to tell when someone was low on their favorite flavor of fruit punch, or when that said punch had too much or too little sugar in it.

But Franny refused to see it my way, and I was tired of the argument. Every time she wanted me to change something, she fell back to *"You let that vampire live here."* I had heard it—or a variation thereof—so many times the past month that my head was spinning.

"Franny, get this through your misty mind. *You have to deal with it.* Aegis lives here. He sleeps with me. Well, technically we have sex in my bedroom. He *sleeps* in his coffin. But whatever the case, this is *my* house and I'll let whoever I want live here." I straightened my shoulders. "Count yourself lucky that I haven't hired an exorcist to deal with you."

"I wish you would! I hate being trapped." But Franny didn't sound like she meant it.

"I could evict you myself, you know. I *could* banish you. Bingo! One easy spell and boom, you'd be out on your ass, wandering the highway like some lost mournful spirit. But did I do that when I found out you were haunting my home? No. I did not."

I paused, suddenly deflating. I wasn't going to exorcise her ass and she knew it. Oh, I was *trying* to sound intimidating. But considering that I was holding a stuffed unicorn under my left arm and a tray of cookies in my right hand, the threat just didn't have the impact that I hoped for.

Franny huffed, then turned and flounced off, the long skirts of her muslin gown sweeping the floor with a ghostly swish as she vanished through the wall. She was still wearing the dress she had died in. Franny had lived around these parts of Bedlam until August 1815, when she died. She had been so wrapped up in reading her book that she missed a step and went tumbling down the staircase, breaking her neck. It was over quickly, but somehow, she had become trapped in the house. I felt sorry for her, but Franny needed to find a sense of humor, and find it quick if she wanted to go on living with me.

Shaking my head, I set the cookies down on the counter and carried the unicorn over to the rocking chair. Made of polished mahogany, the rocker was wide enough to curl up in. I had chosen it specifically for the kitchen. I had always wanted a kitchen big enough to have a rocking chair in and this mansion fit the bill perfectly. As I nestled into the seat, tucking the unicorn onto the table beside the rocker, I closed my eyes. I just needed a little rest. Just a little time out.

"Maddy? Maddy. Oh Maddy, wake up, pretty girl." A sinuous voice echoed through the fog.

I blinked, suddenly aware that someone was kissing my nose. Jumping in my seat, I opened my eyes to find Aegis leaning over me, a grin spreading across those gorgeous lips of his. The tips of his fangs were showing—spotless and glowing white. I'd warned him to watch how much of the whitening toothpaste he used, but television commercials had convinced him that his pearly whites needed to be even brighter. I kept telling him his teeth were practically fluorescent, but they didn't detract from just how pretty the man was. Handsome. Gorgeous. Insert adjective of your choice.

"What the—?" I blinked. "Is it night already?"

Aegis had turned on the light. Outside, the dusk was growing. I had obviously slept away part of the day, and it had to be after sunset for him to be awake.

"Enjoy your nap with Drofur, love?" His voice wrapped around me like a silken scarf, its resonance tickling me. Even though witch's blood was an aphrodisiac for vamps, this particular vampire's voice was an aphrodisiac for me. His voice...his hands...his body...his...

Shaking my head to clear my thoughts before they reached the X-rated stage, I looked down to see that I was holding the unicorn. I must have picked it up again in my sleep. With a blush, I realized that I had been cuddling it. I hastily returned Drofur to his spot on the table.

"Um, yeah. I guess I was more tired than I thought." I cautiously stood, stretching as my knees and back protested the un-horizontal nap they had taken.

He was dressed for his gig, wearing tight leather pants and a leather jacket. His muscled chest was bare, his abs rippling and pale, and he was wearing a thin gold chain around his neck. Even though it was the dead of winter, he wouldn't get cold. Or rather, he was already so cold that the weather wouldn't faze him. Vampires didn't emit body heat.

My breath caught in my throat. I wanted to rub my hands all over him. His hair hung loose around his shoulders, long and dark, and his eyes were the color of rich, black coffee tinged with clouds of cream. When he was aroused or hungry, crimson rings appeared around them. To top it off, he smelled like vanilla musk with a hint of cinnamon, thanks to his shampoo.

Aegis slipped his arms around my waist and pulled me toward him. "You too tired to spend a little time cuddling?" Leaning down—the man was a good seven inches taller than me—he nuzzled my neck, gently nosing behind my ear where he left a trail of butterfly kisses.

Everything in my body tensed, but it was a good tension. I wanted to rip my clothes off and press my breasts against that bare chest of his. My taut nipples pressed against the silk of my tank top. Even through the lace of my bra, the silk seemed to rub them ever so deliciously. Meanwhile, my lower region was starting to clamor, wanting in on the action.

"As long as that cuddling includes sex." I wrapped my arms around his neck and grinned up at him.

"Then we'd better get busy."

He swept me up in his arms. I wasn't a lean woman. I was curvy and busty with thighs that made the floor quake when I was angry. But Aegis carried me as though I was as light as a feather. I laughed, holding on as we headed toward the staircase. My laughter echoed through the far-too-barren living room, and the sight of so much empty space sparked off a random thought.

"We need to buy furniture this week." The furniture from my old condo just wasn't enough to furnish a Victorian mansion, especially one I was turning into a bed and breakfast. I needed to get my ass in gear and start prowling the thrift shops.

Aegis shushed me. "Hush."

He paused on the landing, pressing my back against the wall as he nestled himself between my legs. I wrapped them around his hips. With one hand supporting my butt, he slid the other around my shoulders, then pressed his lips against mine, kissing me so deeply I forgot about furniture and thrift stores and everything else. His tongue gently flickered in and out of my mouth.

I moaned, pressing against him. My breasts were threatening to burst out of the bra all on their own. “Upstairs. Now.”

“At your command.”

And we were on the move again, up to the master bedroom. While it was technically my bedroom, since Aegis and I had different schedules and he didn’t dare sleep above ground just in case of an accident with the curtains, it was all ours when it was time for sex.

He tumbled me onto the bed, wedging himself between my legs as he held my wrists over my head. “Command me, woman.”

A jolt of hunger raced through me, slashing like lightning from my breasts down to my pussy. I wanted out of my clothes. Their restraint was driving me nuts. I closed my eyes, focusing, and the zipper on my jeans began to slowly open. I urged it on, feeling the belt buckle shift as I willed the prong to slip out of the hole.

“You’re very hungry, aren’t you? You want me in you, don’t you?”

His voice echoed through me, like the rich, deep notes of a song. Eyes flashing, he shifted position, sitting back on his knees as he let go of my wrists. Reaching down, he slid my belt out of its loops, tossing it aside. Then, with one swift yank, he pulled my jeans down as I raised my butt and bent my knees. I was going commando beneath, and Aegis let out a growl of delight as he worked the jeans off over my feet. They landed on the floor next to the belt. I sat up, yanking off my top. The hunter green tank joined the pile of clothes, and my bra was the cherry on the top.

Aegis was on his feet, unzipping as he eased off

his leather jeans. His cock sprang to attention, hard and smooth, as cold as the rest of his body. He started to shrug off his leather jacket but I stopped him.

"No. I love the smell of leather." I knelt on the bed, my breasts rising and falling with each breath. The chill of the room shrouded me, and my nipples grew as hard as his shaft.

"And I love your breasts," he said with a low growl. "I love how ripe and round they are, how smooth they feel under my fingers." He grinned. "And I love how they jiggle when I touch them. Your nipples drive me crazy."

I squirmed, wet and hungry for him. "Touch them. Touch me. Please?"

"I'm taking my time, woman. I want to watch you. Lie back and bend your knees. Spread them so I can look at you." His gaze rested greedily on me as I obeyed.

I lay back, spreading my legs as I reached down and slowly rolled a finger around my clit, then spread the lips of my vaj. "You want a taste?"

With a grunt, he dove deep between my legs, pressing his face between my thighs as his tongue worked overtime to swirl over my clitoris. I jumped at his touch, a peal of laughter dancing out of me as my desire began to build.

"Oh gods, oh gods, don't stop!" I fisted his hair as he lapped at me, tonguing my sex until I was dizzy. Catching my breath, I let out a choked shout as he drove me higher and higher. I couldn't stop if I tried. The past six weeks with Aegis had been the best sex of my life. I'd never had it this good, and I'd had my share of lovers, my ex-husband being the worst of the lot. After what had felt like a long, dry desert in my life, everything was growing again, vibrant and humming along like a top-of-the-line vibrator.

"Come on, Maddy, come for me. Come on," he coaxed. His voice muffled by my snatch, he increased the speed of his tongue. He was always careful with his fangs, making certain to keep them at bay when he was eating me out. We'd already had one accident and I didn't care to repeat it.

"I'm coming, trust me I'm co—co—co—" And the words stopped there as I began to come, my orgasm vibrating from my core out through my fingertips. The world exploded with color and then, as the waves rippled in rings and slowly began to subside, I opened my eyes to find a trail of rose petals drifting down around us. They landed on the bed, on my nose, on Aegis's hair.

He laughed softly.

"I love how you bring the roses when you come," he said.

I sighed, settling in beneath him. The roses didn't happen every time, but when they did, I felt like I was dancing in a garden under the moonlight.

Aegis rose up with a steaming look, then nestled between my legs as he drove himself deep inside me. As we began to move in rhythm, his girth stretched me deliciously wide. I let out a soft moan. He rested his head on my breasts and I slid my arms beneath his, embracing him. He thrust deeper, penetrating every inch of me until there was no part left untouched. He slipped one hand down between my legs, tweaking my clit, and that one touch was all it took. I climaxed yet again, and another time as he stiffened, tilting his head back as he let out a long throaty groan.

As he relaxed into my embrace, I drifted and the rose petals kept falling.

At that moment, Bubba landed on the bed beside us and let out a loud *purp*. Aegis glared at the huge orange cat, but then broke into a wide, toothy grin.

I gave the cjinn a shake of the head. "Dude, *really*? Please, we're in the middle of something here."

Bubba snorted then hopped over Aegis's back and jumped off the other side, yowling as he stared out the French doors leading to my balcony. He swatted at the glass, hissed, then turned around and raced out the door into the hall.

"Well, that's enough to dispel the mood, don't you think?" I leaned back, breathing deeply as a wave of laughter raced through me. The past six weeks had been easily the oddest of my life, and the best.

SO, INTRODUCTIONS ALL around. My name is Maudlin Gallowglass. *Maddy* for short. I'm older than the hills—or at least older than most of you. I was born on October 28, 1629. Figure that I'm 387, going on thirty. Nobody could ever accuse me of being mature, though I'm fully grown and a damned powerful witch.

The Gallowglass family has magical roots going back to the days of Stonehenge. You know that folk song "Boys of Bedlam" that a gazillion groups have covered? There's a girl mentioned in it—"Mad Maudlin goes on dirty toes, for to save her shoes from gravel." And the Bedlam in the song wasn't anything like the Bedlam that I live in now.

Yeah, that girl was based on *me*. Nobody in the history books seems sure who wrote the song, although there are claims that someone named Thomas d'Urfey penned it. But I happen to know the truth. Tom (*the* Tom of the song "Mad Tom of Bedlam") was my boyfriend and he wrote it. D'Urfey just swiped it. There was a lot of literary pilfering going on back then.

Tom (my Tom) wrote a number of songs as we escaped England to return to Ireland. We traveled for years, trying to evade the witch hunters. We passed as wandering minstrels and never stayed in one place too long. But it wasn't the witch hunters who finally got him. No, it was the vampires. They trapped us, but I escaped, thanks to him. I've never forgotten his sacrifice. And I remembered the vamps who turned him. They paid. Mad Maudlin made sure.

So yes, I'm Mad Maudlin, though these days I tend to go by just plain Maddy. I left Mad Maudlin in the past, which is the safest place for her. That part of myself can be a lot of fun, but she's scary as hell and not always nice. I've kept her under leash and key for nearly three centuries. The day I let her loose, heaven help whoever I'm targeting.

Six weeks ago, I was living in Seattle in a condo I had won from my ex in our divorce settlement. I was also bored out of my mind. On a drunken dare from my best friend Sandy, I decided to take a look at an old mansion on Bedlam—an island in the San Juans.

The look turned into the decision to buy. From the moment I laid eyes on it, all I could see in the decaying old mansion was a beautiful bed and breakfast. I admit, not all of my reasons always came with the best of intentions. Selling the condo and using the money to buy a dilapidated old house would piss the hell out of my ex, Craig. That alone was enough to make me hand over the check. Anything I could do to thwart his scrawny, pompous ass, the better. But something about the mansion also charmed me.

Moving to Bedlam had been an eye opener. As I said, Bedlam's both an island and a town—in fact, the entire island is the town. Founded by magical folk, it's a wonderland for the Pretcom—the preternatural community. All sorts of Otherkin live here—Weres and shifters, witches and Fae. In other words, just about anybody with magical powers or a supernatural background is welcome, though there were a few humans around, too. Although vampires are kept under strict observation. They aren't exactly welcome, but neither are they shunned. They just have to mind their manners and not feed on the locals. We do have a local vampire queen living here, which is a tad bit scary, but there's not much we can do as long as she follows the rules.

It's not that Otherkin avoid humans. In fact, some of us like humans a lot. Hell, I married one, till that went south. But one bad human doesn't mean they're all bad. However, Bedlam offers us the opportunity to be ourselves without feeling like outsiders. We need a place to call our own. In this corner of the nation, Bedlam is it.

When Sandy convinced me to move back and I bought the house, I wasn't aware that a vampire came attached, as well as a ghost. While I can handle Franny, Aegis and I had a few scuffles about whose house it actually was. We settled the argument in bed and that's all she wrote. Instant connection: instant sparks. We seem to have a connection that goes back a long ways. Past-life stuff, perhaps. But the end result is that he's my boyfriend. He's also a rock star. Or at least an up-and-coming one. I try to balance my natural antipathy toward vamps with my attraction for him.

Franny, of course, is the house ghost. She also came with the mansion and I don't have the heart to chuck her out. And Bubba—well, he came with me. Bubba's a cjinn, but more about that later. He's a little butthead, mostly, but I love him and he loves me, as much as a cjinn can ever love anybody but himself.

End result? The four of us are settling in, trying to learn to live together as one odd little family. Aegis and I are overhauling the mansion into a bed and breakfast fit for a king. Or at least, a guest with a fat wallet. And I've named it "The Bewitching Bedlam Bed and Breakfast." It only seems fit.

I GLANCED AT the clock. It was going on seven-thirty. Outside, the dusk was deepening. "You'd better get a move on. You know that Jack-Az doesn't like the entertainment to show up late."

"Jack-Az can bite me," Aegis said with a smirk. He slid out of bed and wandered over to where his clothes were scattered together with mine.

I couldn't stop staring at his butt, which was one of the finest butts I had ever seen. Tight, muscled... firm ass. *Oh yes.*

"Or rather, I wouldn't mind taking a bite out of him," Aegis continued. "He's a pain to work with."

Jack-Az was the owner of Utopia, Bedlam's biggest nightclub. He wore his name well, although his real name was Johann Azrial Bähr. He was a bear shifter who had been active in both World War I and II. He had a crusty temperament, but he provided free eats on the side, and right now, the Utopia offered a continuing gig for the Boys of Bedlam, Aegis's band.

The Boys of Bedlam were in the process of making a demo tape, but they were having trouble making the connections they needed in order to get it in front of any big-name DJs. They planned on releasing their first CD under their own label but getting airplay, especially among the growing surge of indie bands, was even harder than it had been before the big labels started to fall off in popularity. It didn't help that Sid, the band's bass player, had just had his fifth kid. His wife needed him around a lot, so it was difficult to tour while he was in the throes of being a new father again.

I let out a soft sigh, wrapping the blankets up around my shoulders to keep warm. "Jack-Az has a good reason for his issues. He still suffers from PTSD from World War II. You know how rough it was over there. He lost a lot of family members who were part of the Black Forest Pretcom Resistance."

The Black Forest Pretcom Resistance had been a united group of Otherkin who were connected to the Yugoslavian resistance movements against the Nazis. A lot of them had died, but they had been instrumental in fucking over the German troops who entered the woods. They had helped sabotage Hitler's war machine in ways most people never knew about. They had also run an underground railroad, aiding the escape of a number of humans who were targeted by the Nazis.

Aegis grunted. "I know, and you're right. Jack-Az deserves to be as crusty as he wants, given his service. We could use more like him. I'm just talking trash. I don't mean anything by it." He began to squeeze into his leather pants.

I watched as his balls and dick disappeared under the front of the tight jeans. "Um, aren't you going to shower first?"

"Nope," he said with a wicked grin. "I like having your smell on me, you gorgeous witch. You smell like honey and cream and peaches." He zipped up, then turned around. "Dust me off for the show? It sucks not being able to use a mirror."

I laughed. "At least I can play your personal stylist. Come here, you big lug."

I slid out from beneath the silk sheets. I was happy with Egyptian cotton, but Aegis liked silk. With a critical eye, I circled him. His pants were clean and still a little too new. They hadn't reached that creased-comfort zone yet. His jacket was heavily adorned with hardware—studs, chains, zippers. I adjusted a couple of the zippers and he stroked my face. On his right index finger, he wore a large square ring. Gold, it was engraved with a sunburst pattern on the flat surface, and a carnelian cabochon nestled in the center. The ring was a memento left over from the time when Aegis had been a servant of Apollo.

Aegis had been cast out on the whim of a god, turned away from the sun, which he worshipped, and changed into a vampire—one of the Fallen. But he hadn't let it destroy him, nor would he destroy others through his powers. Not willingly. The other thing Apollo left him besides the ring was his voice. Aegis's voice was as sensual as Jim Morrison's when the lizard king was at his best. Aegis actually looked a lot like Morrison, too—only with longer hair, larger muscles, and a vampire glamour.

"Do I clean up well?" he asked, tapping my nose with his finger.

"You clean up so yummy that I'd yank you back into bed if we had time." Satisfied that he was ready, I stepped back and patted his chest. "You're good to go, gorgeous. Remember, we're having the after-show party here. We may not have much furniture, but we've got the space and it's the first time..."

I paused. I had been about to say it was the first time we had planned a party together, but that sounded way too clingy, considering we had only been together six weeks. But he understood.

"I'm excited too. The boys in the band know you, but now I get to show you off. And maybe this will help the neighbors quit being so prissy about having a vampire for a neighbor." He laughed, then zipped up his coat and headed for the bedroom door. "You'll have everything ready when we get back?"

I nodded. "Sandy's coming over to help." Sandy and I had seen the bottom of way too many wine bottles together. She was the friend who would help me hide the bodies in the middle of the night.

"Don't start the party early, please." He wiggled his eyebrows at me.

Laughing, I threw a pillow at him. "Get out of here. I'm going to shower and dress and then start setting up."

As Aegis darted away from the pillow and slipped around the door, I padded into the bathroom for a shower. The first thing on my renovation list for the mansion had been to hire the Alpha-Pack—the local werewolf pack that owned the main contracting company on the island—to revamp the bathrooms. They had reno'd all six of them first thing after I moved in. Now, in my en suite, I had a huge spa tub, a walk-in shower, and a two-sink vanity.

I turned the water in the shower and slipped beneath the rainshower showerhead as the pulsing side jets beat a welcome tattoo on my body. Leaning my head back, I settled in as the warm water washed over me. The day had been long and chilly, sex had been sweaty, and there was nothing like a shower of warm water and amber-scented soap.

As I loofahed my arms and legs, exfoliating everything I could reach, a faint *click* caught my attention. The bathroom door had just opened.

What the hell? Had Aegis forgotten something? Bubba couldn't open doors, at least not that I knew of. I cautiously wiped away a patch of condensation from the shower door and cupped my eyes to peer out. Sure enough, there was somebody in the bathroom with me, and it wasn't Bubba. No, whoever this was was bipedal, at least.

I considered my options. I was stark nekkid, but I didn't need clothes to use my powers. I could attack first—send out a nasty ball of energy to whap whoever it was, or I could try a paralyzing charm.

The former would hurt anybody who wasn't immune to fire and lightning, but if it was a friend, they'd be fried. Not that most of my friends came creeping into my bathroom, but I wouldn't put it past a few of them. The latter would only work on humans, and there just weren't many humans on Bedlam. As I squinted, trying to figure out my uninvited guest's motives, I detected the scent of musk and wine beneath the lingering fragrance of the amber bath gel I was using.

Hell. Musk? Wine? Those scents were all too familiar. I slammed open the shower door, almost breaking the glass, as I managed to startle the satyr. Standing there large as life, his denim shorts sporting a tent pole that would do any male proud, Ralph Greyhoof was holding my hairbrush in one hand, a plastic baggie in the other.

I stepped out of the shower, planted my hands on my hips, and barked out, "What the hell do you want in my house, Ralph? And what are you doing with my hairbrush? You have ten seconds to answer before I fry your freaking ass right into the hospital."

Chapter 2

RALPH DROPPED THE brush. His erection deflated immediately. With satyrs, *everybody* knew when their cocks were crowing a wake-up call—the scent alone was enough to floor you. Being around a horny satyr was like hanging out with an elk herd during rutting season.

I'd dated one many years ago—a satyr, not an elk—and I'd had one of the sorest pussies around. Satisfied, but sore. Satyrs were huge—they couldn't help it, but not a lot of women dared take them on. There were times when I looked back on that relationship and wondered why I had left him. After the vampires caught my sweet Tom and turned him, I'd let myself off the leash. And when my friends and I finally walked away from the carnage, we had thrown ourselves into playing wild and free, taking multiple lovers and paramours. The wine and magic had run rampant. But after a while, the madness diminished and Sandy, Fata, and I had moved on.

"I'm not doing anything." Ralph Greyhoof shifted his eyes. He was lying, of course. I knew him from way back and I knew that he wasn't prone to telling the truth. Satyrs were smart and they were sneaky. Underhanded? Not necessarily. Sneaky? Always.

He leaned against the vanity, eyeing me the way a hungry kid eyes a candy dish. It suddenly dawned on me that wandering around naked in front of a satyr might not be the best idea. I reached for my robe and slipped it on, belting it tightly.

"Then you tell me what the hell you're doing in my bathroom."

"You didn't answer the door." Ralph frowned, staring at my boobs. Well, at the chest of my bathrobe.

"Eyes on my *face*, Ralph!"

He grumbled, but met my gaze.

"I didn't answer the door because I was *taking a shower*. You don't just walk into someone's house if they don't answer their door, you idiot."

"Sorry." He didn't mean it, of course. "I'll go now." He started to backtrack toward the door.

"Hold it right there." I leaned down to pick up my brush and place it back on the vanity. As I saw the hair in the bristles, it dawned on me just what he had been doing. "You were after some of my hair, weren't you? What are you up to, Ralph?" I shook the brush at him. "And don't you try to bullshit me. I'm one of the most powerful witches on the island and you know better than to fuck with me, Greyhoof. Why were you stealing hair from my brush?"

He froze in his tracks, letting out a sigh that sounded more like a snort. He was tall and imposing, but he was afraid of me and that's the way I wanted to keep it.

Around six-three, his biceps gleamed, and the fur that clung to his goat-like legs was silky, brown, and plush. Ralph was a fairly handsome guy. His eyes were wide and slanted ever so slightly. A rich, dark topaz, they gleamed with Otherkin light. His braid hung down to his butt. He was wearing a pair of khaki shorts and a muscle tank.

"Somebody asked me to." He spread his hands. "Honest. Business has been slow and I figured it couldn't hurt to take a side job."

I tapped my foot. "I don't believe you. You're up to something, Ralph Greyhoof, and I plan on finding out what. But for now, just get out of my house and don't you ever come in again without permission."

He shuffled his hooves, his pretense at innocence falling away. He pressed his lips together but then bluster took over. "Yeah, well quit trying to pinch my customers! We were here before you. You just saunter over here to the island, take up with a vampire, and then try to put us out of business? You're a leech, Maddy Gallowglass. *A leech!*"

"Oh for fuck's sake. Not this again."

Ralph Greyhoof and two of his brothers—George and William—ran a B&B a few miles away. Or rather, a bed-and-brothel, I liked to call it. The satyrs offered more than just a nice room and muffins for breakfast. They catered mostly to women, mostly, and their weekend specials came with a smile and a little sumthin'-sumthin' extra. We weren't really competition, but the Greyhoofs didn't believe it and they were convinced we were aiming to put them out of business, even though the Bewitching Bedlam B&B was a lot more innocuous than the Heart's Desire Inn.

I confiscated his plastic bag and motioned to the door. "Out of my bathroom. Get your ass downstairs to the kitchen and we'll talk."

He gulped—I saw his Adam's apple move—and, after a brief stare down, turned tail and headed downstairs. I followed, deciding I'd better search him for stray strands of my hair before he left. Hair made for powerful magic. Blood was better, but hair worked just fine when you wanted to cast a spell on someone. Which is why I still had a plastic sandwich bag full of hair and bloody tissue from my ex, Craig. While we were married, every time he cut himself shaving, I fished a few of the toilet paper shreds out of the garbage and tucked them away for insurance.

In the kitchen, I put the kettle on for tea and handed Ralph a plate of cookies. "Sit your ass down for a moment. You do realize what my boyfriend would think if he found out a satyr crashed my shower in the middle of the night? And what he might do for payback?" I was feeling particularly snarky. Might as well make him sweat.

And sweat he did. Ralph turned an ugly shade of green. "You wouldn't really do that, would you,

Maddy? Come on. We go back too far for that sort of torment." He fiddled with one of the cookies before setting it down with a grumpy sigh. "Listen. I really don't know who the chick was, but she offered me five hundred for some of your hair. I wasn't going to lay a whammy on you—I know better than that. But it's the off-season. And this old decaying hunk of house is looking mighty nice now. Too good to ignore for tourists. You're going to ruin our business."

"I am not. We have two entirely different types of clientele." I pursed my lips, not wanting to feel sorry for the lecher, but I couldn't help it. Ralph and his brothers had dreamed big since the day I met them, which was shortly after I joined the Moonrise Coven. They never quite reached those dreams. They were always looking for the next big thing, the next get-rich-quick scheme. Their inn was the most practical thing they had ever done in their lives.

Relenting, I shrugged. "Fine, I'll have mercy on you. But dude, you knock next time you come over. Or ring the bell. And if there's no answer and it's unlocked, stay out. And I swear, if you find out the name of whoever paid you to fetch my hair and you don't tell me, I'll turn you into a hamster and give you to Bubba as a chew toy. Get the idea?" I poured our tea.

"Yeah, I get it. If it helps, the woman who hired me is a blond bombshell. I swear, if somebody had figured out cloning, this dame could be a duplicate of Marilyn." He arched his eyebrows and the scent of musk rose again.

"Monroe or Manson?" I knew just how to bait him.

Ralph let out a sputter, but then relaxed and laughed. "Either, for my tastes. But no, Monroe. She's tall, has some sort of allure about her." He leaned forward. "I think she's a vampire, Maddy."

Vampire? That was new. Aegis was the newest to come out of the coffin about his existence. There were probably fewer than thirty vampires on the island, and most of them belonged to Essie Vanderbilt's nest. She just happened to be one of the regional vampire queens, and kept aloof, though cordial, relations with the community.

"New?"

He nodded. "I don't remember seeing her around. She wasn't wearing the mark of the local nest, and most of the loners are well-known. I don't remember her name. You'd think she would have told me, but I can't recall. But she's got everything that counts."

I snorted. To a satyr, that meant readily available sex organs. "Dude, you already slept with her?"

Ralph threw half of his cookie at me. "Stereotypes, always with the stereotypes. No, I did *not* sleep with her. I draw the line with vampires. Unlike some *witches* I know." He touched his finger to his nose, nodding at me.

"Leave my sex life out of this. Aegis is a wonderful man, even if he's dead."

"He's a vampire. They're all the same, in the end—dead and clammy. But no, I didn't mean I slept with her. She has money and isn't afraid to use it." He shrugged. "This is going to sound silly to you, but the woman can carry a tune. We sang together for a good two hours. I think she was bored, but she humored me. Not very many people around here will take the time to sing with us. Including that boyfriend of yours."

The only thing satyrs liked as much as sex was music. Money was good, but they loved their music. And then it hit me. Aegis had been a servant of Apollo, who had been in a major fracas with Pan, the god of the satyrs. They'd basically created the first Olympian Idol contest, so to speak, and Apollo won. Pan had never forgotten the slight. It made sense that Ralph wouldn't like Aegis, even if Aegis hadn't become one of the Fallen.

It was hard to fault Ralph for being suckered in. Music to a satyr was like gold to a leprechaun or a big fat juicy steak to a werewolf.

I let out a long sigh. "Empty your pockets before you go."

"Damn it, Maddy. Oh, all right." Ralph emptied his pockets. A switchblade, a couple grape lollipops, three condoms, twenty-five dollars and some change, and a set of lock picks.

"Pull up your shirt."

As he flashed me, I realized that Ralph had put on about twenty pounds since I'd last seen him. He was still incredibly built, but with a little padding around the edges. But nothing there to say he'd managed to actually get my hair out of the brush. I had no intention of patting him down. I knew where that would lead. For *him*. Not for me.

"All right. You're clean, as far as I can tell. But

I'm warning you, Ralph. If this woman actually does get hold of my hair—or any other anchor—I'll know where to look. And I'll bring Aegis with me and he'll take it out of you in blood, and after that, I *will* turn you into a nanny goat who's constantly in heat. Got it?"

Ralph nodded, eyes wide. All pretense was gone and he just looked grateful to be escaping with his skin intact. "I'll go now."

"You do that." I saw him to the door and locked it, considering putting a reinforcement spell on the lock. But that would make it harder for Aegis when he came home. I glanced at the clock. I still had to get ready for the after-party.

After-party! Crap. I raced back upstairs to get dressed.

By the time I decided on what I wanted to wear—a black Bohemian gauze skirt with a skull-patterned corset, a silver-colored belt, and black lace-up leather boots—Sandy had arrived. Franny peeked around the corner of the door to my bedroom. I'd warded it heavily so she could only get in if there was an emergency, and she knew better than to fake one.

"Your friend is here. The blonde." She sniffed, affecting a long-suffering tone.

"You don't like Aegis because he's a vampire. What the hell is wrong with Sandy?"

"She's not very lady-like."

"Neither am I. Go bother Bubba. He's always up for a good spar." I shooed her away. Then, wrapping a silver and black shawl around my shoulders, I headed downstairs.

Franny was nowhere to be seen, but Sandy was petting Bubba, taking care to steer clear of his belly. Cjinns were sneaky. While they were all cat on the outside, in their heart and soul they were djinns and they granted wishes based on belly-rubs and how persnickety their mood was.

A happy and purring cjinn? Might be magnanimous. An irritated cjinn would twist your words into the worst possible meaning. Trouble was, they could read emotions and—I suspected—thoughts, to a degree. If you offhandedly were talking to a friend while petting a cjinn's belly and you happened to say, "I wish I had a million bucks," you might very well find yourself the owner of a very large herd of elk. Mostly, it was safest to avoid the stomach area, especially when Bubba offered his fuzzy tum-tum up for adoration.

"You look good." Sandy gathered up Bubba, kissed him on the nose, and gently tossed him on the sofa. He gave her the stink-eye and wandered off. "In fact, you look good enough to eat. Hope Aegis has been topping off the tank at the blood bank lately."

I snorted. The local blood bank also took donations for vampires who didn't want to drink from humans. Aegis used it more often now, given how I felt about him dining on our friends. "Yeah, he has. And you look good, too."

Sandy Clauson was five-nine, thin, blond, and seldom showed up for anything other than parties in yoga pants and a crop top. She had the abs for it but despite the new-age getup, she was as experienced a witch as I was. We had been in the same coven for years, and friends for what seemed like forever.

THE MOONRISE COVEN had been around since 1950. I had been one of the founding members, along with Sandy, and Linda Realmwood, whom we agreed would take the role of High Priestess, given neither Sandy nor I wanted the responsibility. Linda had the power to hold the title and the wisdom to wield it.

Linda's great-great-grandmother had originally been from Norway before arriving in Newfoundland around 1000 CE. Over the years, her descendants moved southwestward into what was now the United States, long before Columbus ever set foot on native soil. The family intermarried with Native Americans, and eventually, Linda's mother-to-be, Greta, married Mohe, a Cherokee brave from the AniWaya Clan. Mohe brought Greta into the tribe as his wife and in 1797, Greta gave birth to a daughter, Linda, and gave her her own family name—Realmwood—as was her family's custom. Linda took on the wolf spirit for her animal guardian, given her father's tribe was the Wolf tribe, and she learned her mother's magic.

Linda had also been elected mayor of Bedlam in 1995 and nobody would let her even think of retiring. She did a good job and everybody trusted her.

"SO WHAT'S THE theme of this shindig?" Sandy wandered over to the bar and poured herself a snifter of brandy. "Want one?"

"You have to ask? Of course I want one. And tonight is a pre-Solstice party for the band and their families. I'm making eggnog, so let the brandy flow." As I accepted the drink and gently swished the drink, warming the glass in my hand, Sandy glanced around.

"So where's the food?"

I grinned. "You know I don't cook beyond a few cookies or a boxed cake. The caterer will be here in about twenty minutes." I paused, then said, "I was in the shower earlier. I heard something in the bathroom and when I peeked out, I found Ralph Greyhoof trying to steal hair from my brush."

Sandy stared at me. "Is he still alive?"

"Yeah, and he's lucky he is. Thing is, he told me some chick paid him to do it. And get this. She paid him both with money and a sing-along. Have you heard of any strange vamps moving into the area lately? He thinks she was a vampire."

"No, but this doesn't sound good at all." Sandy scowled. "Maddy, you *know* what hair's used for. You think Ralph might be lying? That he was going to pay somebody to throw a whammy on you?"

"Well, at first I did. My thought was that he wanted to hex the B&B. But the more he talked about the woman—I'm kind of convinced he might be telling the truth." I motioned for her to follow me into the kitchen.

"Don't be too sure. The Greyhoofs are an old family, but they're crafty. I don't know that I'd trust anything Ralph said. Be careful, Maddy."

She made a good point. The Greyhoofs have been on Bedlam for more than a hundred years, and they were known for rabble-rousing and causing general havoc. They were in jail so often that Delia—the sheriff—joked about putting in a revolving door for them.

"There is that. Well, I'll look into it more tomorrow. I guess I'd better tell Aegis, even though I wasn't going to. If he found out on his own, Ralph would be a few pints low before anybody could intervene. Now, help me set up these tables?"

Aegis had brought up three long tables up from the basement. The dining room had plenty of space for them, since we didn't have a formal table yet. The buffet would taste just as good on metal and plastic as it would on solid oak.

As we wrestled them through the kitchen door, Franny reappeared. She stood to one side, frowning. Half of her was still inside the wall next to the stairwell, and her arms were crossed as she stared at us with a pointed look of disdain.

"Those are ugly. When I was alive, my mother had a beautiful cherry wood table. You should buy something like that." She tsked at me.

"Franny, can you just give it a rest for once? You do nothing but complain all day. What—besides painting the kitchen pink—will make you happy?" Exasperated, I swung on her, wanting nothing more than to exorcise her right then and there.

Franny jerked back, as if I'd slapped her. "You know, I can *help* you if you'd give me a chance. Just because I'm a ghost doesn't mean I can't do anything. It gets boring just standing around watching everybody else go about their business." She arched her back and pulled out a fan. If she had been hiding it, I had no idea where and I wasn't going to ask. In an affected voice, she added, "I can do a lot of things that you don't know about."

I wanted to shoot back, "Besides complain?" but decided to drop it for the night. I was tired of sparring with her and truth was, I suddenly felt sheepish. After all, I had the advantage. For one thing, I was a witch. For another, I was still alive. Franny was just an unlucky spirit who—for whatever reason—couldn't move on. And it must suck to be stuck in one house for eternity. Come to think of it, I didn't even *know* whether I could exorcise her. There were so many variables involved.

"I'm sorry—" I started to say, but she vanished.

Sandy arched her eyebrows. "Sensitive much?"

"I guess being trapped in a house over two hundred years *would* tend to set a person on edge. I really need to find out more about her story. I haven't had much of a chance to do anything else but work on this house." I paused, trying to think about it from Franny's perspective. "She lived here when she was alive, I do know that much. And she died by falling down the stairs while reading a book. I suppose it really does hurt to see the home she grew up in being gutted and changed so much."

"Either that, or she's just a grouch. Here, help me tip this upright."

Sandy had opened the table we were carrying

and unfolded the legs. We set it up and then went back for the other two. Once they were standing, I found the tablecloths—long, green linens—and we were arranging them as the caterers arrived. Sandy and I retreated to the living room, giving them control of the kitchen and dining room.

The caterers had no more set up the food when the door opened and Aegis strode in, followed by the band members and their families. I decided I could wait till later to tell him about Ralph as he swung me into his arms and gave me a long kiss. But as his lips touched mine, I could sense that something was up. He felt...*nervous*.

"Is something wrong?" I murmured.

Aegis shifted, just enough to tell me I had hit a chord.

"Why do you ask?"

"I don't know. It's been an odd evening."

"Don't worry about it. Nothing that I can't handle. Band stuff." And he went back to kissing me.

Keth, the drummer, passed by, clapping Aegis on the shoulder.

"Get a room, dude." But he laughed as he said it. Keth was half-satyr, half-human, with a spiked Mohawk. His ears were stretched with heavy gauges and he was heavily tattooed. Residual horns poked out of his head, but they weren't fully formed and they never would be, given his heritage. He had feet rather than hooves, but he was a very hairy man.

"Hey Maddy, thanks for hosting the spread." He immediately headed over to the tables of food and began to pile a plate high.

Sid was there, sans wife and kids. "Sylvia sends her love, Maddy. She's still tired. I told her to stay home with the kids and nanny and watch TV."

"How's the baby?" I wasn't really geared toward maternal feelings but I cared about Sid and Sylvia. However, I had the feeling she could use more than one nanny. With five very active Fae children, the stress had to be high. But I decided to forgo offering unsolicited advice. Sid couldn't afford to hire more help. Not all of the Fae were rolling in dough. Especially the artists and musicians. Actually, a number of those who chose to live in the human world instead of their own seemed to find it rough going.

"The baby's a handful, all right. She's already causing havoc." He beamed, looking proud as a peacock. Sid and his wife were aiming for ten kids, and I couldn't imagine the mayhem that was going to generate. But they loved the bustle.

As everybody poured into the dining room, gathering around the spread, Aegis slid his arm around my waist. "You did a fantastic job."

"The caterers did most of the work." I nestled into his embrace, still feeling unsettled. My radar was buzzing and I wasn't sure what I was picking up on. "But yeah, things seem to be going over well. How did the show go?"

A slight but subtle tensing of his arm told me I was right. He was concerned about something. "Everything went fine. Why?"

I forced myself to relax. "I just wondered."

He didn't answer, just kissed me on the head and moved over to talk to Jack-Az.

I headed into the living room where Sandy was leaning against the wall, watching the interplay. While she was a socialite, my best buddy was also extremely observant and I trusted her judgment. I joined her, drink in one hand and a cookie I'd liberated off of somebody's plate in the other.

Lowering my voice, I asked, "Does Aegis seem tense to you?"

She glanced over at him, watching for a moment. "Yeah, he does. So do his band mates."

I was about to say something when I heard a yowl from upstairs. It was Bubba, and he sounded pissed or hurt.

"Oh hell, what's going on?"

I shoved my drink in Sandy's free hand and darted up the staircase. Bubba might be a little turd at times, but he was *my* little fuzzy turd. I followed the parade of hisses that came tumbling down the stairs. As I slammed open the door to my bedroom, I caught sight of Bubba, arched up like a Halloween cat. He was in front of the French doors leading out onto the brand-new balcony. I'd gone tumbling off the old one when the railing gave way weeks ago, so that was one of the first things I'd asked the Alpha-Pack to fix.

"What's going on? What's out there, Bub?" I cupped my hands to the windowpane, peering out into the icy night.

It was snowing outside, and didn't look like it was going to stop any time soon. A number of Winter Fae lived on the island and they attracted all that went along with the Winter Court. Bedlam was located on the northernmost tip of the San

Juan Islands, northwest of Ferndale. As a result of all the magical energy and the positioning, winters here were a lot harsher than on the southern islands. This storm, fresh off the westerly winds, was blanketing us with snow.

The twinkle of faerie lights shimmered from my balcony. I loved them, and kept them up year-round, but in the snow, they glowed with a gentle radiance that always made me feel calmer. Except right now, calm wasn't quite the word, with Bubba hissing like a wildcat.

"What's out there, Bub?" I leaned against the window, cupping the glass as I pressed my face against it. I couldn't see anything, but Bubba seemed positive there was something out there. "What do you see?"

He glanced up at me. *"Mrowf."*

That wasn't good. I knew that meow. He had constantly used it on my ex. It usually meant *Enemy at the gate!*

"Is there someone out there who's dangerous, Bubba?" I knelt beside him, glancing back out the window. I tried to make out any movements outside. But only the snow seemed to be moving—falling fast and thick.

Bubba nosed the window and I followed his gaze. In the faint glow of the lights on the snow, I could see what looked like footprints in the snow. Someone had been outside my bedroom on the balcony. They weren't *my* footprints. I hadn't been out there since morning and the snow had covered what prints I had left.

"Mrowf." Bubba was louder this time, sounding

pissed. His eyes flashed and I could feel the magic rising.

"Let me get—" I stopped as I turned to see Aegis and Sandy edging into the room.

"Hey, Bubba's upset. Someone was out on the balcony. I can see the footprints."

"Do you think it was Ralph?" Sandy pressed her face against the glass.

I winced. I had hoped to wait for a better time to tell Aegis that Ralph Greyhoof had seen me naked. Somehow, I didn't think that would go over very well.

"Ralph? Ralph who and why would he be outside your bedroom window?" Sure enough, Aegis didn't sound happy, and he didn't even know who we were talking about yet.

I cleared my throat. "I don't think those are his prints. They look like shoe prints, not hoof prints."

"Are you talking about Ralph Greyhoof? Why would he be outside your bedroom window?" There was an edge in his voice that I had only heard the first time we had met. But then, it had been mixed with arousal. Now he just sounded pissed.

"Um...I was going to tell you about that. Ralph showed up in the bathroom as I was taking a shower—"

"Bathroom? You were in the shower? If he touched one hair on your head I'll drain him dry, and he'll feel every drop leave his body." Aegis whirled, stalking to the door.

"Get back here, you big lug. Listen to me. Ralph didn't touch me. He was trying to steal hair out of my hairbrush." I paused. That didn't sound much better, given what it meant.

Aegis slowed, then turned. "Why would he be doing that? Answer me before I charge over to the Heart's Desire and light a fire under Ralph's balls."

"I don't know, to be honest. He said he was doing it for some vamp chick who paid him to." I watched Aegis closely, suddenly thinking that maybe, since he was from the *fang-me* set, Aegis might have some clue about who the strange vamp was.

Aegis frozen, then glanced out the window. "Stay inside. I'm going to have a look outside." Abruptly, he turned and stalked out of the room.

I turned to Sandy. "Something's going on. Those prints out there are shoes, and they look like about the size of a woman's footprints. Bubba was having a hissy fit when I came in." I turned back to the cjinn, eyeing him carefully. "Bub, is there still somebody outside?"

He looked at me, the pale gold of his eyes shining. He let out a whimper of a mew, then moved closer to me, rubbing his head against my leg. Sometimes, Bubba was a hellion. Other times, he seemed very much just a scared kitty-cat.

I leaned down and stroked his head, then scooped him up in my arms. "Bub, if there's something scary out there, Aegis will find it."

"There's something out there in the snow." Sandy reached for the handle on the French doors and before I could stop her, she opened the door, darting outside, then back in. She was holding a red rose. "What's this?"

I stared at the flower. "What the hell is going on?"

"I don't know, but somebody is bringing you flowers. Maybe Aegis?"

Bewildered, I shook my head. "Lock those doors. Until we know whether Aegis finds anybody out there, it's best to stay inside. Can you go back down to the party and keep things running smoothly?"

She nodded, handing me the rose and heading for the stairs.

As I sat on the bed, holding Bubba close to me, a noise near the hall door made me jump. I whirled around, but it was just Franny, standing in the doorway with a concerned look.

"Franny, did you see anything out there?" I nodded toward the balcony.

She shrugged. "I couldn't have, now could I? You banned me from your bedroom. But Maudlin, something's wrong. There's a strange energy afoot and I'm not comfortable. It's making me shiver in my shroud. You should be careful." She sounded like she actually cared.

"You think something is wrong, too? Do you know what it is?" Carrying Bubba, I headed toward the door.

She moved back to allow me room to exit. I could have just passed through her, but by now, Franny knew how much I hated doing that. Not only was her energy unearthly cold, but it just gave me the creeps.

"I don't know what it is, no. But there's an unsettled energy around the house. We may have our differences, but this isn't anything to joke around with. I have a horrible feeling that something's going to go terribly wrong. Please, be careful?"

When a ghost was asking me to watch my step, I knew that things had taken a bad turn. "Thanks, Franny. I promise. Would you stay here and keep an eye on the bedroom with Bubba? You can come in the room." I disabled the wards against her with a flick of the wrist. "Bubba can generally take care of himself but until we know what's going on, I don't want to take any chances."

"Of course. Thank you for asking." She silently drifted into my bedroom and stood by the window, with Bubba sitting by the hem of her gown.

As I rejoined the party below, Aegis returned, a dusting of snow on his shoulders. The flakes clung to him. He had no body heat to melt them off. I glanced around to make sure no one could overhear us.

"What did you find?" I wasn't sure what I was expecting, but he shook his head.

"Nothing. I didn't find anything out there. But don't leave the doors or windows unlocked tonight. Come on, let's go talk to the guests."

He stared at me, unblinking, and for the first time since we had met, I was nervous. He was lying and I could sense it. But there wasn't much I could do.

"Fine. But we need to talk later." I looped my arm through his and plastered a smile on my face. As we rejoined the party, the evening slid into a mire of doubt and shadow.

Chapter 3

BY THE END of the night, I was exhausted, and Aegis didn't want to talk. In fact, he seemed preoccupied to the point where I took Bubba and went upstairs to bed by myself. We had occasional nights where we didn't have sex, especially if we had played around during the early evening, but if he was home, we usually cuddled for a bit before I dropped off at around midnight. Scheduling my days around his nights wasn't always easy, but we had done our best to synch up. But tonight, I decided it wasn't worth opening a can of worms, and chalked it up to a grumpy day.

Next morning, I made sure that the basement was secure before heading out for the day. We had rigged up a mechanism where Aegis could bar it from the inside so that nobody could get in. He had a secret passage through which he could escape if the house was on fire or some other nightmare like that, but nobody besides us knew about it. We hadn't hired the Alpha-Pack for that particular renovation. Instead, Aegis installed it himself and if he said it was secure, I trusted him. It was his life that was at stake.

I fed Bubba, then puttered around the house while debating over attempting to make pancakes. But I knew that my cooking skills weren't up to the task. In all of the years I'd been alive, I had always managed to avoid being the one stuck in the kitchen.

Instead, I dug out the leftover cookies from the party, along with a couple deviled eggs that were tucked in the back of the fridge, and I added a thick slice of cheddar. In a fit of inspiration, I mashed up the eggs and spread them on a piece of toast, then added the cheese for an impromptu egg sandwich. After that, I finished off a half-dozen chocolate peanut-butter chip cookies, then drank the last few swallows in the quart of milk I found in the fridge. I had never stocked milk until I started living with Aegis, but he liked it, and so I kept it around now.

Bubba meandered past, giving me the side eye as I stood there, eating in front of the refrigerator door.

"What? You eat off the floor. My manners aren't any worse than that."

He sniffed, eyeing the milk in my hands. *"Mrow?"*

"No, I'm not giving you any milk, it's not good for you. You know what it does to your digestion. The cat box is a horrendous mess and you end up urping for several days." I tossed the empty milk carton in the recycling bin. "Besides, we're out. I'll pick you up some treats when I'm out this afternoon."

Bubba leaped up on the counter and stared at me with that innocent look of his. He was gorgeous, with his long flowing ginger fur and wide, winsome eyes. *"Mrowf?"*

I stopped, letting out a short sigh. "No, I don't know who was on the balcony, but I think Aegis found something. He's not saying anything, though. But it wasn't Ralph. I know that much."

Bubba considered this for a moment, then wandered off into the other room. I watched his tail pluming as the drafts in the old mansion ruffled through it.

The caterers had cleaned up after the party, so there really wasn't anything to clean, and if there had been, Aegis would have done the dishes while I was asleep. He usually left breakfast for me to eat, but given the amount of leftovers I knew would be in the fridge, I had told him not to bother the previous night. The man could cook and bake like a pro.

Finally, I scribbled out my to-do list for the day—a never-ending trail of shopping and planning—and settled in for a morning's work on turning the mansion into a place where people would want to come stay.

BY ONE-THIRTY, my head was spinning from numbers-crunching. I squinted, seeing double as I turned off the ten-key. Time to go shopping. I had so many things I had to buy before we opened the next week that I was starting to panic.

Shouldering my purse, I told Bubba I was headed into town and firmly locked the door. As I tromped through the snow to my car, my fur-trimmed coat barely keeping the cold at bay, it occurred to me that I loved my new life, even when there were glitches.

My mansion was on the outskirts of Bedlam, but given how small the island was—twenty-six miles long and from two miles wide on the ends to fifteen miles wide at the center—driving into the town didn't take very long.

Grateful I had the forethought to buy snow tires for my CR-V, I cautiously navigated Yew Tree Road toward the still-icy Thornbush Drive that would lead me into town. Obviously Harold Winsket had overslept. The chief of trash collection, he was also our snowplow operator during winter. When he couldn't make it, Skerrit Tomas, his assistant, took over. Both of them were ferret shifters, and they were usually on the spot about their work. But the roads were covered in snow and ice, and the banks were only growing deeper.

As I eased down Thornbush Drive into the town square, I found myself smiling. Living in Bedlam made me happy.

Over the years the architecture had changed, but some of the old buildings were originals, going back to the early days of the island. The post office, city hall, and police station were a combination of red brick and gray stone—the same on the outside as they had been during the 1800s. Oh, they had electric lights now, and heating and plumbing, but the architecture stood true to form, and the buildings rose from under their cover of snow, full of old-world charm and strength. I had my doubts that they would survive a major earthquake, but then again, if the big one hit along the Cascadia Subduction Zone, we were *all* going to be running for cover.

Bedlam was a tidy town anyway, but she *really* spruced up for the holiday season. Multicolored lights encircled every tree along Main Street, and wreaths hung from the lampposts, shimmering with the brightly colored faerie lights. Downtown proper was built up around the central square, which acted like a gigantic roundabout.

In the center of the square itself was the city fountain, with a massive sculpture of a cat sitting on a crescent moon in the center. The water had been turned off because of the freezing temperatures, and a layer of snow dusted the cat's ears and head, and the horns of the moon. There were four Yule trees, one at each corner of the fountain, and shoppers milled through the square, though no one lingered on the benches in this weather.

I found a parking spot in front of McGee's Apothecary and, bracing myself against the chill, slid out of the car into the biting wind. Snowflakes were blowing every which way as I hurried into the shop. I needed to stock up on ingredients for several of my spells, and I also wanted to get some of Andy McGee's elixir. It was the best tonic in the world, better than any multivitamin for energy and general vitality. I wasn't sure what he put in it—he had developed a secret recipe—but it worked.

Andy's daughter, Beth, was behind the counter when I opened the door. At the jangling of bells, she glanced up from her computer screen.

"Hey, Maddy. What brings you to town on a morning like this?" Her frown of concentration vanished, replaced by a wide smile. The girl was pretty enough, but more than that—she had the nature of a healer and just standing near her made anybody feel better.

I jammed my hands in my pockets. I'd forgotten my gloves in the car and just the short jaunt from the curb to the shop had left me chilled.

"I need some of Andy's elixir, along with some other spell components."

"One bottle or two?" She turned to the shelf behind her, to a row of bottles with old-fashioned labels affixed to them. They were reminiscent of tonic bottles from the early twentieth century.

"Might as well take two."

"Two it is." She pulled out a pad of paper and a pen. "Now, what else can I get you?"

"I also need an ounce each of Muddle leaf, gooseberry root, sassafras grass, chopped valerian, coltsfoot, and two ounces of comfrey leaf. Two pounds of Dead Sea salt, a packet of graveyard dust, and a bottle of War water." I glanced at my list. "Oh, and if you still sell those incredible chocolate thunder bars, I want three."

Not only did Andy make the best elixir, he also

made one of the best chocolate bars I had ever eaten. Nobody could say the man wasn't talented with mixing things. He was one of the best alchemists in Bedlam, and he was one of the few humans. His daughter showed similar talents, even though she was only in her thirties.

As Beth bustled around the shop gathering my purchases, I took a seat in the small reading nook next to the window. Various magazines were scattered on the table—*Dazzle*, *Star-Crossed*, *Spell-Caster's Monthly*, and *The Otherkin Gazette*. The daily *Bedlam Crier* was on the table, too, and I picked it up to glance through the news. There wasn't much—Bedlam was a fairly quiet community as far as sensationalism went, but I noticed a prominent ad for the Heart's Desire Inn on the third page. Ralph and his brothers weren't sparing any expense, it seemed.

"Here you go." Beth finished weighing out my herbs and slid the plastic bags into a paper one. "I put the tonic in a separate bag to avoid any possibility of getting your herbs wet."

I fit my credit card into the chip reader and waited, then entered my PIN when it prompted me. "Thanks, Beth. I have some shopping for the Solstice to do. Merry Yule, in case I don't see you before then."

She handed me my bags and receipt. "Blessed Yule to you, also. Don't leave that Muddle leaf around where it can be confused for oregano, or you'll have a few weeks of trying to sort out all the confusion."

I locked the bags in the car, then walked the

half block to Art World, where I hunted through the prints until I found a copy of "Woman, Reading." It was an Impressionist-inspired painting by a relatively unknown artist of a woman wandering through a meadow, a book in her hand. Franny had seen it in a catalog I had been looking through and had loved it. While I drew the line at painting the kitchen pink, I decided I could give her this for Yule and maybe bring a little joy into her life. While the clerk was wrapping up the print for me, I flipped through another stack.

I was mulling over a painting of a rose garden when my phone beeped at me. Pulling it out, I saw a text had come in from a number I didn't recognize. Frowning, I opened it to see a picture that stopped me cold.

"What the hell?"

"Excuse me?" The gallery clerk looked over at me from where she was wrapping my painting.

"Nothing," I murmured, turning away and looking at the text again. The text was a photo of a painting, that much was obvious. And the painting was of Aegis, his arm around a striking blonde. They were holding goblets of blood, raised as if to toast the artist.

I caught my breath. Who had painted this? And who had sent it to me? I thought about asking the clerk but decided that wasn't the wisest idea. I started to text back WHO ARE YOU? WHY DID YOU SEND ME THIS? then stopped.

The representative smiled at me. "Will this be all?"

My heart in my throat, I nodded. "Yeah, please

ring me up."

She quickly began tallying up the painting and tax. "All right, here's your total."

"Thanks." I handed him my credit card and then, clutching the print for Franny, headed back outside.

What the hell was a painting of Aegis and a blond woman doing on my phone? And then, I stopped and glanced at the text again. The woman looked very much like the vampire Ralph had described to me. The one who supposedly paid him to swipe my hair.

"Crap." I didn't know whether to text the person back or not. Whoever sent it definitely wanted to make sure I saw it, but the phone number had a different area code. That didn't necessarily mean much, given the way people moved around. My phone still had a Seattle area code. Breathing heavily, I decided to pay a visit to Ralph later in the afternoon to see if he could confirm whether it was the same woman. Or to find out if he had been the one to send the photo to me. I'd avoid texting back until after I talked to Sandy.

Fretting, I moved on to French Pair—a boutique that carried lingerie. Aegis's favorite color was purple, so I shuffled through the teddies till I found a bustier and cute boy shorts in a rich plum shade. The bustier was jacquard, with a richly embroidered print in black on it. I held it up, trying to assess whether it would fit over my boobs or not. I was more than well endowed and it made some tops a bit problematic.

"Choosing a gift that keeps on giving?" Sandy's

voice rang out behind me. “I saw you through the window so I decided to join you before lunch.”

We had agreed to eat at the Blue Jinn Diner down the street.

I laughed. “I’m trying to. Do you think Aegis will like this?” I turned around, holding up the bustier.

“If he doesn’t, then he’s not the hot-blooded...” She stopped, then laughed. “Let me rephrase that. If he doesn’t, then he’s colder than... Oh fuck it. Yeah, I think he’ll like it.”

I glanced around the rest of the shop, spying a table of microfiber high-legged briefs. “I need some new panties. I love this brand. They’re the most comfortable thing next to going commando.” I sorted through the collection, choosing four pairs of blue, three plum, and two hunter green. I added two pairs of burgundy and three pairs of black panties to the pile. “There, two weeks’ worth.”

Sandy picked up a pair, running her hand over the material. “Nice. No seam lines to dig in.”

“They last for a long time, too. And they don’t fade.” My stomach chose that moment to rumble. “Come on, let me pay for all this and then we’ll go eat. I’ve got something to tell you about but I don’t want to get into it here.”

As I paid for the clothes, my worries came flooding back. “Sandy, do you know a good private investigator?”

She gave me a sharp look. “Why?”

“No reason.” I shrugged. “I may have some questions. Anyway, let’s go. I’ll tell you all about it over lunch. After lunch I was planning on shopping for furniture. If I’m planning on opening the B&B late next week, I *have* to finish decking the place out and I haven't a clue what I want at this point."

Bags in hand, we hurried through the falling snow. The storm had picked up substantially from just thirty minutes ago. "I'll drive. We'll swing back to pick up your car after lunch." I shoved the bags into the back seat with the others and started up the engine.

As we waited for the car to warm up, I pulled out my phone.

"Have you ever seen this picture before? Somebody texted this to me. It's a painting—but I have no idea who sent it to me." I held out the phone.

Sandy stared at it, then shook her head. "No, I haven't. But that's Aegis. Who's the woman?"

"I have no idea. I want to know when it was painted and who she is, and who the hell decided to text it to me."

"Well, by the style of her dress I'd say it was painted during the late 1980s." Sandy's pursed her lips as she enlarged the photo. "She's a real looker. Expensive, too. That haircut's so precise you could shave your legs on the edge."

"Thanks, I needed that visual." I leaned over to glance at the picture again. "She's wearing an expensive dress, though. That's a Donna Laurenz, unless I miss my guess."

"I think you're right." She snapped her fingers. "I have every *Styalista* published. I know I saw that dress in there. I'll have Lihi get on it."

"You don't have to bother her—" I started to say, but Sandy formed a ring with her index finger and thumb and raised it to her mouth, whistling sharply. A moment later, a homunculus appeared. Twelve inches tall, she looked like a cross between a bat and a woman, with leathery wings and large ears. She was wearing a pink halter top and a pair of leather shorts with a hole cut in back for her long, rat-like tail. Lihi was cute more than anything, but I knew better than to underestimate her. Homunculi were dangerous if you crossed them, but Lihi was bound to Sandy by a mutual contract, so I wasn't all that worried.

"Lihi, see this?" Sandy showed the homunculus the picture.

Lihi nodded. "What do you need, Mistress?"

"Please go through my back issues of *Styalista* and find this dress. I want to know what issue it's from—what month and year. Also the designer's name and if the story says anything about someone who may have bought the original."

"As you will." Lihi vanished as quickly as she had come.

"She's cute." I started the car. "How long has she been with you? I can't remember."

"About four years. We agreed to a seven-year contract to begin with. She's handy and her pay comes easy. She loves crystals, and since she can't enter this realm without being summoned, she can't go hunting them herself. So I promised her ten quartz crystals per month, with a bonus of an amethyst and citrine at the end of the first year, and other gems at the end of other years." Sandy grinned as she leaned back.

"You got off easy." It seemed to me like Sandy was getting the best of the deal.

She snorted. "Not so much. She eats like a trucker. I go through a lot more food than you might think. And in her world, those ten crystals per month? Are quite a hefty payment. But we get along and I'm pretty sure we'll both want to renew when the seven years are over. She's incredibly handy and I like her sense of humor, though it takes some getting used to.

"So, who do you think the woman in the painting is?" Sandy asked as I turned left on Backslide Street—aptly named, given the gradient. I grimaced, coaxing the car up the steep hill.

"I don't know. But given she appears to be a vampire by the tips of those fangs showing, I'd better find out, and find out quick. If Ralph confirms she's the same one who hired him, then I need to talk to Aegis. I'm sure as hell not looking forward to that conversation."

We topped the hill and turned onto Exxo Street. From there it was a block to the Blue Jinn. Easing into a parking space, I turned off the ignition. As the car settled, Lihi appeared again, her wings fluttering just enough to keep her aloft above Sandy's lap.

"I found the information you asked for. The issue with that dress in it was released in October of 1987 and it's a Donna Laurenz original. No copies were made." The homunculus looked extremely pleased with herself.

"Good job, Lihi. Go enjoy yourself the rest of the day. I won't be needing you till tomorrow, so take some time and have fun." Sandy waved her off, and Lihi vanished with a smile on her face. "I told you, a Laurenz. 1987. If there were no copies, then whoever is wearing that dress in the painting bought the original."

"I wonder how we could find out the name of whoever bought it. I doubt the designer—or her company—would release confidential records like that." The wheels of my brain were spinning as we entered the Blue Jinn.

"We have a reservation. Gallowglass."

The hostess ticked us off her list and led us into the depths of the restaurant. The Blue Jinn was a fancy steakhouse with a lounge. The bar, open from four p.m. till midnight, sported a stage for live music and the occasional dinner theater. We passed by the lounge to a booth near the back with a window overlooking the patio. The hostess handed us our menus.

"Your server will be with you in a few moments. Can I start you off with drinks and appetizers, or do you need a few minutes?"

I didn't feel like alcohol. "Peppermint mocha. For an appetizer, I'd like a bowl of your New England clam chowder."

Sandy ordered a cup of lemon tea and the lobster bisque. As soon as the hostess left, she leaned across the table. "I think you need to talk to Aegis about this, and soon. Seriously, Maddy. You two have something good going. He's not going to ruin it by—" She paused as Rose Williams, a member of our coven, hurried over to our booth.

"Maddy, I don't want to interrupt your lunch, but I think you should know that the Greyhoofs are spreading rumors about you." She shoved her phone toward me. "Read what he said about you on Flitterbug." Flitterbug was a social networking site for the Pretcom. I had very little to do with it. Social media in general irritated the hell out of me.

I reluctantly took her phone and glanced at the "flit"—as they called the posts. There, George Greyhoof had written:

> DON'T BE DECEIVED BY THE ILLUSIONARY ALLURE OF BEWITCHING BEDLAM. FOR TRUE COMFORT, CHECK IN AT THE HEART'S DESIRE INN, WHERE WE CATER TO ALL YOUR NEEDS—BOTH THE SUBLIME AND CARNAL.

"Damn it." I scanned through the rest of his posts for the week, only to find several less-than-flattering mentions of the Bewitching Bedlam. Including the insinuation that Aegis would feed off our guests. "I'll box their ears."

Sandy took the phone from me and read through the notifications. She silently handed it back to Rose. At that moment, the waitress brought our soup and drinks.

"Would you like to order now?"

I wanted to bark "No, go away!" but bit my tongue. The waitress hadn't done anything wrong. Motioning to Rose to stick around for a moment, I glanced at the menu again.

"Grilled cheese with cheddar, a side of steamed asparagus, and fries, please."

Sandy handed her menu to the waitress. "BLT on whole wheat, a side salad, and onion rings."

The waitress jotted down our orders, took our menus, and left. As soon as she was gone, I turned back to Rose.

"How long has he been spreading stuff around like this?"

"Since they first realized you were serious about opening a bed and breakfast. At first, I didn't think anything about it. I thought he would stop, or something. But apparently he's out to cause you more trouble than I first thought."

"Have you heard anything else?" Just how far had the Greyhoof boys gone to smear my reputation?

Rose ducked her head. "I should have told you all of this earlier. Last week, I overheard Ralph badmouthing you and Aegis to a couple from out of town. He warned them not to book a room at the Bewitching Bedlam because your 'boy toy' might end up having dessert 'on the house.' I interrupted him and told him to watch what he said, but he blew me off. After seeing George's flit, it occurred to me they might really be trying to sabotage your business. I decided I had better tell you."

My temper rising, I tried to keep my voice steady. "I'm glad you told me, even if I am pissed. Thanks, Rose. I'll see you at the Esbat on Wednesday." The Moonrise Coven held rituals on the Esbats—the full moons—as well as the Sabbats, and our eight High Holy days. I handed her phone back to her.

She excused herself and returned to her table.

I kept my tongue in check until she was out of earshot. "Sandy, I swear, I'm going to roast me some goat. I need to have a little *chat* with the Greyhoof boys." I pulled out my phone and brought up the picture of the painting. “I first thought Ralph was trying to gather some of my hair to put a hex on the Bewitching Bedlam, and now I think I’m right. I don’t know how this woman fits into the picture—no pun intended. Maybe she’s a vampire who used to be a witch?”

“That would be bad. I wonder. But how are Aegis and Ralph connected? It’s not like they’re best buddies. They barely talk.”

“I don’t know, but there has to be some link.” I shoved the phone back in my pocket and let out an exasperated sigh. “Let’s focus on lunch. I really don’t want an ulcer, and that’s all I’m going to get if I talk any more about this while we’re eating.”

“Sure.” Sandy held up her mug of tea. “Here’s to old friends and good food. With everything else going on in the world, we need all the support we can get.”

“Heaven’s truth to that,” I murmured, saluting her back as we settled into other topics.

AFTER LUNCH, WE stopped in at the Calou Bakery. I had phoned in an order for three loaves of Witches’ Bread, and had received a text that they were ready. The Calou was owned by a local hearth witch named Glenna, who supplied most of the wedding cakes and birthday cakes in town. She was a natural born baker, and the magic she wove into her food was apparent from the first bite.

As we entered the shop, a bright, warm little

bakery with three tables and two benches for customers who were waiting their turn, I took a number. We were headed over to one of the side benches when I froze. Ralph Greyhoof was sitting there, blowing a gum bubble almost as big as his head.

When he saw me, Ralph swallowed what must have been a monster wad and stumbled to his feet—hooves, clearing his throat.

"Maddy. Hey." He shifted his gaze as I loomed over him, cutting off any chance of a retreat he might have without going right through me.

I held out my phone, bringing up the picture. "Is this the woman you were talking about?"

He straightened his shoulders, which told me I was right on the money.

"Yeah...um... Where did you get that?"

"None of your business. You *sure* you don't remember her name?"

He shook his head, slowly. A lie and I knew it.

"You're lying. You damned well *do* remember her name. Give it to me now. Somebody's trying to mess with me and I want to know who and why. And you're involved, you mangy satyr. First you show up in my bathroom, sneaking around trying to steal my hair. Then I hear you and your brothers are trying to ruin my business before I even manage to open the doors. What the *fuck* are you up to, Ralph?" I wasn't known for having an even temper, and Ralph's eyes widened as he pushed himself back against the wall.

"Take it easy, Maddy—"

"I'll take it easy all over your furry ass, you idiot.

Tell me what the hell's going on!"

Ralph's musky scent flared as he narrowed his eyes. He lurched to his feet.

"If you can't take the heat, stay out of the fire. And if you can't handle competition, stay out of the bed-and-breakfast business. The Heart's Desire has been around for three decades and now you barge in, determined to yank our clients away from us. Who the hell do you think you are?" His nose was pinched and his face was getting red.

I gave him a withering stare. "Are you *serious*? I'm not after your clientele. I'm not running a *whorehouse* at the Bewitching Bedlam. Your 'clients' are horny hardups. My B&B is out for the tourists—not sex-starved satyr-fets."

"Maddy, calm down—Glenna is coming out from the back." Sandy tugged on my sleeve.

I froze. Sandy was right. This wasn't the right place to start an altercation. Turning away, I intended to apologize to Glenna when Ralph shoved me from behind. I lurched forward, into the crowd who had been staring at us. One of the men kindly caught me before I fell but not before Ralph stomped forward, his eyes blazing.

"You shut your mouth, Maudlin Gallowglass, or I'll shut it for you. I swear, I'll make sure your business goes under and you with it!" He was raving now, his arms flailing wildly as he did his best impression of a windmill gone amok.

"Break it up."

I knew who it was, before I even turned around. Sure enough, Derek Lindsey broke through the crowd. A member of the Majestic Mountain

Squad—a league of search-and-rescue witches who specialized in healing on the island of Bedlam—he was also one of the senior officers in Bedlam's sheriff's department.

Derek turned to Ralph. "Did you just threaten Maudlin?"

Ralph sputtered, but instantly deflated, backing away. "It's all talk. Just a friendly little spat between competitors."

"That's not what it sounded like to me," Derek said. "Ralph, get out. You come back later and I don't want to hear another peep out of you. You already got on the sheriff's bad side with that last bender you went on. You'll be cooling it off in a cell if she catches word that you've been raising hell again."

Ralph muttered something unintelligible, but grabbed his jacket and stomped out of the bakery.

I stepped delicately to the side. "I'm sorry, Lieutenant Lindsey."

"Just watch out. The Greyhoofs have been in and out of trouble for years. They're not the calmest heads in town." With that, he tipped his hat and took his place in line again.

Sandy let out a soft breath beside me. "Maddy, you should be careful. I don't trust Ralph and his brothers. They're always up to no good."

"I don't know. I think they're more bluster than brawn, to be honest. But I'll be careful. I promise." But something told me that Ralph and his brothers weren't going to let this drop.

Chapter 4

AFTER DROPPING OFF Sandy at her car, I headed for my last stop before going home.

Bjorn Kitsa, a fox shifter—also known as a kitsune—was my real estate agent and friend. He was flamboyant, gay, and fabulous. Bjorn wore designer suits to tennis matches, he drove a Jaguar, but beneath that snobby, elitist exterior, he had a heart of gold. He worked with the local food bank, was on the board of a nonprofit children's cancer society, and had personally paid off four mortgages belonging to aging widows who would otherwise have been thrown out of their homes. The latter was only known to a few of us, and he had pledged us to secrecy.

Bjorn was six-two, lean and fit, and he had a shocking head of red hair that tumbled to mid-back. He had his father's striking green eyes, and his mother's porcelain complexion. His mother had been Norwegian, his father was Irish. He wore both heritages with pride.

"Maddy, love. What's up?" he asked as I peeked into his office. He owned the Bedlam Realty office and was determined that every customer who walked through the door would be treated with respect and leave satisfied, even if he determined he couldn't help them. To that end, Bjorn had endeared himself to other real estate agents around the area and they sent a surprising amount of business his way.

"I just want to talk over a few of the licensing aspects of owning a B&B—make certain that I have everything filled out correctly. You have some time?"

"For you, I have all the time in the world." He motioned to the chair opposite his and we dove into business.

An hour later, I slid into my car, ready to head home. But all the way, I had the strange feeling I was being followed. I glanced in my rear mirror several times, but saw nothing.

As I pulled into my driveway, a call came in from Rose. Surprised to hear from her again so soon, I answered the phone.

"Maddy, I have a big favor to ask you. Can I come over later tonight? I need your help with a spell. I just got word that my sister is missing and you're one of the best at Finding spells."

Technically, she was right, and the plea in her voice was more than I could stand. I could talk to Aegis about the picture later. Right now, a covenmate needed my help, and a missing sister took precedence over a business dispute.

"Sure, come over around eight o'clock. Bring something with you that she touched, or a picture of her. We'll see what we can do." With her thanks still ringing in my ears, I gathered my purchases and headed inside. The sun had already set—it was after four-thirty—and I was surprised to find a note from Aegis.

Had to go out early. Will head straight to rehearsal tonight. Don't wait up for me. Love, ~Aegis

I stared at the paper, wondering if I should join him after Rose arrived. But I was still irked about the picture and my confrontation with Ralph had done nothing to soothe my mood. I decided to savor a long bubble bath, eat a leisurely dinner, and then help Rose. Then, if I wanted to, I'd crash their rehearsal.

By the time I saw Rose out the door—Finding spell in hand—I was too tired to bother going out again. Twenty-five degrees and fresh snow convinced me to forget about everything for the night and head upstairs to bed, where I cuddled with Bubba under the quilt. For once, I slept like the dead.

I WOKE TO find a dozen roses arranged in a vase by my bed, along with a box of chocolates and a handwritten note that said, "I love you. Aegis."

Stretching, I blinked as a ray of sunlight splashed through the French doors to wash across my bed. Blue sky winked through the windows, and for once, I was thrilled to see the hint of sunshine.

"What time is it?" I glanced down at Bubba, who was licking one paw. He rolled over on his back, exposing his belly as he let out a rumbling purr. "No, I am not rubbing your belly. But you look like you've been fed. Did Aegis feed you, Bub?"

"Purp." The trilling purr rumbled through his meow.

"He did? I assume he went to bed on time." One look at the sunbeam and I changed that to "I *hope* he went to bed."

"*Mrow,*" Bubba answered in the affirmative.

"Good." My irritation from the evening before had evaporated. I loved the gloom and rain of the area, but the sun was a welcome sight for a change. I slid from beneath the covers and padded into the bathroom for a shower, cringing at the icy chill on the floor.

This time, I locked the bathroom door.

After I was warm, clean, and smelling like peppermint, I dressed in a pair of comfortable black jeans that didn't sausage-squeeze my ample butt and thighs and a plum V-neck sweater. I fastened a black leather belt around my waist and slipped into a pair of black suede slouch boots. They were almost flat with good traction, and they came up to mid-calf over my jeans. Side zippers allowed me to easily pull them off and on.

I clattered downstairs, humming to myself. Before I had breakfast, I decided to go out and pick up the paper. The paperboy always threw it into the backyard rather than bringing it around front. At first I thought it had something to do with him being afraid of Aegis, but given vampires slept in the daylight, it was probably just laziness.

"Bubba, I'm going to grab the paper. I'll be right back."

"Mrow." Bubba was lounging in a sunbeam, lazily batting a catnip toy. I wasn't sure how old the cjinn was—we had met around seventy-five years back—but he seemed content to mostly act like a cat.

I opened the sliding door that led from the kitchen out to the patio. As I stepped out into the cold, crystalline morning, scanning for the paper, I realized there was something in the yard, near the back fence. I couldn't quite make out what it was, so I began to wade through the fresh snow until I reached a point where I could see clearly. There, frozen and surrounded by a stain of red frozen ice, lay Rose, dead as could be.

AFTER THAT, THINGS got a little fuzzy. It wasn't that I had never seen a dead body. You don't live close to four hundred years without running into a few corpses here and there, and I admit, I was responsible for more than a few of them. But facing the death of a friend was a far different experience. I stood there, unable to process what I was seeing as a whole. Instead, I noticed the frozen pool of blood surrounding her. The way her coat spread out meant she hadn't buttoned it shut against the cold. The curious turn of one ankle—if she was alive, it would hurt like hell, so she must have twisted it fighting back. A crow was perched on a branch, eyeing Rose with speculative eyes, and I waved it away.

"Tell the Morrígan she can wait," I said hoarsely. "And if you aren't her servant, then get the fuck out of my yard." Crows were harbingers of the Morrígan, but they were also opportunistic scavengers.

The crow cocked its head and flew away. I slowly crossed the snow to Rose, kneeling beside her. She wasn't a friend on the scale that Sandy was, but she *was* a coven-mate and I liked her a lot. Finding her dead in my yard was as big a shock as I had had in a long time.

I tried to make sure that I didn't touch anything near her so I wouldn't contaminate the crime scene, but it was obvious she had been there for a while. The blood around her had frozen and she was covered with snow. I reached out, intending on feeling for a pulse, but then stopped. I knew she was dead. Without a word, I rose and pulled out my cell phone.

My first call was to Sandy. The moment she came on the line, I blurted out, "Can you come over? I just found Rose dead in my yard."

After a frozen pause, she exploded. "What the hell? What happened? Did she have an accident?"

"I think she was murdered." I stared down at the body, unable to look away. It was almost as though

I was afraid she'd vanish if I closed my eyes.

"Get away from there! The murderer may come back. Have you called the cops yet?"

"No, but I will right after this. Please, come over. I'll go inside, but Sandy, I think she's been out here since last night." I rang off, promising to phone her back if anything else happened before she got here.

On the way back to the house, I called the police. Delia Walters was the sheriff. She was a werewolf, and exceptionally good at ferreting out secrets. There weren't many unsolved crimes in Bedlam, and people generally thought twice before pulling some stupid stunt they could get arrested for. She had been sheriff for the past twenty years, taking over from her grandfather, who had finally retired.

Inside, I searched for something to keep myself busy. I put the kettle on for tea and made some toast to calm my stomach. I was just pouring the boiling water into the teapot when the doorbell rang.

"Where's the body?" Delia was a flurry of movement. She was short but sturdy, and her tawny hair was caught back in a tidy braid. Delia was all business. She was so focused on her work that she had rejected getting married or having children.

"Out back. It's Rose Williams." I caught the surprise on her face.

"Rose? Who could want *her* dead? Have you told anybody else about this?"

I could see the wheels turning in her head.

"I have no idea, and I only told Sandy. She's on her way over." I showed her through the kitchen. "I just made tea. Would you like a cup?"

"After I have a look around. This isn't a social call."

Yep, blunt to the point.

"Right. I didn't even think." Actually, that was the truth. I was running on autopilot and I realized that I was suffering a mild shock. "Out here." This time, I stopped to shrug into my coat before leading Delia out to Rose.

She stopped me about six yards away. "Those are your footprints?"

I nodded. "Yes. I didn't see any others around when I came out here. Even Rose's were covered up, so I'm assuming she's been here since she left my house last night."

Delia motioned for me to stay back as she used my footprints to get to the body. She knelt and felt for a pulse. "Dead, all right. Did you touch anything?"

"No. I was going to check for a pulse but then thought that the chances of her being alive were pretty minute." I wanted to sit down, but even the nearby bench was covered with snow. I wiped it off anyway and gingerly sat on the edge.

Delia frowned, looking intently at Rose. Then she stared at me for a moment until I felt uncomfortably scrutinized. "You're wearing the same coat, it looks like."

"Right. We joked about it a week or so ago. I guess we have similar tastes." I paused, then lowered my voice. "*Had*...similar tastes."

Standing up, Delia glanced around the yard. "So, the backyard. That your driveway? I see three cars."

"The CR-V is mine, the black Corvette belongs to Aegis, and the silver hatchback is Rose's." I shrugged. "That pretty much guarantees she was here all night. Look at the snow buildup on all of our cars. Aegis's has the least amount. He was at a show. I guess he must have thought Rose stayed over."

Delia stood, glancing at her watch. "The coroner should be here any minute." She was still staring at Rose's body. "You know, from this angle, she and you could be indistinguishable. She has long dark hair like you do, you're both about the same height, and you're wearing the same coat. She was in your yard." She drifted off, leaving the thought unfinished, but I knew what she was getting at.

"Are you saying that you think that whoever murdered her thought she was me? That I was the intended target?" The thought hadn't crossed my mind but now it was implanted firmly into my brain, and I pulled my coat tighter. "Who would want to murder me?" But even as I said it, I had to admit that I'd led a checkered-enough past that there were more than enough people who would be happy to see me take a nosedive.

"Who would want to murder Rose? The girl was young and well-liked in the community." Delia's phone beeped and she glanced at it, then texted something. "The coroner is here. I told Jif to come around through the side gate. He's brought his team."

Within moments, the coroner and his forensics team had taken over the backyard. I answered their questions one by one. *Why had Rose been here? When did she leave? Had I noticed anything odd? When did Aegis return home? Did he come through the backyard, usually?*

"He gets back late from shows and rehearsals. He might have come in by the front door, but it's more likely that he came through his private entrance, which means he wouldn't be crossing through the backyard." I refrained from telling them that the entrance to his secret passage was near the garage, which was detached from the house, over by the cars. It wasn't safe for anybody to know the location for a vampire's private entrance.

"We'll talk to him when he wakes up tonight. If I need him to, he can show me his private entrance at that time." Delia understood why I was being obtuse. Werewolves and vampires really didn't like each other—the old-wives' tales were true—but they worked together as need be.

"Right." As I watched, the forensics team took photographs, then slowly turned Rose over. The blood had come from her stomach, and it was frozen into a sheet of ice attached to her shirt. The team carefully broke the ice away, bagging it in case there was any evidence that might disappear if the ice melted before they got back to the hospital. As they separated the ice from her skin, a massive gash appeared in her stomach.

"Well, we know where she bled out."

"Yeah," I said, drawing a deep breath. The wound was ugly and vicious. "Is the knife still there?" I couldn't see a blade anywhere, but maybe it had been lodged in the snow beneath her.

"Nope," one of the men said. "Nothing that we can see. We'll have to go through the yard to see if the murderer dropped anything."

"That's fine," I said, staring at Rose's astonished expression. Her death mask was heartbreaking. "I can't believe someone murdered her in my yard. This is going to break her family's heart. They're already facing the disappearance of one daughter." Rose was one of the rare people who had been born onto the island. She was still quite young—at least for a witch—at only sixty-seven. But she had been talented and quick to learn.

"What the hell?" Sandy appeared from the kitchen, coming out the sliding-glass doors. She stopped, gaping as she watched the men examining Rose. "Oh good gods. Somebody *stabbed* her?"

"Apparently so, but please keep this to yourself," the sheriff said. "Let me make the official announcement. I don't want you or Maddy talking to anybody about the death yet. We need to keep as much information private as possible so that we have a leg up on the murderer." Delia tucked her notepad and pencil in her pocket, then nodded toward the kitchen. "How about that tea? I'd like to ask you both some more questions about Rose. The boys can finish up here just fine."

As we tromped back into the kitchen, I realized I was shivering and it was from more than the cold. The sight of Rose's face, and the realization that she was well and truly dead, had finally hit. As the shock wore off, my nerves were fraying.

Sandy must have noticed, because she steered me over to the kitchen table and motioned for

Delia to join me. "I'll bring the tea. You both look like you could use some food. Do you have any cookies or cake?" She poked her head in one of the cupboards.

"Yeah, there are cookies in the cookie jar over there—the one shaped like a black cat." I slid onto the banquette below the window that looked outside. The kitchen table had four chairs around it, and the banquette provided room for two more.

Sandy brought over the tea and cookies, then cups and saucers from the cupboard. After she poured our tea, she settled down opposite me. Delia was to my right.

"I was telling Maddy here that, in the dark, with the same coat, she and Rose could be mistaken for one another." Delia sipped the tea and, grimacing, pulled the sugar bowl over and scooped two heaping spoons into her cup.

Sandy looked from Delia to me, then back at Delia. "Are you saying you think Maddy was the actual target? That Rose somehow got in the way and was mistaken for her?"

"The thought crossed my mind, and now it's nagging at me. I usually find that when that happens, I'm on to something. Do either of you know anything about Rose's private life? Does she have a boyfriend? Was anybody bothering her? Stalking her, maybe?"

"Sandy knows her better than I do. I knew Rose from being in the same coven, but we usually get right to work at the meetings. We talk socially after for a while, but until I moved here a few weeks back, I didn't have much of a chance to see her."

Sandy nodded. "That's true. Rose has always been private. She lives—lived—with her mother and father, and I don't think she's been dating anybody for a while. Her parents might know."

"What about past boyfriends? Any of them ever show up at the coven meetings unannounced?" Delia was taking notes as she drank her tea.

I lifted my cup, breathing deeply as the steam of the peppermint filled my senses. I closed my eyes, willing it to take away the chill. I was cold to the bone, not just from being outside, but from the shock, and now the thought that I might have been the intended victim was making the cold settle in worse.

"No, not that I can remember. Most people are pretty respectful about the meetings. I think the last person Rose was seriously dating moved to the Bay Area." Sandy squinted. Worry lines crisscrossed her forehead. "You'd have to ask her parents if she was seeing anybody new. Rose might actually have a diary somewhere. We encourage all our coven members to write down their experiences."

"You said she was here asking help for a spell?" Delia turned back to me.

"Yes, she asked me to help her create a Finding spell. Her sister has gone missing and their family is worried sick. When she got here, she explained that her sister had moved to New York. Two weeks ago, all communications suddenly stopped. They contacted the police there, but there's no clue of where Lavender—Rose's sister—went. The Williamses filed a missing person's report but there are so many missing people in the city that the cops don't have time to hunt down every adult who vanishes."

"Why did she ask you to create the spell? Why didn't she do it?"

"Because I'm good at it and Rose knew that. She and her family are too emotionally invested in the situation. While she was here, I created a Finding spell specifically aimed at finding Lavender. Rose was taking it home so that she and her parents could cast it. Their lineage is kitchen witchery—they don't do hardcore magic." I stopped. "Wait, did she have the spell with her? She should have had a paper with the instructions all written out, and a small bag of spell components on her. I gave her everything she'd need."

"Let me talk to Jif." Delia headed out back where the forensics team seemed to be wrapping up things.

Sandy leaned across the table. "She's right. I can feel it, Maddy. Whoever killed Rose thought she was *you*. Mark my words, somebody's out to get you."

I didn't want to agree, but it was looking like that might be the case.

Delia returned, rubbing her hands together. "Colder out there than a witch's tit. No offense intended," she added, grinning. "Well, they found her purse, her wallet, the note, and spell components. All her identification was there. In fact, it looks like robbery wasn't the motive, because her credit cards and cash were still in her purse."

"The spell wouldn't be worth stealing. It was

geared toward someone in particular. And if somebody really needed a Finding spell and couldn't afford it, I'd work one up for them anyway. Everybody knows that—at least everybody who has had any contact with our coven. It's not like I'm a total stranger to Bedlam." I didn't like the direction this was taking.

Delia made a few more notes, then asked, "How about you? Anything you want to tell me about Ralph Greyhoof?"

Startled, I blinked. "What? I don't think he had anything to do with this. I mean, yes, he was here Saturday and yes, I did find him in my bathroom while I was taking a shower, but..." Then, I realized she was talking about the incident at the Calou Bakery, where Derek Lindsey had broken up our fight.

"You mean that wasn't the first time you and Ralph got into it? Tell me everything that happened." By the tone of her voice, I knew she wasn't going to take no for an answer.

I let out a long sigh. "Ralph showed up in my bathroom Saturday morning. I caught him trying to steal hair out of my hairbrush and put the fear of the gods in him."

Delia's gaze flickered. "Even I know what that means and I don't work with magic. So, what happened?"

"We got into an argument. I accused him of trying to throw a hex on the B&B and he said that he had been paid to steal my hair by a woman that he thought was a vampire." I realized that I had better tell her the whole story. I told her about the woman and showed her the anonymous text of the painting with her picture in it. Dreading that this might drag Aegis into the mess, I tried to skim over the fact that he was in the painting, but Delia noticed.

"How much do you know about your boyfriend?"

"As much as I need to right now." I prickled. I didn't like the direction the conversation was suddenly going.

"Hold on." She moved away, pulling out her cell phone. When she returned, she said, "I put out an APB on Ralph Greyhoof and called in for a warrant to search his house and the inn. If he's really that angry about you opening up a bed and breakfast, then there's no telling what he might do."

"Ralph isn't the kind to hurt somebody else. Trust me, I know." I didn't want yet another reason for the Greyhoof family to hate me. And as mean as Ralph could be, he wasn't a murderer.

"You let me be the judge of that." She stopped as her phone rang. "Hold on."

While she was over by the stove, talking, I leaned toward Sandy. "We can't let this get out of hand. Even if somebody is targeting me, that's no reason to assume it's Ralph. Hell, he's a perv, and he's shady as hell in some ways, but I don't think he's a murderer. He wouldn't kill me over the fact that I'm running a B&B, would he?"

Sandy pressed her lips together, then shrugged. "You know satyrs. They get wound up and go off all half-cocked. They're so full of hormones that it's hard to predict what they're going to do. I wouldn't put much past them. Hell, I gather that Ralph and his brother George had a big to-do over a woman a couple years back and Ralph put George in the hospital. Rammed him with those damned horns of his. Of course, George didn't press charges, and they left the hospital arm in arm, but if he's capable of that, who knows what he might do if he really believes you're out to ruin his business."

Delia returned. "They just picked up Ralph. I've sent someone to search his house. I'm going in to have a little talk with him now, so you need to keep quiet about this for the time being." She finished her tea in one gulp, then snagged a couple of the cookies, biting into one. "Until we figure this out, you should be cautious," she said, wiping crumbs off her mouth. "If somebody *is* out to kill you and it's not Ralph, then whoever it is, they're still out there. For now, watch your step, Maudlin. I'll talk to Rose's parents after I speak with Ralph. I'll be in touch."

As she left, I noticed that Rose's body was gone from out back but team members were still combing through the yard, looking for evidence. I poured another cup of tea and sat back, wondering what the hell to do next.

"It seems to me that we have two separate issues here. Three, rather. First: why did Ralph try to steal your hair and did he really do so at the behest of the blonde in the painting? Second: who *is* the woman in the painting and why is Aegis with her? Third: who killed Rose?" Sandy used a napkin to wipe up a few drops of spilled tea.

"More than three. If the person who killed Rose was actually aiming for me, why do they want me dead?" Obviously, this question was top in my mind. I had been threatened before, but for the past couple hundred years, nobody had tried to act on it. I'd been on the run from witch hunters at one time. They would have first tortured, then killed me if they had managed to catch me. But the witch hunters were long dead for the most part, and it wasn't legal to kill witches anymore. At least, not in the US, and not in the UK.

"Is there any way you've met this blonde and just don't remember?" Sandy brought up the picture on my phone. "Doesn't she ring *any* bells?"

I slowly shook my head. "No. I honestly don't have a clue who she is."

"Well, if you want my opinion, you should put a stronger lock on the door, get rid of the vampire, and find some strapping bodyguard to watch over you." Franny appeared in the middle of the table, making me jump.

"Crap!" Sandy almost tipped over her chair.

Franny laughed. "Scared of little old me?" But then she stopped, staring over Sandy's shoulder at the picture. "I haven't seen her in a while."

"You know who that woman is?" I stared at Franny.

"Not really, but I've seen her. She came to visit a couple times before you moved in. She's Aegis's ex-girlfriend, Rachel."

And with that, she moved out from the table into the center of the room.

Chapter 5

"AEGIS'S EX-GIRLFRIEND? WHAT the hell? Why didn't you tell me about her before?" Even as I said it, I realized how ridiculous that sounded. Franny didn't know what had been going on.

"I assumed that he told you about her. It's not like he's fresh out of the cradle. Aegis *has* been around a few thousand years. I figured you knew all about his past liaisons." Hands on her hips, Franny glared at me.

"Right, right." I took a deep breath and tried to calm down. "You had no way of knowing, Franny. I'm sorry. But we've been trying to figure out who this woman is since yesterday."

"Oh. Well, you're right, I didn't know. But I'm happy I could help." Franny seemed to be mollified. In fact, she looked downright jolly. I realized she didn't get many opportunities to feel useful anymore.

"Franny, if you see her in this house, tell me. Please." I wanted to ask her to leave so Sandy and I could discuss what we had just found out, but that would be rude, especially since she had just helped us out. And maybe, just maybe, Franny could be of more help.

"So. *Rachel*, huh? Do you also happen to know her last name?" Sandy seemed to be on the same page I was.

"Oh, no. Vampires don't always use their last names, you know." Franny was veering into eerily cheerful territory. The grin plastered across her face looked rather manic. The idea of a bipolar ghost intimidated me.

"So she *is* a vampire? That would mesh with what Ralph said." I bit my lip, worrying it between my teeth. "I had better let Delia know about this. Franny, is there anything else about Rachel that might help us? Maybe where she lives?" Then, quickly, I added, "She never lived *here*, did she? With Aegis?"

Franny shook her head. "No. I'd know if she did. I think they had already broken up when he came to live here. I heard Rachel keep begging him to take her back. Well, ordering him. She likes to be in charge. I also heard her talking about Essie Vanderbilt. Apparently they didn't like each other very much."

"None of that is good news." Sandy pushed her tea away. "We need something stronger than tea for this." She moved to the fridge and pulled out a bottle of champagne that was half-full. Pouring two flutes of the sparkling wine, she handed one to me. "To Rose. May Delia find whoever the hell killed her."

"May the gods hear your words. To Rose." I upended the drink. The bubbles tickled my nose and stung my lip where I had accidentally drawn blood. I paused. "If she's trying to get Aegis back, Rachel has plenty of reason to want to get rid of me."

"Yeah. She can't be too happy if she knows about the two of you." Sandy paled. "They should check Rose for bite marks."

I reached for my phone, intending to call Delia, but just then I noticed a commotion outside, near the bushes. One of the forensics team seemed to have found something. He was holding it up, talking loudly to his buddies. I stuffed my phone back in my pocket and tromped through the snow, intent on knowing everything I could about Rose's murder. The tech had already started to bag it before I managed to cross the distance between us, but even from where I stood, I could make out what he was holding.

He turned around as I approached. "I've called Sheriff Walters. She'll be back in about half an hour."

Quickly, I backtracked inside the house. "Damn it, he found a set of panpipes."

"Ralph's?" Sandy's eyes widened.

"Ten to one, yes."

"Could Delia be right? Could Ralph have killed Rose, thinking she was you?"

"No. I refuse to believe he would do that. Ralph's *not* a killer. We have to tell Delia about Rachel. She's on her way. Until she gets here, I guess we just wait." I could call her but since she was coming back, it seemed easier to wait. The matter was getting entirely too convoluted, entirely too quickly.

A thought struck me. "Franny, I know you can't go outside, but by any chance were you looking out the back window last night? Did you see anybody out there? Maybe the person who attacked Rose?"

She moved to the window, looking out. "Just because I'm a ghost doesn't mean I have spectacular vision. Nor does it mean that I'm always spying on everybody." But then, she let out a long sigh. "No, I didn't notice anything. I wish I had. I liked Rose. She was sweet and polite to me." Franny sounded wistful. "Do you think she might come back here as a ghost? I haven't seen her but that doesn't mean she won't wake up pretty soon."

"I hope to hell not. The coven will hold a ceremony for her so she's free to move on."

Franny shrugged. "I have to admit, since you bought the house, at least I've had people to talk to. Aegis wouldn't talk to me at all before you got here. He tried to pretend that I didn't exist. The same with Rachel. But you...*you* acknowledge my presence."

I winced, thinking it wasn't possible for her to sound any lonelier.

"That's because you're the best house ghost I could hope for." I forced a smile. "Thanks to you, we know about Rachel, even if we don't know where to find her." I stopped myself. Franny wasn't an oracle, and she wasn't a crystal ball and I didn't want to make her feel guilty. Guilt like that usually didn't do anybody any good. "I'm sorry. I didn't mean it to sound like that. I know very well that you aren't here to keep track of everything that happens. And I'm sorry you had to spend so many years alone."

Franny moved over to sit on the banquette. At least, she did a good job of appearing like she was sitting down, though we could see the seat right through her. "That's all right. I also realize that it's hard for people to think of me as a real person. Get slapped with the label of ghost and people assume you have no feelings, or that you're just some misty vaporous rerun."

Sandy gave me a sideways glance. I could tell she was thinking what I was—Franny sorely needed friends, and maybe she had been such a pain in the ass because she was so lonely. "It must be very difficult going through your days as a spirit. Has anybody tried to free you before?"

Franny shrugged. "Oh yes, several times. But it seems that there's something keeping me bound to the house. Nobody's ever taken the time to figure out just what it is. And I certainly don't know or I'd be gone by now."

Curious, I asked, "What do you remember from your last days, and right after you...right after the accident?" Even though we all knew she was dead, saying it to her face felt wrong.

She closed her eyes, then wistfully said, "I remember telling my mother I wasn't going to marry the man she had chosen for me. And then I ran to my room. I was reading a book. I did so love to read—it wasn't new, but I hadn't read it yet. I remember very well—the book was *Clermont*, by one of my favorite authors. Regina Maria Roche. She was a bestseller at the time, you know. Anyway,

I was so wrapped up in the book that when the dinner bell rang, I continued to read as I headed downstairs. But I didn't see that one of the serving girls had dropped a piece of coal on the stair and I stepped on it and tumbled down—all the way down." She paused, wiping a hand across her eyes. "The staircase didn't have a railing or carpet like it does now."

I winced. The thought of tumbling down the stairs like that was horrifying. The staircase was steep, though wide.

"As I dropped my book and found myself falling, I remember being shocked—as though I had discovered some terrifying new thing and didn't know what to make of it. After that, I remember one sharp pain, and then everything went black. I don't know how long later, but I woke up and I was standing on the staircase, but nobody seemed to realize I was there."

"That must have been horrible," Sandy said.

Franny nodded. "It was. My mother...my grandmother and sisters...my father—they all ignored me when I tried to talk to them. I couldn't go outside. When I went into the parlor I saw a casket, and there was my body in it. After that, it got misty again until I was standing in the kitchen and somebody else was there. The kitchen was different and I realized that I was dead, and that I was in the house but my family was gone."

"What did you do?"

"I tried to contact the woman, but she couldn't seem to see me. People came and went. The house changed hands several times. Some saw me and were afraid. Others saw me but couldn't talk to me. Either way, until you moved in, I pretty much lived an isolated life. Afterlife?" She cocked her head. "Do you know why I'm trapped here? I'm not sure what waits beyond these walls, but I'd like to find out."

I thought of what it must be like to be a ghost, trapped without anybody to talk to. Franny had an active and curious mind. She had died reading. The thought of her stuck without anything to do but able to remain as congenial as she was made me terribly sad.

"I don't know why, but when I get things sorted out with Rose's death, I'll see what I can find out. Would you like that?" It felt like over the years *somebody* should have at least looked into it.

She clapped her hands. "Would you? Really? Oh, thank you, Maudlin. I take back every mean thing I thought about you because you wouldn't paint the kitchen pink." She paused. "Somebody's coming up the front walkway. I'll excuse myself, if you don't mind."

And, before I could say a word, she vanished.

It was Delia. She gave me a polite nod, then headed out to the back where she talked to her men and looked at the panpipes. A few minutes later, she came back inside and sat down at the kitchen table. "I suppose you've figured out who they belong to?"

"I saw, yes. Panpipes."

"They're engraved. Those things don't come cheap."

"Ralph's?" I wanted her to say "No," but she

nodded.

"Yeah, they have his name on them. And they have blood on them. We'll have it analyzed, but ten to one it's Rose's blood. I think we have our killer. And we have a motive." She scuffed the toe of her boot on the floor. "I was hoping it wouldn't be him. I've always liked Ralph, even though he and his brothers are hotheads."

"I have more information for you to check out. I found out who the woman in the picture is." I told her what Franny had said. "So, she's got motive to hurt me, too. You should check Rose's body for fang marks."

"We beat you to it. Nothing. She was stabbed at close range and bled out from those wounds. Not a fang mark on her. No, I think her killer is someone who's still alive." Delia pushed herself to her feet. "Okay, I need to head to the station so I can question Ralph. I can't know for certain, but I'm pretty sure you're safe now."

This was all moving a little too fast for my taste. "If Rachel was involved, she might still be after me."

"There's no evidence of a vampire attack on Rose. I can't hunt down a vamp because she wants your boyfriend. We have no proof yet that Ralph was commissioned to steal your hair."

"Why would he say that if it wasn't true?"

"To throw suspicion off of himself and onto somebody else. If he wanted your hair to have a hex worked against you, it would make sense to say somebody paid him to do it when you caught him in the act." She was beginning to look a little irritated and I realized she thought I was questioning her judgment.

"But how could he describe her in such detail?"

"He told you a blond pretty woman asked him. He threw in the idea that she *might* be a vampire—he didn't know for sure. That's vague enough to chalk up to coincidence. And when you showed him the picture, what better chance to divert the attention to somebody else?"

"But it doesn't track—"

Sounding downright grumpy now, Delia stood, adjusting her jacket. "It tracks well enough for me to arrest him. I have to go. I advise you to remain cautious but don't get paranoid. I'll call you after I talk to Ralph. Meanwhile, steer clear of the Greyhoof brothers. They might all be in on this." With a glowering frown, before I could say another word, she turned and headed out to the backyard to her forensics team, who was wrapping up their search.

I looked over at Sandy. "I know Ralph didn't do it."

"Okay. I'll back you on that. But how are you going to prove it?"

I shrugged. "I have no idea. I guess I'll wait to see what Ralph tells her and go from there. Meanwhile, I need to talk to Aegis about Rachel. How do I bring her up?"

The last thing I wanted was to start the ex-from-hell discussion. He knew about Craig, but I had purposely left things vague so that Aegis couldn't decide my ex needed an etiquette lesson. I felt fine sending a whammy or two Craig's way. But sending a vampire to do my dirty business was a whole different ball of wax.

I glanced at the clock. It was almost noon. The entire morning had been spent steeped in death, but my stomach was rumbling and I was feeling a little light-headed. The champagne hadn't helped, either, although one glass barely tickled my nose.

"I need food. I'm tempted to go out to lunch but the news about Rose's death has probably spread and I really don't want to answer any questions." I opened the fridge. "Want some eggs? I'm not much of a cook but I can fry an egg."

"No, and neither do you. Let me take care of lunch." Sandy pulled out her phone. "Alex, can you run over to the Clam Shack for me? We want two large orders of fish and chips. Bring them over to the Bewitching Bedlam—yes, Maddy's place. Also, two side salads and two cups of clam chowder." She paused. "Why not? Rolls sound good too. And love, if you could make that order stat, there's a twenty-dollar tip in it for you."

Alex was Sandy's personal assistant. Sandy was independently wealthy. Her ex owned a four-star hotel and restaurant, and together, they had parlayed that into a chain of upscale eateries before Bart came out and found his soul mate in a twenty-two-year-old waiter.

After they divorced, the pair remained friends. Sandy was the CEO and on the board of directors of the corporation, and the divorce settlement was more than fair. She spent most of her time in private study and volunteering for several local charities. She also volunteered for the local literary foundation and ran book drives to buy new books for low-income children.

She tucked her phone back in her pocket. "Lunch is on the way. Now, why don't you go wash your face and I'll make us a couple of hot rum toddies."

"Not all problems can be solved with a drink," I said, but grinned. We had been party-hearty buddies for a long time and I didn't foresee that stopping any time soon. "Make mine spiced, okay?"

As I retreated to the powder room, I thought about Ralph. Could he actually be behind Rose's murder? Was he so mad at me that he would kill in order to save the Heart's Desire Inn? But that didn't make sense. Even if I cut into his business, he and his brothers offered plenty of services that I didn't—and I never planned to. There were other hotels and motels on the island. It wasn't like I was the only upstart. Ralph hadn't gone off at them.

But—they weren't just a hop and a skip from his inn. And what if his business was already on the decline? The economy didn't offer as much incentive for travel lately. And suppose some of the Pretcom visitors were here on official business? It would look better to their superiors to stay at a respectable bed and breakfast than at what amounted to an orgiastic brothel. Really, when you got down to the core of matters, the Heart's Desire was one giant lovely brothel for both men and women.

Shaking my head, I tried to clear my thoughts. There were too many variables. I needed to let it go until I knew more. And knowing more included finding out all I could about Rachel. A flash of jealousy raced through me. She was a gorgeous drop-dead blond bombshell. Somehow, I hadn't thought of Aegis as preferring that type, but really, what did I know about his past?

Trying to wash away my worries, I splashed water on my face, taking care not to smear my eyeliner. As I headed back in to the kitchen, it struck me that the afternoon was going to feel like it lasted forever, with sunset a world away.

ALEX BROUGHT OUR lunch and Sandy made me sit down to eat. I wanted to gobble down the food and then head over to the sheriff's office to find out what was going on with Ralph, but Sandy sternly shook her finger at me and backed me into a chair.

Capitulating, I tried to relax and enjoy the food.

"I wonder if Delia took care of notifying Rose's family yet." Sandy poked at her fish with her fork.

"I hadn't even thought about her family. That makes me feel horrible. I'm a selfish person, Sandy." I felt like a heel. Here I was, concerned about how all this affected me when I should be thinking about Rose's family. They had to be going through hell right now. "Should we call them?"

"I'd ask Delia first. We don't want to spring it on them before they've been notified. We can go visit them afterward." Sandy frowned as I pulled out my phone. "Put that away. We can ask her after lunch. Right now you just sit and eat and try to keep yourself from obsessing."

"Easier said than done." I glanced at the clock. It was almost one o'clock. "This sucks. The only thing I had to worry about the other day was what style sofa I should buy. Grand opening's coming up in less than ten days and I still have to furnish half the house. Then one of our coven-mates is found murdered on *my* lawn, my boyfriend suddenly has an ex-girlfriend who might—or might not—be back in town and out to steal him back. And a bunch of horny satyrs are trying to shut down my business by badmouthing me all over the internet."

"We could try to do a Divining spell on Miss Rachel. If you like." Sandy cocked an eyebrow at me. I knew that look. She was egging me on.

"I like how you think." I grinned at her. "We do have several hours before sunset, so we can't very well ask Aegis for help right now. And Delia told us not to call her until she has something for us." I popped a French fry in my mouth, contemplating the idea. The more I thought about it, the better it sounded. "Why not? What have we got to lose?"

Bubba leaped up on my lap. *"Mrowf."*

I looked down at him, ruffling the fur on his head. "No, you cannot help."

"*M'rrow...m'rrow.*" He was being awfully insistent, but the last thing we needed was a cjinn messing around with our magic. Our spells were volatile enough without his help.

"No, you are not allowed in Circle. Sorry, Bub, I love you but no matter how much you play the sympathy card, you're not invited."

"Mmmf." He twitched his tail, flicking it hard against the table. Then, with a deliberately snide

look at me, he stretched up so his front paws were by my plate, grabbed a piece of fish, and darted off my lap, racing around the corner into the living room.

"Hey—" I stopped. It wasn't worth the chase. He'd have scarfed down the food before I could catch him, and it seemed a fair consolation prize.

"You spoil him."

"If he was just a cat, yes, I'd say he's spoiled. But remember, beneath that fuzzy smirk lies a very twisted sense of humor. Bubba likes getting his own way and when he doesn't, he tries to find a way to repay you. A piece of stolen fish is a small price for refusing to let him in on our Circle. Now, if you're serious about this, let's finish lunch and get busy. It's a whole lot better than just sitting around waiting."

Casting a Divining spell didn't offer too many chances for backfiring. Besides, I rather liked taking things into my own hands and the idea of being proactive was always high on my list.

We cleared away the dishes and headed into the parlor, where I shut the door to keep Bubba out. Sandy cleared off the coffee table while I gathered a white candle, a bowl of water that had been charged under the new moon, a crystal ball, and some sea salt. After we arranged everything, Sandy tossed a handful of the salt into the water while I touched the wick of the candle with my finger and whispered, *"Light,"* igniting a steady flame. Sandy cast a quick Circle to keep any astral eavesdroppers from peeking in, as I leaned over the bowl and blew across it.

Breath to water, water to mirror,
Bring that we seek to see so clear.

Sandy sat beside me, leaning in to watch. As the water began to churn into miniature waves throughout the crystal bowl, I brought the image of Rachel's face to my mind and narrowed my attention, focusing only on her.

I seek to know all that I can,
About a specific woman.
Mirror, mirror, water-born,
Hear me and inform.

Then, letting out a long breath, I held my palm over the bowl. The water calmed into a smooth, glassy surface, reflective like any mirror. I pulled my hand back and we waited, watching for any sign of a message.

A moment passed, then another, before finally things began to shift. Rachel's face formed in the water, and then vanished, followed by the image of an old gothic house on the other side of town. Both Sandy and I immediately recognized it.

I groaned. "I do not want to go there."

"I don't either." Sandy frowned. "Ask the mirror if that's the only chance we have to find out what we need."

I frowned, trying to fit the question to a rhyme. The Divining spell worked in rhymes and only rhymes. You could make a near rhyme and get away with it, but if it wasn't a poem, the mirror wouldn't cough up any info.

Mirror, mirror, you show a house,
Is this the only route we can,
Find out about this louse,
Who once dated my man?

Sandy snorted. "Wow. Such eloquence."

"I never claimed to be a poet. *You* make up something, if you don't like it. Anyway, it's not like we're doing a formal incantation. Spells on the fly always come out wonk—" I stopped, motioning for her to be quiet. The mirror was stirring again, revealing yet another image. This time it was of a woman that both of us recognized and neither of us really wanted to see.

"Crap," Sandy said. "Looks like you have a visit to make."

"I'm debating whether it's worth it, especially since Franny said Rachel didn't like Essie very much." Paying a visit on Essie Vanderbilt, the vampire queen of the Pacific Northwest, was the last thing I wanted to do.

Essie lived in a mansion that was reminiscent of the Addams Family house and basically held court from there. Her court was subject to the laws of Bedlam, however, and unlike a number of vampire courts around the nation, Linda, the High Priestess of our coven, kept a strict eye on Essie and her vamps. As vampires went, Essie didn't seem a bad sort, but she liked to play up the ghoulish aspects of her people and always seemed to be skirting just to the right side of the law. There were occasional skirmishes, but Essie always made sure they never quite broke the treaties they had with Bedlam.

"Aegis isn't going to like it if I go visit her. For one thing, he doesn't like her. He told me he thinks she's a pretentious ass. For another, he said that—as far as he knows—while they tend to keep up appearances, Essie isn't as upstanding as the cops want to believe."

Sandy gave me a keen look. "If the vamps aren't keeping to their treaties, they really shouldn't be allowed to live here. Did you ask Aegis if he talked to Linda about this?"

I gave her a long look. "What do *you* think? I'm pretty sure if he did, Essie would find some way to take revenge on him for selling her out. I don't blame him in the least for wanting to keep his mouth shut." But even as I said it, I realized I was crossing a line. If Essie was involved in shady dealings, Linda needed to know, and so did Delia.

"You really don't mean that, do you?" Sandy paused, then, worrying her lip, continued. "I'm going to say something and you aren't going to like it. You let Craig beat you down and change you. You were with him less than ten years and you ended up knuckling under to a blowhard human. And I *do* mean blowhard. You just rediscovered your core, Maddy. You can't let this happen again. Even though Aegis is a vampire and not a human, you have to stick up for yourself and your beliefs this time. Don't let him push you into anything that isn't comfortable."

She was right—I didn't want to hear it. But she was also right in that I needed to avoid falling into the same trap. I had been at a real low point when I met Craig and he took advantage of me. And I had let it happen.

I took a deep breath and let it out slowly. "It really stings to hear you say that. But you're also right about the fact that I have to watch myself. I will say this, though. Aegis has never asked me to cover up anything. He implied that Essie isn't quite as aboveboard as she seems but he's never said anything outright. I'm the one who didn't pursue it. I guess it's easier not to know something and therefore not be responsible for that knowledge. I'll talk to him later tonight. We have to get all this out in the open. But I think I should pay a visit to Essie first. The mirror's pointing us in that direction and it seldom gives wrong advice."

Sandy took my hands. "Maddy, you once were the terror of both villages and the vampires that preyed on them. You were a force that nobody wanted to cross. I'm *not* asking you to become Mad Maudlin again. But you can't swing to the opposite side of the pendulum. You can't let yourself avoid conflict because you're afraid of who you once were. You can be strong, you can rule your life the way you want to without losing control."

As I gazed into her eyes, I said, "This is why you're my best friend. You've always been there for me, *Cassandra*. And you were by my side when we went hunting."

Sandy had been Cassandra during those dark days. She was as wild and rough as I was, and together with Fata Morgana, we hunted down the fiends that were threatening to take over the country, even as we played at crossroads with the witch hunters. We partied harder than all the gods combined. Finally, we decided to come to America. Sandy came west first, and she was the reason I followed. While she settled in Bedlam, I had chosen Seattle.

"Okay. I know you're right. I'll let Mad Maudlin off her leash. Just a little bit." I grinned at her. "Maybe a touch of her craziness is just what the modern world needs. Is just what *I* need."

"Good." Her eyes sparkled. "And don't worry. If I see you swinging too far, I'll let you know. Now, let's get over to Essie's before Aegis wakes up and tries to argue you out of the idea. I need to stop at the post office first, anyway."

As I shrugged into my coat, I wondered about the wisdom of approaching Essie before I talked to Aegis, but impatiently brushed it away. Either way, I needed to know what I was up against. And if he was angry at me for checking up on his ex-girlfriend, then he'd better have a good explanation for why she was in town. As we headed out the door, I tossed one of Bubba's toys into the living room for him.

"Bub, I'm headed out. Keep an eye on the place for me."

"*Mrowf*" was all Bubba had to say in return.

Chapter 6

THE POST OFFICE was slammed. By the time we got through the line, Sandy thought of a couple of other errands she needed to run. When we finally pulled into Essie's driveway, it was already four-thirty. The sun had set and the winter dusk gave the estate a desolate air. It wasn't the same sense of abandonment that my own home had given off when I first set eyes on it. No, Essie's house was deliberately set to look foreboding. If I didn't know that a vampire lived inside, along with her other nest-mates, I would have pegged the place as the haven of an emo-goth family, overdone and melodramatic. But given that the occupants had the bite—literally—to back up the bark, I decided to keep my opinion to myself.

"So, Essie's lair." Sandy stared at the house as I cut the motor and leaned back in my seat.

"Yeah. You ever been here?" I felt like a kid in

a movie who was about to be dared into throwing stones at the creepy old lady's house.

"Do you think I'd keep it from you if I had?" She eyed the place, sounding nervous now that we were here. "They say Essie's freakshow scary."

"That's what they used to say about me, doll." I stared at the house. Making up my mind, I opened my door and stepped out into the drifting snowbanks. Apparently, Essie didn't believe in shoveling her walkway. Of course, given how many visitors voluntarily showed up here, I doubt if she had to worry about lawsuits.

Sandy reluctantly joined me. The yard was fenced, and a gate opened onto the sidewalk leading up to the house. The whole place had an air of desolation, but I had a suspicion it was contrived and not out of neglect. The trees loomed over the mansion—they needed a good trimming and I suppressed a snort. Essie wouldn't appreciate the shadows they provided if one of them came down on her roof. By the looks of the branches, none of them had been trimmed in a long time, and it was doubtful she had hired an arborist to check the stability of their roots.

Sandy pushed close to me. "You think she likes being a vampire?"

"I think we can make bank on that." Skirting the worst of the snow piles on the pathway, we finally reached the porch. The steps were icy and I began to wonder just how much of a test this was. A *You really want to visit me? Prove it* sort of thing.

When we were finally standing in front of the door of the plantation-style house, I glanced at

Sandy. She looked even less thrilled than I was to be here. It wasn't like Essie could hurt us. She knew that her vampire nest was on watch. But she *could* make life uncomfortable.

"All right, let's do this." I looked for a doorbell, but there was only a gargoyle knocker. Shaking my head—the woman was a walking stereotype—I lifted it and knocked. The concussion echoed from within, a thudding noise that reverberated through the heavy door, making it sound like I was using a battering ram. I waited for a moment, then knocked again.

"Nobody's home, let's go," Sandy said, sounding gleeful.

But at that moment, the great door swung open. A butler, of all people, studied us gravely, then gave a little bow, just enough to show respect. "May I help you?"

"My name is Maudlin Gallowglass and this is Cassandra Clauson. We're from the Moonrise Coven and we need to speak with Essie." I decided it was a good time to stand on formality here. Sandy flashed me a quick grin, then cleared her throat and straightened her shoulders.

"Certainly. I'll tell the mistress you're here. Please follow me." He stepped back, ushering us into a gloom-ridden parlor replete with heavy velvet drapes and dark, boxy furniture. I had the feeling I'd stepped back two hundred years in time, given the mood of the room. "Please wait here and do not venture into the rest of the house. We have a few younger members who aren't fully trained in their manners yet." And with that dire warning, the butler vanished, shutting the door behind him. I heard the faint *click* of a lock.

"Think he's locking us in for our own safety?" I asked.

"I don't really want to find out," Sandy said. She shook her head, turning slowly. "I feel like we've landed in the worst B-movie ever. I mean, really, this might have been the fashion in eighteenth-century Scotland out on the windswept moors, but give me a break. Unless Essie's a closet goth girl."

"It does seem a little too on the nose, doesn't it? I wonder what she's like?" I glanced around. "Rachel didn't seem to be all that—" I froze at the sound of swishing from outside the door. Holding up my hand to forestall Sandy from saying anything, I said in a loud, clear voice, "We'll just find out what we need to know and then be on our way." I gave Sandy a studied look and she inclined her head to say she understood.

"What are you making for dinner tonight?"

"Making? *Me?* Nothing. But I think Aegis is frying up a chicken." I cocked my head, straining to hear anything else.

A moment later the door opened and Essie, Queen of the Pacific Northwest Vampires, stepped through. She was wearing a long red and gold dress that looked like it was made out of a Persian rug. Her vibrant red hair was piled high on her head in an elaborate coif of swirls and curls. It must have taken hours to achieve that look, and I wondered if it was lacquered into place with a bottle of hairspray. Even the tendrils coiling down the sides of her face were motionless.

"Good evening, Ms. Gallowglass and Ms. Clauson. I am Essie Vanderbilt. How may I be of service?" She motioned to the sofa. "Please, sit. Would you like some tea? I can have one of my servants fetch you some."

As she took her place in a black velvet wing chair, I sat on the sofa, Sandy sitting next to me. "No, thank you. I appreciate you seeing us on such short notice."

She smiled, but there was no warmth behind those cool brown eyes or the rich crimson of her smiling lips. "Of course. Remember, it is the law of your coven that I be available if you have need to ask me questions. I cannot refuse."

She was correct. The Moonrise Coven could make things extremely uncomfortable and unsafe for the local vampires if need be. But Linda continually reminded us that we should work with the vampires, but never, ever trust them. Of course, I was caught between a rock and a hard place when it came to Aegis, but I preferred to overlook that issue.

"I've come to ask you about a possible member of your nest. I need to know everything I can find out about her. Her name is Rachel. Here's a picture of a painting that was done of her." I held out my phone, the photo of the painting pulled up.

Essie glanced at it, a cool smile on her lips. "Ah yes, Rachel. She is, I believe, the ex-paramour of your boyfriend, Ms. Gallowglass?"

I tried not to blink or show any emotion. "Yeah, she is. Is she a part of your nest?"

"No. She's not allowed in my nest. She's a rogue,

coming and going as she will, but not protected under rights of any treaties I make. She's unwelcome in my court." Strictly all business. With perhaps, a touch of warning behind the words.

Well, that was clear enough. No love lost between the two.

"Do you know if she's currently on the island?" I caught Essie's gaze and held it, even though I knew that wasn't exactly the best idea.

Her eyes pierced my thoughts and I had the sudden feeling she could read right into me. After a brief pause, she said flatly, "Yes, she's around. She asked for an audience, but I refused."

"You refused to even talk to her? May I ask why?"

"I don't like rogues, for one thing. Your boyfriend is also a rogue but *he* doesn't cause trouble for the Fallen. Rachel, on the other hand, has been a problem in the past. A word of caution, Mad Maudlin."

I must have looked startled because she let out a snort.

"Of course we know who you are. Who you *were*. When one of the most dangerous vampire hunters from the past shows up to live in our neighborhood, it pays to know all we can. I'm well aware of what you and your...friends...were capable of. Though that may be in the past, I advise you to watch out for Rachel. She's aligned to no one but her own desires. And when she decides she wants something, she's like a crazed rottweiler."

Her dark eyes flashing, she leaned toward me, placing an icy hand on my own. "Rachel is obsessed with Aegis. I warn you because she's likely to stop at nothing to win him back. And I do not want my nest indicted along with her. We have no truck with her."

I studied Essie. Even though she was cooperating, it was obvious she wasn't happy about doing so. There was something more there, though I doubted we could pry it out of Essie. But when she said Rachel's name, there was a flash of ruthlessness there that I recognized. It was the ruthlessness when one talked about a hated rival. Essie reminded me of a snake in a cage—coiled and ready to strike if given the opportunity. But so far, she was smart enough to play by the rules.

"Thank you for your candor."

"Have you been having problems with her?" Essie flashed another one of her cold smiles. "Perhaps we could help?"

I decided to forgo the offer. Something told me to keep quiet about Ralph trying to steal my hair, and Rachel putting him up to it. No sense in giving out any information that might be used as a weapon against me, and I had no doubt Essie could figure out how to twist it.

"Nothing to speak of." Motioning to Sandy, I stood. "We won't take up any more of your time. Again, thank you for your help."

Essie's eyes glittered as she stood, her long skirts swishing with every movement. "Any time you feel the need, drop in for a visit. And tell your beau that he's welcome here in my nest. Aegis would be a feather in *any* nest's cap." She tilted her head to the side, a cunning look on her face, then glided out of the room.

Sandy was about to say something but I shook my head as the butler showed us out and walked us back to our car. "Thank you, Madame Gallowglass. Madame Clause. Both of you have a good evening." He shut Sandy's door for her, then stepped back on the sidewalk, shading his eyes to watch as we drove away.

I let out a soft breath as the house vanished behind us into the gloom of early dusk. "What kind of freaky-assed bitch is she? I felt like we were one second away from becoming dinner."

"Yeah, she did seem ready to bite at any minute."

"So, the rumors about Essie and Rachel not getting along seem true."

"Yes, but she'd jump at having Aegis in her nest. You heard her. *Aegis would be a feather in any nest's cap...* I wonder what makes him so special." Sandy paused. "Not that he isn't special. But—oh, you *know* what I mean."

"I think because he has a record of leaving his victims alive, and he's also got a lot of sex appeal and charm."

"You're right. He would be a good front man for them. You know, *We're not so scary after all. Look at the hunky guy. He may drink off you but he'll leave you alive.*"

"Good point. But I doubt that Essie could ever lure him into her court. For one thing, Aegis has been around a lot longer than she is. For another, he's not so much into the goth look except when it comes to his leathers for the band." Although I sounded confident, the truth was that I wasn't so sure of myself. Given Aegis had entirely neglected to tell me about Rachel or that she was back in town—and I couldn't help but believe that he knew she was around—it led me to wonder just what else I didn't know about him.

"What now?" Sandy rested her forehead against the window, staring out into the gloom. "I'd rather not hang around her house. I don't trust Essie any more than I trust a warlock."

"You think she's an oath breaker?"

"I think she skews the truth to suit her. And I know she was holding back something. You don't hate somebody as much as she hates Rachel without a reason. I wish Linda would have given a lot more consideration to the possible dangers before writing up the treaties with her."

I found myself agreeing with her. Essie was a slippery slope, and I wasn't looking forward to any future dealings I had to have with her.

As I parked next to her car where she had left it in the parking lot near the French Pair, I turned to her. "I suppose I'd better go home and talk to Aegis. I doubt you want to be there for the fireworks I envision."

Sandy hesitated. "Are you sure you want to be alone? I can't help but think..." She paused again, obviously uncomfortable.

"What is it? Out with it."

"He's a *vampire*, Maddy. You remember what they're like? Even with the good ones, one misstep, one flare-up, and they can drain you before you blink. Or break your neck. Or worse— Do what they did to Tom—"

"Stop. I don't want to go there. I really don't."

"I'll shut up about that subject, but face it. You are going to tell him you've been checking up on him. On his ex-girlfriend. Given all the weirdness that's happened today, are you sure that you want to be alone?" She lightly touched my arm. "Remember, Rose was murdered in your yard. Somebody's out to get you and we both know that we're thinking it might be Rachel. Ralph may have been getting the hair from your brush for her, but we both know that he's not really a killer."

I pressed my lips shut, staring out the window as the snow began to fall again, silent and in thick flakes. "I know. I agree that Rachel may have it in for me." I stopped again, processing the flood of thoughts cascading through my brain. Finally, I shrugged. "Come over, then. Delia is going to want to talk to Aegis tonight, she said, so it's not like it's going to be a private evening. Maybe it's best if we put everything out on the table."

"I'll follow you over." Sandy slipped out of the car, shutting the door and motioning for me to lock it.

I locked the doors and waited till she was safely in hers, then started the engine again. With Sandy on my heels, I eased out of the parking lot and cautiously headed for home. I wasn't looking forward to the conversations that awaited me there.

THE LIGHTS WERE on when I got home, and I shivered, waiting for Sandy to pull in behind me. Together we headed for the kitchen door, through the yard where I had found Rose. The snow was lightly covering over the spot where she had been lying, and as we passed by, both Sandy and I paused, staring at the ground.

"We need to talk to her parents. And the coven needs to meet to discuss how we want to handle the Cord Cutting ceremony and if we want to open to a new member. Linda has to have heard by now." I steeled myself, glancing up at the Bewitching Bedlam. "I hate to say this—it sounds so crass, but I just realized what a mess this could make with our opening. *Come to the B&B and get murdered...* Damn it, why does everything have to get muddled like this?" The full weight of what had happened and the potential ramifications were hitting home. "Now I wonder, maybe Ralph did do this. It *could* hurt my business really bad."

"I didn't think about that, either."

"Well, let's go. No use putting this off any longer." I strode ahead and unlocked the door into the kitchen.

Aegis was sitting there, in the rocking chair. As he saw me, he leapt to his feet.

"Where were you? Why didn't you leave a note? I've been worried sick about whether you were okay or lying dead in some alley!" He grabbed me, kissing me soundly, and then pushing me back by my shoulders. "Don't you scare me like that again!"

I stared at him, my fears beginning to melt. "You heard about Rose, then?"

"Heard about her? The sheriff called and told me she's on her way out to talk to me about the dead woman found in my yard. I panicked, thinking maybe it was you, but then she mentioned Rose's name. What were you thinking, not leaving a note?" His eyes were filled with concern, and Bubba came bouncing up onto the counter beside him.

"You could have asked Bubba—" I started to say, but Aegis wrapped me in his arms, kissing me again. I searched his eyes as I came up for air, questioning him—looking for anything that might say he was putting on a show, but saw nothing but concern and love in his face.

"You know I can't speak cjinn all that well." He glanced over at Sandy. "I'm supposing you came with her to make sure I didn't do anything particularly nasty." His tone was sour, but he smiled to take the sting off his words.

"Do you blame me for worrying?" Sandy dropped into a chair and crossed her legs. "How about a drink?"

"Help yourself," Aegis said, nodding toward the refrigerator. "There's wine. And no, I suppose I don't. I was worried enough for the both of us." He let go of me and I slipped out of my coat.

"Pour me a glass too, Sandy." I draped my coat over the back of a chair and dropped into the rocking chair. "How long till Delia gets here?"

"She should be here within the hour. She called about twenty minutes ago. I had been up for about half an hour. I couldn't find you anywhere, and then I went outside and saw that the yard looked like it had been excavated—at least the snow had. I had no clue of what was going down until she called me." Over his shoulder, he added, "Ralph killed her, Delia said?"

I hesitated, wondering how to bring up Rachel. Sandy did it for me.

"We need to talk about Rachel, Aegis. She's in town, and we found out today that she's the woman who Ralph says paid him to retrieve some of Maddy's hair."

Aegis froze, then turned around very slowly. His eyes were luminous, glowing with a crimson tint. He silently moved to the kitchen island where he hoisted himself onto the counter, sitting very still.

"How do you know about Rachel?"

I let out a long breath. "Someone sent me this anonymous text yesterday." I held out my phone. "Franny saw it and identified the woman as your ex-girlfriend, a vampire named Rachel. I showed it to Ralph and he said it was the woman who paid him to gather my hair. We went out to Essie's this evening and she verified that Rachel is back in town and looking to get you back. She said Rachel is trouble." I held his gaze, trying to read his mood.

Aegis glanced over at Sandy. "I assume you're here to make sure I don't go all fang-banger on her?" His tone was snide, but she didn't flinch.

"You got it. Aegis, I like you but you need to get it through your thick skull. *We don't know you that well.* Regardless of the fact that you're fucking my friend—that you two have made a love connection—the reality remains that we don't know your background or what you have done over the past...

what...couple thousand years? Three thousand?" She shrugged. "If you think I'm going to let Maddy walk into potential danger alone, then you must not think I'm much of a friend."

He stared at her for a moment, then turned back to me. "Sandy's right, you know. You can't let your feelings for me cloud your vision. Essie's right. Rachel is dangerous and she's no fool. She's also off the wall fucking crazy and she's been stalking me for years."

I was torn, not wanting to cross-examine him in front of Sandy. But we had passed the point of diplomacy. "Why didn't you tell me about her?"

He shrugged. "I didn't know she was here until last week. I was trying to figure out how to tell you about her when things began to happen. When I went out to check on the noise that startled Bubba the other night, I smelled her. I realized she was hanging around the house and it scared me because she's never forgiven me for breaking up with her. I'd forgotten that we posed for that painting. And I forgot that Franny knew about Rachel."

I wanted to ask him the most important question of all. Well, it really wasn't the most important, but to my heart it was. But Aegis took one look at my face and slid off the counter, walking carefully over to me. He tipped my chin up, so I was looking into his eyes.

"I don't love her anymore. I don't know if I ever really did. And the last thing I want is for her to be part of my life again. She's crazy and dangerous and if I had had any clue what kind of sociopath she was, I would never have taken up with her in the first place. Since I met you, Maudlin Gallowglass, there hasn't been another woman who could turn my head. Nor do I expect there will be." There was such conviction in his voice that I couldn't help but believe him.

"Thank you."

"For what?" He looked confused. "I screwed up, I admit it. I should have known that Rachel might come looking for me one of these days. I put you in danger with my silence."

"For not making me ask. For not trying to make me feel like I have no right to know about her." I remembered what Sandy had said. I had been Mad Maudlin, respected and feared. I held tight to that memory, straightening my shoulders. "Because if you had tried to brush me off..."

"You'd make me leave. I understand. But Maddy, do you really think Ralph killed Rose? He might be working in cahoots with Rachel, but I never pegged him for a killer. While Rose's death is going to impact the business, I just can't see him attacking your coven-mate."

"There's something that I don't think Delia told you. Rose was wearing the same kind of coat I was. She has long dark hair. In the gloom..."

Understanding dawned in his eyes. "She could have been you. But wasn't she killed today? In the sunlight?"

I shook my head. "She was killed last night when she left here. That's why Delia wants to talk to you. When you came home—"

Sandy shifted. "What Delia's going to ask you is how, when you returned home, you managed to miss Rose's body."

The doorbell rang then, and I broke away, going to answer. Delia was standing there, along with one of her deputies. I ushered them in.

"Aegis is waiting," I said. "I have some more information that might have some bearing on the case."

"Don't you want to know if we caught Ralph?" Delia asked, following me back into the kitchen.

"I don't think he did it—"

"He's in jail, Maddy. He confessed. He said that he was tricked into it by the woman he keeps talking about, that she said she could help him destroy his competition." She pulled out her notebook. "I just have some routine questions," she added, turning to greet Aegis. "Hello—mighty fine band you have there. I caught your show last week at the Utopia. Good sound."

"Thanks." Aegis frowned. "You say Ralph confessed?"

"That doesn't make sense. When I talked to him, he acted like normal—like he always does. If he killed Rose, do you think he would have stood there arguing with me in the bakery? If he thought Rose was me, don't you think that he would have been surprised to see me?" Nothing made sense, not even why Delia was taking Ralph's word at face value.

She bit her lip. "Tell me what else you found out. For the record, I don't know if Ralph's telling the truth, but not many people confess to murders they don't commit, and Ralph's not the self-sacrificing type."

That was true enough. Satyrs, in general, didn't think much about others. They were fun-loving and brave, but I wouldn't count on them to have my back unless they were a good friend.

"Okay. I went out and talked to Essie." I laid out everything about Rachel that Essie had told me. Aegis chimed in to fill in the blanks.

Delia frowned. "So this Rachel is around. Ralph might just be working with her. Or there's another possibility. I'll have my men check Ralph for bite marks. He might be under thrall. If that's the case, then he'd do anything for her and she could use him as a fall guy."

"True. Satyrs can be mesmerized by a vampire as much as anybody." As a witch, I was immune to the charm a vampire's gaze caused, but just about anybody—witch or not—was subject to thrall, the state of euphoria and slavish devotion that a vampire's bite could produce.

Aegis shook his head. "I wouldn't put it past Rachel to sneak around Bedlam trying to produce an army of slaves. She always longed to be worshipped. Anybody who refused to put her on a pedestal ran the risk of becoming lunch. I release those whom I drink from so they aren't bound, but Rachel never did. *When* she left them alive, she left them pining for her."

"How long were you with her? We need to know everything we can about her. It sounds like she's not just a danger to Maddy, but to Bedlam proper." Delia was taking notes furiously, but I had the feeling she was watching Aegis very closely even though her focus seemed to be on her notepad.

His gaze clouded over. Finally, he shrugged and looked directly at me. "I first met Rachel in 1925. She was a dancer at one of the burlesque joints. The moment I set eyes on her, I knew she was special. I just wish I had never walked into that music hall, because that's the last day I ever felt fully free."

Chapter 7

"I MET HER in New York. She was dancing at a place called the Moxy Music & Theatre Hall. It was cold out, I think. The snow was thick and even though I didn't feel the chill, it seemed bleak and dark. I was new in the city—I had come over in steerage to prevent exposure to the sun, and it also gave me an ample amount of people to drink off of during the night. I hid out and slept during the day. Anyway, I was fresh to the city and trying to find my way. I had worn out my welcome in Greece, and England was feeling old and tired. America promised wide spaces and new vistas."

I understood, and I knew Sandy did, as well. Those of us in the Pretcom were long-lived, so we had to keep things fresh. We had to turn over our lives and reinvent ourselves more than once to stay focused. The Fae didn't seem to feel the passing of time as harshly as we did, and Elves were best at handling long expanses of time. But shifters and Weres, witches and vamps—we all needed to shake the dust loose now and then.

"I ducked into the Moxy, just to see what was there. And she was on the stage. Rachel. She went by the name Desire—her stage name. She was dancing. But it wasn't bump and grind. No, she used her glamour to enthrall her watchers. I could see it even though I wasn't pulled in by it, but the aura gave her away. I knew she was one of the Fallen. A vampire like me."

I didn't want to hear this and yet, I had to. I had to face the fact that Aegis had had other loves—like I had—and that they had been to him what my sweet Tom had been to me. Aegis must have sensed what I was feeling, because he smiled at me.

"Glamour's very real, but it's not the core of what true attraction is. Anyway, she must have felt the shift in energy as I came in, because she looked directly at me from up there on the stage and that was it. I waited till after she was finished and we took up together that very night. Rachel knew her own way and she was a shrewd businesswoman. Nobody ever got one over on her. But there was a side of her that I couldn't accept. She was ruthless and a user. She liked bloodwhores and sycophants, and for people to grovel in front of her."

A chill raced down my back. "She likes power."

He shook his head. "She *craves* it. I think it's an actual addiction for her."

"Where did Rachel originally come from?" Delia asked.

Aegis frowned. "She's from an old Romany family. She's not as old as I am, but she's at least four or five hundred. She comes from the Old Country and keeps to her family's customs. Her mother was one of the Strega. When Rachel was turned, her mother tried to stake her. Rachel killed her entire family, but she holds to their beliefs about vengeance. Once you cross her, you're forever on her list."

"When did you break up?" My stomach was knotting up. I had known Strega in my time. Some of them were good people, but like every other group, some of them were dangerous and vicious. In fact, I may have run across her long ago and not realized it. Whatever the case, Rachel was a first-class threat and if what Aegis was saying was true, she'd be a danger for life. The Strega never forgot. They nursed their grudges like dragons nursed gold.

"In early 1990, she crossed the line. I knew she didn't leave all of her victims alive but I managed to look the other way, until I found her drinking the blood of ten-year-old twins. Granted, we were in the middle of nowhere, and there were only scattered families around. We'd gone on a stupid road trip and ended up in the Midwest. When I discovered she had slaughtered an entire family, including the twins, she laughed in my face. She said I was an idiot and that Apollo was right to cast me out—that I wasn't worth keeping around."

I winced, trying not to picture the carnage. But that alone convinced me that Aegis and I had to have a talk about my past.

"And *you've* never killed a child?" Delia sounded skeptical. The question seemed cruel, even for her. Although werewolves and vamps didn't mix, I understood. Given the millennia Aegis had lived, I understood her line of reasoning.

Aegis straightened, staring directly at the sheriff. "Never. I've *never* killed a child. And I've never ruthlessly murdered to feed. Vampires don't need to kill their food supply. It doesn't make sense, anyway. The only time I've killed anyone is when they were attempting to destroy me. And I have killed a few other vampires. Once, I found one attacking a pregnant woman. Another time, I followed one of the Fallen into an alley to find that he had enthralled five or six young girls—all under their teen years. He wasn't just using them for blood. He died that night and I made sure the girls ended up in the hospital. Nobody ever knew how they got there, but I made sure they were found before I left."

Delia flipped her notepad shut and leaned back. "Why does Rachel want you back? Why not move on to the next catch?"

Aegis shifted, looking uncomfortable. "I'm the only one who ever left her. Everybody else, she's either killed or dumped. I'm the one who walked away, and that bruised her ego. It was worse when she found out that I had come to Bedlam, a town where the vampires answer to the witches. Rachel refuses to kneel before anyone who isn't one of the Fallen royalty. She'd be happy for the entire world to be enslaved."

"She really is a piece of work, isn't she?" Sandy

snorted. "Megalomaniac, narcissistic. It's a wonder she's not running for president."

"Too much paperwork and not enough autonomy," Aegis said, breaking the tension with a laugh. "After a while, her temper tantrums would cease to be welcome." He sobered again. "But seriously, check Ralph for fang marks. She'll have to have bitten him for him to fall under thrall. I'm betting you find them."

"Even so, I can't let him go if he's the one who actually murdered Rose. Even if he did it under her orders, we'll have to prosecute them both. The best I can offer is that he'll need a good lawyer." Delia let out a long sigh. "He'll be up on charges under both state law as well as having to answer to the Bedlam Tribunal. The latter may be far harsher on him than the former." She stood, glancing out the window. "Vampires don't leave fingerprints, do they?"

"Yes, they do, but most often you won't find them in any record because the majority of us are older than the fingerprint databases. If they *could* match some of the prints left in unsolved murders to vampires, they might solve a number of cold cases." He gave her a shrug. "What can you do?"

"Last question. Do you know where she's staying?"

I wanted to know that answer, as well.

But Aegis just shook his head. "If I did, she wouldn't be the problem she is, Sheriff."

And that ended that. Delia gathered her things and left, enjoining us to be cautious until everything was sorted out. "If she's angry at you for taking up with Maddy, then Maddy isn't the only one in danger."

Aegis grudgingly agreed. "I guess that makes sense."

"You know it does. Now, I'm going to see what I can find out. Maybe I'll pay a visit to Linda and ask for her take on this." Delia glanced over at Sandy and me. "Don't you two go calling her before I can get there."

"We won't, but whatever you're planning, do it tonight. We have ritual tomorrow night and Linda's going to have to know everything before we cast Circle. We can't keep any secrets like this away from her, not when we're talking the level of magic we of the Inner Court perform."

Those of us who made up the Inner Court ran magical energy that could backfire with incredible volatility, and the spells we worked in private for the protection of Bedlam and the prosperity of its inhabitants were best performed with no hidden agendas or worries. While we didn't advertise what we did, it was generally known that we weren't good people to mess with. Obviously, Rachel hadn't gotten the message.

Delia scowled. "*Magic.*" She shuddered. "Gives me the creeps. But I understand. I'll stop over there tonight and talk to her." As she headed toward the door, she added, "Given what you've told me, don't go outside alone after sunset. Aegis, that goes for you, vampire or not." She closed the door behind her before we could say another word.

"Well." I leaned back in my chair. "This thing has blown way out of proportion." I felt grumbly and out of sorts. It wasn't Aegis's fault, but the thought kept running through my head that it would have been so much easier if he had decided to be a loner when Apollo kicked him out of service, rather than making his reputation as a playboy who won women over before breaking their hearts.

Aegis glanced at Sandy. "If you don't mind, I'd like to talk to Maddy. Alone. I'll walk you to your car."

"That's rude—" I started to say, but Sandy cut me off.

"He's right. You two need to discuss this without me being in the way. Besides which, I want to go home and eat, and then prepare for tomorrow night. I'm suddenly very tired, and if I coax him, Alex might just give me a massage." She purred over the name.

"I know you're dating your assistant. Don't you try to hide it from me." I laughed as she stood. Aegis held her coat for her and she slid into it.

"What's the harm in that? He's free. I'm free. I hired him because he does a great job, but he's far handier than I thought, and I'm not being slimy here. I never have to micromanage him, he doesn't take advantage of me, and best of all, he didn't *need* the job, so he won't play fast and loose trying to make more work for himself. Alex accepted the job because he thought it would be interesting, and he donates half his salary to charity." She beamed. "I think I might have found a keeper this time."

I couldn't even begin to count how many times Sandy had said that over the years, but it had to be into the triple digits by now. She simply wasn't a woman who settled down easily, but she had managed through several long-term relationships including the last marriage, ending most of them amicably before moving on to new pastures.

"I'll call you tomorrow morning. We need to talk about the ritual tomorrow night, anyway. Be careful driving home and have Alex meet you at the car."

"Rachel isn't after me," Sandy said, laughing off my concern.

"No, but if she's out for me, she'll be more than willing to strike at those I love. And woman, you are my right hand."

As Aegis walked Sandy out the door and across the lawn I thought about my relationship with Sandy. We had been together longer than anybody I knew—she had known my Tom. She had held my hand when the vampires turned him. She held my hand as I wept, and ran beside me when I ran mad. She and Fata Morgana had hunted the countryside with me. Along the way somewhere, Fata had vanished and we had lost touch with her. But Sandy, she was there through all the ups and downs of my life, and I tried to return the favor. We were sisters of the heart, blood bound by choice, and I couldn't have a better friend.

Aegis returned a few moments later. "She's off safely. Even a vampire would have trouble keeping up with her, though I swear, it's so icy I hope to hell she slows down."

I snorted. "Sandy has a Hasty spell in her repertoire that she's modified to work on her car.

The one caveat is that no one will be harmed by it. If she's in danger, it will slow her down, or if anybody else is in danger from her driving, it will also slow her down. The spell also takes over when she's drunk, so she puts the car on autopilot so she can safely get around."

"It won't be long before she can buy a self-driving car and save the magical energy." Aegis stopped by the kitchen island. "I guess—you want to talk?"

"I'm thinking we'd better. And it's not just about Rachel. Aegis, there are things about me you should know. I don't know if anything out of my past will crop up to make your life a living hell, but there's always the chance. And there are things I did that I have to be honest about." My voice was shaking, and I realized this was one of those crossroads in a relationship, where futures were decided.

He motioned for me to follow him. "We can build a fire in the parlor. You want to go in there? Somehow, I'm thinking this conversation is better left out of the bedroom."

"I'm thinking you're right." I poured myself a glass of wine and followed him into the parlor. As I knelt by the stack of kindling and logs in the fireplace, Bubba hesitantly wandered into the room. I held out my fingers to the wood, but then decided not to waste the energy. Instead, I grabbed one of the long fireplace matches, struck it against the brick, and lit the fire.

As I curled up on the sofa with my glass, Bubba sat patiently in front of me.

"Mur?"

"Hey, Bub. You lonely?" I patted my lap and Bubba jumped up, curling softly in my lap. I stroked his fur gently, my fingers sliding over his sleek, plush coat. Lifting him gently, I kissed his head before settling him back in my lap.

Aegis was also carrying a glass of wine. The lamps were off, but I had strung faerie lights all around the room, winding them with a glittering garland, and Aegis plugged them in before sitting down in the recliner closest to the sofa. He leaned forward, cupping the goblet as he rested his elbows on his knees.

"So, who goes first?" Then, before I could answer, he said, "Ask me anything you want to know. Anything. I won't be upset."

I contemplated the possibilities. How could you cram several thousand years into a few questions? The answer was that you couldn't, of course. And really, what did I need to know?

"All right. The most obvious one you answered, but I want to hear it again. Do you still have feelings left for Rachel? Has all of this stirred up any unrequited desires?"

He paused, taking his time. "To say I don't have any feelings for her would be a lie. But they aren't the ones you fear. I'm angry at her. I'm tired of her chasing me—and before you ask, this isn't the first time she's tracked me down. But the last time was a year ago, when I came to live here. That must be when Franny saw us. Rachel tracked me down to beg me to come back to her. I told her to leave me alone. I told her I never wanted to see her again. I thought she left, and maybe she did. But she's back now."

"She's really crazy, isn't she?"

"Yes, and in a bad way. Actually, I wouldn't even call her crazy. She's just narcissistic, vain, and... evil. Rachel is an evil woman, Maddy. She's the stereotype that makes people afraid of the Fallen. Oh, we are definitely a frightening lot, but she gives rise to all the nightmares about what we can do." His voice trailed off, sounding forlorn. "She's the monster I never wanted to become. I never want to become."

I sucked in a deep breath. "Maybe I'd better go next. I need to tell you about who I was. About who you're dating. Because Aegis, there was a time when I could have become exactly what Rachel is. The two people who kept me from going that far were a friend named Fata Morgana, and Sandy. But even they couldn't have stopped me if I hadn't been ready to stop."

As the shadows enveloped the room, I moved Bubba to the sofa beside me. I began to pace, unable to sit still. I was about to open an old wound that I hoped was scabbed over so deep that it would never see the light of day again.

"TOM WAS MY love and I was his. We kept on the run because the witch hunters during that time were dangerous and they were everywhere. Some were agents of the church, others were just bounty hunters, but they sought out my kind to put us to death as enemies. They were afraid of our power. They were afraid of what we stood for—the gods and lands we had shepherded before they drove through and took over."

"I remember those days. From a different perspective, of course. Few knew about my kind, or believed we were real."

"The witch hunters were after us, and so we ran. There were so many on the move back then. Those who could see the future coming tried to find shelter. They had visions of the fires blazing, the stones being piled on the bodies, the rack and the iron maiden." I closed my eyes, remembering the fear that had run through the Pretcom back then as witches and Fae and Weres did their best to hide from the fanatical zealots who sought us out.

Aegis nodded. "I kept to myself, hiding in the night in the bigger cities, moving on before anybody ever figured out that the Fallen were among them." He paused. "Tell me about Tom."

I smiled softly, remembering.

"Tom had a voice as sweet as yours is dark. He could sing, and so we posed as wandering minstrels, staying in each village a month here, a month there, until somebody would notice that things had a way of happening around us. When you're a witch, magic is as natural as breathing. You can't just turn it off."

I worried my lip. "Long story short, because the story lasted for years, one night we were out in the woods and we thought we were alone. We didn't realize we had been followed by a group of vampires."

Aegis froze. "Crap. I didn't know that. What happened, Maddy?"

I closed my eyes, pausing by the fireplace as I leaned my head against the wall. The smell of fresh cedar from the boughs swagged across the wooden mantel filled my senses.

"I keep these memories locked away because they're as fresh as they were then when I take them out to examine them. Tom and I in the woods, making magic together, weaving a spell to heal one of the village girls who reminded Tom of his niece. She would never know why her leg healed up so quickly—and her parents would attribute it to prayers. But we would know, and most important, she would live and grow strong. Life for the handicapped was usually a death sentence during those days.

"The sparkles of magic were bright that evening, brilliant and flaring around us in a silence brought about by the weight of the energy. Everything seemed suspended in a lovely haze, and then it collapsed as the vamps descended. Tom was closest to them, and they caught him. As he struggled, he screamed for me to run, to get away.

"I didn't want to, but he summoned up every ounce of power he had and I turned to find a unicorn standing beside me, a bright Fae warrior on its back. She reached down and grabbed my arm, hauling me up with her, and we were off, vanishing into the mists. The next moment, we were in a Barrow Mound, and I curled on the floor, weeping."

Shaking, I gulped down a deep breath, then

sipped from my wine and crossed to the window, staring out into the snow.

"When they let me out, I realized that twenty years had passed by. The Fae had kept me with them that long, so that I would be safe. Oh, legends had grown up around my disappearance, but I don't know if anybody really believed it. I cloaked up, disguising myself, and began to search for Tom. I found out that he had been turned. He was a vampire."

Aegis rubbed his forehead. "Maddy."

The pain I kept suppressed in a little box in my heart welled over the sides and I started to rock back and forth, holding myself, trying to push back the angry tears.

"I still loved him, even more than before because he had saved me. Tom had used every ounce of his power to summon the warrior—she owed him a favor—to make certain I escaped. Time in the Barrow moved indeterminably and when I left, it was as though only a day had passed for me. Twenty years, but to me, it felt like twenty hours. I emerged from the Barrow to find Sandy waiting for me. She told me Tom was one of the fiends, feared like few other vamps. In that moment, I truly became Mad Maudlin."

"You hunted them down?"

"Oh, yes." I met his gaze. "I sought them out, all right. Together with Cassandra—Sandy—and Fata Morgana, I raged through the land, seeking every vampire I could. They feared me, they whispered my name in secret. I killed so many of them, driving the plague of vampires back from the towns.

Even the witch hunters gave me a wide berth, terrified to anger me. I took out my share of them, too. But the vampires? I shadowed them. Haunted them. I destroyed every one of their hiding places I could find. I drove them into the sunlight. And then, I ran wild. Sandy and Fata and I decided that we would bedevil the demons. We would make them understand what it was to fear."

"When did you stop?" His voice was soft and I suddenly realized that, if anybody would understand what I had been through, it was Aegis.

"We found a huge nest of them—an entire village. I encircled it with flames. Then, as the sun set and the vampires began to rise, I sent the flames inward and destroyed every single vamp there. We fought, of course—there were some who got through the flames—but between the three of us, we devastated them. When I realized that my Tom had not been there—I thought he was—I broke. I had wanted to free him, and it seemed like that was the one vampire kept from me."

I was weeping now, not wanting to face Aegis.

He quietly held out his arms. I wanted to run to him, to bury myself in his love, but the guilt overwhelmed me. I had lost my love to the vampires, and now...now I was falling for one. Mad Maudlin would have killed Aegis on sight, but I had fallen in love with him.

I let out a shuddering breath and straightened my shoulders. "That night ended my hunting days. We left the village and the three of us lost ourselves in a whirlwind of parties and booze and drugs. I did my best to sever myself from the carnage. I tried to leave my anger behind, which meant leaving my love for Tom behind. Because the pain of losing him—the horror of knowing he was still out there, killing for blood—had almost driven me out of my mind."

"But you never really quit loving him. And you didn't harm anyone who didn't deserve it."

I studied the floor. "I still love him, even though I shoved that love into a tiny corner of my heart and taped a caution sign over it. But he was vicious, he was vicious—like Rachel. He became a crazed monster. If I saw him today, as much as it hurts, I'd stake him. Because Tom turned into a fiend set on destroying others."

"You have nothing to apologize for. You did what you needed to."

I shrugged. "I know. And to be honest, I don't regret my actions. I won't be a hypocrite and wring my hands and say *I'm so sorry*. The only thing I truly regret was losing my Tom, and never being able to send him to rest."

He pulled me to him, holding my shoulders gently as I looked up at him, tears streaming.

"You have to understand this about me, Aegis. I'm not ashamed of what I did. Of what I was. I hunted your kind. I killed them with glee and joy in my heart. I played judge, jury, and executioner willingly. Given the choice, I'd do it all over again. I *am* Mad Maudlin, and I can't ever deny the truth of what I did. Because she's still a part of me, like it or not."

"Do you miss that wild ride?" A faint smile crinkled at the side of his lips. And in those words,

I distinctly heard that he—too—had his own wild past.

I gave a hoarse laugh. "Not so much. And I wasn't alone, thank gods. Sandy was with me, and Fata Morgana. They had the foresight to rein me in when it became necessary. And afterward? We partied like it was 1999."

Aegis seemed to be digesting everything I had just thrown at him. "I'm glad you told me. We all have our baggage. We've all done things that aren't so pretty." He paused, then asked, "You remember when I told you that Apollo threw me out because I dared to love one of his servants whom he also took a shine to?"

I nodded. "Yeah, but I know that you don't like to talk about it, so I try to leave it alone."

He hung his head. "I wasn't entirely truthful. Mostly, but not completely."

"What did you do?" I looked at my glass. It was empty and I wanted more wine.

He took my glass. "Let me refill these and then I'll tell you. I promise, it wasn't horrible, but it wasn't good, either." As he headed into the kitchen, I returned to the sofa, where I curled up in the corner and stared at the flames burning in the fireplace.

It felt good, actually, to have that off my conscience. Keeping that secret from him had been weighing on me. I didn't want him to think I was someone I wasn't—someone with a crystal clear past. He was a vampire. I had killed his kind ruthlessly. But regardless of what he decided to do, I had been truthful with him.

Aegis handed me my glass, along with a sandwich. "I thought you could use a little something to eat. It's ham and Swiss."

Just that small act told me that he wasn't ready to throw in the towel on us, at least not yet. Gratefully, I accepted it, biting into the spicy mustard. "Thank you. I needed this." Pausing to chew, I waited until he was sitting down again. "How do you feel about what I told you?"

"You mean, that you were a famous vampire hunter? That you killed scores of the Fallen?"

I nodded, holding my breath. The flames in the fireplace crackled and popped in the silence that hung between us.

Aegis caught my gaze and held it. "I'm glad you finally decided to tell me. I've known since I first met you and I've been waiting for you to talk about it. But I didn't want to push you."

"What?" I jerked, straightening up. "You knew?"

"Yes, love. I knew. And what you did. It wasn't just out of revenge. You saved thousands of people from being hurt. The vampires then, they were a lot less civilized. Most of them didn't give a damn about humans." He paused, then reached out. "Maddy, love. I knew all about your past. That doesn't change how I feel about you."

I held his hands in mine, gazing into his eyes, suddenly realizing that he was accepting me—all of me. It was almost too much to take in. Feelings warred within me, and I managed to push them to the side for a moment. I had to examine them one by one, to sort through the mosh pit of emotion that was racing through me.

Swallowing, I whispered, "So, tell me your dread secrets, my love."

He seemed to understand, because he smiled, just the corners of his lips lifting. "My turn, then. Here it is my most dreadful secret. It's true that I fell for a servant of Apollo. And that she returned my love. I don't know what we thought would eventually happen, but we were doing our best to keep it hidden. But Theo, a man I thought was my best friend, found out about us. I don't know whether he was jealous, or whether he was just in a mood, because he told Apollo about us."

I sucked in a deep breath. "Betrayal's never easy."

"No, it isn't. And for a long time, his actions broke my belief in friendship. Apollo sent Astra and me into the dungeons while he decided how to punish us. I had other friends, though. One of them let me out with my promise that I'd return to my cell before Apollo found out. I snuck into Theo's room while he slept and I killed him." Aegis's smile vanished. "I was willing to face Apollo's wrath, but Theo had put Astra in danger. For that, I could never forgive him. I slit his throat while he slept."

I had actually expected much worse. "What happened next?"

"I stood by my word and went back to my cell. The next day, Apollo turned me into one of the Fallen. He never mentioned Theo's death. And part of my punishment was that I never found out what he did to Astra. I've done many cruel things since then, but I don't take harming others lightly.

Theo, however? I do not regret killing him. Sometimes, I wonder what happened to Astra. Then I think, perhaps it's best I don't know."

As he fell silent, I squeezed his hand. "We're a pair, aren't we? Mad Maudlin and Aegis the Fallen."

He leaned down, his lips seeking mine. "I love you, Maudlin—whether you're mad or not. From now on, no hidden secrets. I know other parts of our lives will come up. Secrets we might not think important will come to light. But if these are the worst, then we're weathering the storm well." And with that, he laid me back on the sofa and began to undress me.

Chapter 8

HIS LIPS WERE soft against mine as he brushed my hair back from my face, his fingers lingering on my cheek. The flames from the fireplace brightened, the sparks crackling as they consumed the wood. My breath caught in my chest, and I shifted, allowing him to slide his hands beneath my shirt. A cool ripple raced up my spine from the chill of his fingers. I still wasn't used to his touch, and part of me hoped I never would be. The thrill was still new and even though old loves were often the best, that vibrant sense of still being in the *Getting-to-know-you* phase appealed to me on so many levels. I slid my legs apart, the material of my jeans chafing at me as he nestled his hips between them. I moaned softly.

"I want to feel your skin against my fingers," I whispered. "I want to touch you, to feel you inside me."

"Do you want to go up to your bed?" His voice was muffled as he buried his nose in my hair, nuzzling my neck.

"No. Here, by the fire." I didn't want to traipse all the way upstairs. The sofa was comfortable and all I wanted was to ride him, to connect body to body, heart to heart.

He pushed himself away from me, sitting up, and began to strip off his shirt. I scrambled to my knees, yanking off my own top. As I unbuckled my jeans and stood to shimmy out of them, Aegis tossed his pants across the room, then threw several of the large sofa pillows on the floor.

Turning to me, he stood at full attention, a lascivious look spreading across his face. Oh, he was smoking, all right. One look was all it took to make my blood pulse heavily in my throat. His chest was taut, his muscles finely developed but he wasn't too bulky. Just the right amount to fill out a muscle shirt nicely. He had a thin layer of hair on his chest and I was grateful he had never shaved it because I liked my men with a little chest hair, not all smooth and shiny. Although bald wasn't bad...a bald scalp was one thing. A blank chest devoid of hair was another.

Shaking my thoughts away from his chest, I followed his muscled abs down toward the V of his waist, biting my lip as my gaze reached his groin. My mouth watered as I took him in, all firm and swollen, waiting for me.

"Is that all for me?" I whispered, suddenly realizing how corny I sounded. I blushed, hoping I hadn't destroyed the mood.

"Oh, Maddy, it's *all* for you. Want me to give it to you now?" His eyes were twinkling and he looked ready to laugh, but then the energy shifted and he began to stalk me around the room. I backed away, not afraid, but daring him onward.

"You want me, come and get me."

We had played this game before, though it really wasn't a game. He was the hunter and I was his quarry, and yet the hunter was actually the hunted.

Gaze locked with his, I slowly crept around the sofa. Aegis responded, darting around the other way. I paused as he headed toward me, then side-stepped to behind the desk, my blood racing as he grunted and shifted direction.

"You can't get away from me," he said, his eyes bright.

"Ah, but are you worthy to catch me?" I ducked behind the chair and around the other side as he made a lunge for me. "Come on, show me what you're made of."

We went on this way, cat and mouse, vampire and witch, lover and lover until I was panting, aching to feel him inside me. He was hungry, I could feel it—not for my blood but my body. As I rounded the sofa, he leapt over the top, landing in front of me. I turned to run, but he caught me in his arms, pulling me toward him, and I melted, my breasts heavy and aching for his touch. As I pressed against his chest, he swept me up in his arms and tossed me on the pillows that we had scattered in our foreplay. I leaned back on the thickest, bending my right knee and ever so slightly spreading my legs.

"Touch yourself," he said, his voice rough.

My sex was wet and I reached down and slowly trailed my fingers over the thatch between my legs. "You mean like this?"

I fingered myself, slowly circling the raised nub of my sex, luxuriating in both the feel of my finger and the sense of him watching me. Conscious of my breasts, I began to breathe rhythmically as I picked up the pace. I raised my other knee, spreading my legs wider as I reached lower, sliding one finger inside me as I let out a little moan.

Aegis dropped to his knees, staring. I brought my other hand up to trace one of my nipples, pinching it so hard that I gasped. Closing my eyes, I focused on my body, my breath quickening as I became more aroused.

"You're so fucking sexy, Maddy." The hunger was thick in his voice, and I recognized it as both desire and thirst. Witches' blood was an aphrodisiac to vampires, almost an intoxicant. Aegis had never drunk from me, but I knew he fought the longing.

"If I'm so sexy, what are you doing way up there?"

That did it. He dove for me, burying his head between my thighs as he pushed my hand out of the way. His tongue fluttered over my clit and I arched my back, gasping as he quickened the pace. The frantic lapping drove away all thoughts of anything but the feel of his tongue rasping against me, the roughness jolting me toward a climax that I didn't expect so soon. I came, almost spiraling out of my body, then slammed back in as he came up between my legs to grasp one of my breasts between his lips, worrying the nipple like a dog might worry a favorite bone. He pressed his cock against me, and all I could think about was feeling him inside me.

"Fuck me, Aegis. Fuck me, *now*."

As I arched up toward him, he drove himself inside me, swiveling for better position. I wrapped my legs around his back, pulling him tighter. He was thick and hard, cool as ice and the chill penetrated my body as he hunted, thrusting as deeply as he could. I squirmed beneath him, dizzy from the pleasure.

But still, I could sense what he wanted—to drink from me. To taste my blood.

"Aegis—" I started, ready to capitulate, to give him what he so very much wanted.

"No," he whispered back, stopping inside me, holding me close. "I know what you're going to say. Don't even think about it. I refuse to drink from you. Maddy, I want you, all of you, but I won't take anything from you that you aren't ready to give. Blood is the most sacred of elixirs. It's life force and energy. I won't take that from you unless...until..." Pausing, he leaned down and kissed me, long and deep. He lingered on my lips, reaching up to softly caress my cheek. "Love me, Maddy. Love me and let me love you, and that's enough."

And then, he started moving again, slowly building his strokes, thrusting deep as we lost ourselves in the rhythm of our bodies.

BY THE TIME I woke up, Aegis was gone to his lair. I drowsily remembered him escorting me upstairs, where I promptly fell asleep the moment my head hit the pillow. I blinked, pushing myself to a sitting position, squinting as I glanced out the French doors leading onto my balcony. Even from here, I could see the snow falling heavy and thick. I pulled the blankets up around my neck, not wanting to get out of bed into the chill that pervaded the room.

"Murp?" Bubba bounced onto the bed, landing solidly by my side.

"I'm getting up, yes. You'll get your food. Just give me a moment." I yawned, stretching, then pulled Bubba to me and scratched him behind the ears. He purred, shifting so that I could reach the good spots. The next moment, he was drooling on my arm. Happy drool, I called it, when his cat nature overtook his cjinn nature and he reveled in all things feline. "You like that, don't you? Hmm, boy? Good boy."

He rolled out of my arms and onto his back, exposing his belly. I thought for a moment about rubbing it and wishing Rachel voted off the island but, considering the potential for backfire, I decided to forgo that little pleasure.

"Thanks for the offer, Bub, but I don't think that's a good idea. Come on, let me get dressed and then we'll head downstairs." I bit the bullet, throwing back the covers. The chill of the morning hit me full force and I groaned, shivering as I made my way to the bathroom where I turned on the shower full force. As the room began to fill with steam, I made sure my bedroom door was locked. Ralph might be in jail, but his stunt had left me paranoid. With Aegis asleep, I didn't want to have to face any new unwanted visitors.

"Bubba, dude, can you watch the door for me?"

"M'rrow." He took up his post, guarding the door with a stare so intense it was almost comical. He had a way of frowning that reminded me of a grumpy troll.

I wasn't sure what he could do if something came through, but I wouldn't put it past him to have a repertoire of attacks, even if he just latched onto an ankle and bit. Feeling a little more secure, I draped my robe over the back of my vanity chair and stepped under the steaming water. The pulse beat down on my back, and I finally began to loosen up. My body felt sore—and it wasn't just from wild monkey sex with Aegis. Apparently, I was holding onto far too much tension. My muscles were all knotted up. I turned the showerhead to "pulse" and let the throbbing water pound against the back of my neck and shoulder blades. It wasn't quite as good as a massage, but it helped.

Ten minutes later, I lathered up my hair and rinsed it out, then turned off the water and cautiously emerged from the shower. Wrapping a towel around me, I lowered myself to the chair, leaning my elbows on the granite counter. Running over things in my mind, I took stock of the situation.

One: I needed to furnish the Bewitching Bedlam so I could open on time.

Two: I had to assess the damage Rose's death had caused to my reputation and start deflecting any collateral damage. Speaking of Rose, I had to—three—go see her parents. I'd call Sandy in a little while and go over that.

Four: the coven was having a meeting tonight, since we were on the verge of a full moon, and I needed to prepare for the Esbat.

Five: I should talk to Delia and ask her what she learned from Linda.

Six: Ralph was sitting in jail for a crime I was pretty sure that he didn't commit, and I felt like there had to be some way I could help prove him innocent. But a little niggle of doubt flickered in the back of my mind. What if he *had* killed Rose? Even if he had been in thrall, he would be the one to face the harshest part of the punishment. If we caught the vampire—my guess was Rachel—who enthralled him, the Moonrise Coven could mete out its own punishment. But still, the law of the land would see Ralph punished far harsher than her, if he had been her triggerman.

All of these thoughts jumbling together in my mind, I combed out my hair and began to dry it. By the time I had my makeup on and my hair done, the warmth from the steam was wearing away. I slid into my robe and padded back into the bedroom. Deciding jeans and a turtleneck would work well for the day, I dressed and pulled on a pair of rumble boots. I clattered downstairs to feed Bubba and get some breakfast. It was time to start the day.

"DAMN IT." I was staring at my computer.

"What's wrong?" Franny appeared beside me.

I steadied myself. I was starting to get used to her popping in and out.

"I haven't checked my email in several days and now I find two cancellations for our opening weekend. We only have one guest room left booked." I gnawed on my pencil, trying to decide how best to approach this. I scribbled down a note to refund their deposit and stared glumly at the screen.

"Do you think they heard about Rose's death yesterday?"

"Yes. No. I don't know. They're both locals from Bedlam, so my guess is probably. Either that or Ralph's trash-talking campaign is working. Either way, it sucks."

I glanced at my reservation planner. Hoping our one remaining guest wouldn't take it into her head to cancel as well, I jammed the planner back on the shelf above my desk and quickly glanced over the rest of my to-do list. Except for furniture, the inn was pretty much ready to open. We still needed a lot of landscaping done, but that wouldn't happen till the spring.

"Is there anything I can do?" Franny's offer was tentative, but it was the first time she had shown any interest in the bed and breakfast and she seemed genuinely concerned.

"Thanks, Franny. I appreciate the offer, but unless you can scare up customers or quench the rumors going around, I don't think so. But thank you."

"All right. But if you need anything. Well, I'll let you think." Franny silently vanished.

As I sat back, deciding what to do next, my phone rang.

"Yo, Maddy." Sandy's voice was perky but breathless. "I thought we could go over to talk to Rose's parents this afternoon. I really don't want to wait much longer."

I rubbed my forehead. A headache was rapidly brewing. "You're right." I glanced at the clock. "It's ten now. I need to run a few errands. Meet you at the Blue Jinn at noon?"

"Sounds good. We can take your car—you're better at driving in the snow than I am—and you can drop me off at the diner afterward. Listen, I've been thinking about where Rachel could be staying and I have a couple ideas. I'll run them by you on the way to the Williamses' house."

I knew exactly what that meant. "You aren't thinking we should perhaps pay a visit to her if we can find her, are you? That I should unleash *Mad Maudlin: Vampire Hunter* again?" Visions of old crypts and mausoleums and creeping through a cobweb-shrouded labyrinth flashed through my mind.

"Why not? Rachel can't do anything to us during the day, can she? And if we can find her and stake her, well, problem solved." Sandy sounded so matter of fact that I hated to burst her bubble.

"Aren't you forgetting the treaty Linda set up with Essie?"

"That doesn't cover Rachel since she's not part of Essie's court."

"True, but even though by rights we could take her out, we just can't go around staking vampires right and left. How do you think that's going to go down if we just willy-nilly stake somebody we *think* is behind this? We have no real proof right now."

Sandy snorted. "Proof, schmoof. For one thing, Essie herself said that Rachel's not welcome in her court. And second, we both know that Rachel's the ultimate reason Rose is dead. So we find her, stake her, and say nothing. Nobody's going to know. There won't be any proof left behind except a pile of ashes, and those are easy enough to clear away."

I pressed my lips together, mulling over the idea. It would take care of the issue, and it wasn't like I didn't have the experience behind me. But this was different. If I staked Rachel without ever telling Aegis and he later found out, it could destroy our relationship. And the truth was, we didn't have any proof.

"Sandy, this isn't the 1700s. We have to do this through the proper channels."

"I think the *proper channel* may find her hands tied. At least hear me out."

Letting out a long sigh, I caved. "All right. We'll talk this afternoon. Meanwhile, I need to dash. I have to cast a quick Prosperity spell and then I have a couple errands to run. We had two cancellations this morning. I have to ensure that we don't end up closing our doors before we even open them. I love this house, but I never intended to just live here and do nothing."

After I got off the phone, I retreated to the library, which I had turned into my ritual room. This was one room that was fully furnished. Every direction had its own altar on a square table.

To the north, the altar was covered with a green cloth, and held a small oak chest, open and filled with malachite and smoky quartz, with tiger's eye and hematite, and strings of peridot and citrine. A brass pentacle sat on the table, and statues of a wolf, bear, and stag.

To the east, my altar had a sphere of lapis lazuli, along with clear quartz and apatite, celestite and blue calcite. The crystals rested on a pale yellow cloth. A fan made of raven and owl feathers was propped next to a small censer with a smudge stick in it. And figurines of an owl, raven, and hawk faced toward the east.

My altar cloth for the southern altar was burgundy, and the altar was decked out in carnelian and garnet, with the bones and skin of a snake, a statue of a salamander, and a wand fashioned of copper and crystals.

And to the west, the cloth was blue, and the stones were pearl and aquamarine, rainbow moonstone and selenite. A crystal bowl filled with Moon Water rested on the altar, along with statues of a dolphin, salmon, and shark. I had found a piece of driftwood and it sat at the base of the bowl.

In the center of the room was a round table where I worked my magic and read the bones.

On it sat one of my crystal balls and a candelabra with three candles in it—one red, one black, and one white. While most of the built-in shelves were filled with books, I had reserved an entire section for my spell components. Now, I sorted through them, selecting a piece of parchment paper, some Dragon's Blood ink and a calligraphy pen, a vial of Prosperity oil, and a bottle of Uncrossing Water. I set them on the center table, then lit the candles.

I had put my Uncrossing Water in a plant mister, and now I walked the Circle widdershins—counterclockwise—spraying it every few feet to mist the air. It cleared out the lingering cobwebs of energy from other spells and from anybody who might be passing through on the astral and etheric realms. While I could have smudged the space, the Uncrossing Water was stronger—it also issued a stern warning to stay out if not invited. Once I was done, I removed my sword from the wall where it hung on stag-shaped sword hangers. Facing the north, I held out the sword and slowly turned, casting the Circle.

Between the worlds, in sacred space, I cast this Circle 'round,
I weave this web of magic strong, I center it and ground
The energy, that it might hold against all with harm's intent,
I call upon great Arianrhod, that she will, her magic send.
I call the spirits of the Earth, to ground the magic's flow.

I call the spirits of the Air, sweep through with winds that blow.
I call the spirits of the Flame, burn brightly with your fuel.
I call the spirits of the Waves, temper, cleanse, and cool.
This Circle cast, the magic dance, visions let me see,
Between the worlds, I do stand. As I will, So Mote It Be.

The Circle settled. As the hum of magic flowed around me, I replaced my sword on the wall and took my place at the table. I stared at the parchment for a moment, trying to think of the best way to word the spell. Finally, dipping my pen in the Dragon's Blood ink, I etched several runes on the parchment and then, in the center, wrote:

Bring abundance to this dwelling.
Keep the coffers always swelling.
Radiate a welcome light,
Bring the guests both day and night.
With purses full and smiling ways,
Let them book their relaxing stays.
So Mote It Be.

After the ink dried, I dabbed a drop of the Prosperity oil on all four corners, then placed my hands over the paper and focused my energy into it, chanting the incantation three times. As the energy settled, I placed the paper on the altar to the north, and opened the Circle. That should hopefully counter some of the bad press the Bewitching Bedlam was getting.

Returning to the kitchen, I gathered my keys and purse and coat, and headed out for the day.

FIRST STOP: THE sheriff's office. I needed to feel out Delia for her take on what was going on. The Bedlam Town Hall was a large, brick building on the opposite side of town. The sheriff's office, fire department, county clerk, courthouse, utilities office, mayor's office, and library were all contained within the sprawling stone building. Built over a hundred years ago, the Bedlam Town Hall was a beautiful monstrosity of brick, stone, and masonry.

I parked in the lot and, zipping my jacket against the chill, dashed through the snow that continued to fall to the side stairs leading to the nearest entrance. The hallway wasn't exactly crowded, but there were more people hurrying through the building than I would have expected. Maybe there was a run on building permits or something.

The hall intersected with another shortly after the entrance and I turned left. To my left was the library. To the right, City Hall. I continued straight, toward the wing that sprawled out in the back section. There, was the fire department, the courthouse, and the sheriff's office. As I headed straight toward Delia's office, I caught sight of Joel Purdy—the fire marshal. He was a werebear, and the president of the Bedlam Arborists Society. We had talked briefly when I was hunting for a landscaper, but he recommended waiting till spring, promising to hook me up with a gardener who was also a landscape designer. We waved as I hung a right and pushed through the swinging doors leading into the sheriff's office.

Delia was standing beside the receptionist, who was also the dispatcher, reading off of a tablet. They both looked up as I entered.

"Maddy, I'm glad you're here. But give me a couple minutes, please. Just take a seat over in the waiting room and I'll be with you in a moment." She wiggled her fingers toward a seating area.

I gave her a quick nod and sat on the microfiber sofa. As I ran my hand along the arm, I realized I liked the feel of the material. Hmm, maybe I should consider microfiber instead of leather for the living room. It wouldn't be sweaty during summer, and microfiber was easy to clean. As I jotted a note to myself about it, I realized that a text had come in earlier that I hadn't noticed. I didn't recognize the number as I opened the message.

There, in bold letters, it read: DURHOLM HALL. TUNNELS. BE CAUTIOUS. SHE'S NOT ALONE.

I stared at it for a moment, trying to figure out who had sent it and exactly what it meant. There was no greeting, no other words. The number was the same one that I had received the text of the painting from.

WHO IS THIS? I texted back and waited. Nothing. I tried calling the number but nobody picked up and there was no voice mail to leave a message.

As I puzzled over the text, it clicked in my head. *Of course*. The text had to be about Rachel—it couldn't be about anybody else, could it? Straining to remember anything I might have heard about a Durholm Hall, I didn't notice Delia was standing beside me until she spoke.

"Maddy? Maddy?" Delia's voice penetrated the fog of my thoughts.

I jerked my head up. "Oh! I'm sorry, I thought you were going to be longer."

Delia grinned. "Nah. Not much cooking around here today. I just had to clarify something with Bernice. Come on back to my office." She led me through the maze of desks, then through a door with a frosted window. Stenciled on the window was her name, along with the word "Sheriff" below it.

As I settled into the chair opposite her desk, she poured a cup of coffee and offered me one.

"Thanks. Milk and two sugars, please."

Delia fixed my coffee, handing it to me when she was done. "So, what brings you here?"

"I wanted to find out how your talk with Linda went. Also, I wanted to ask about Ralph. I kind of want to see him, but I'm not sure if that would violate protocol." Truth was, I wanted to snoop around as much as possible, but I wasn't going to tell her that, nor was I going to mention the text I had gotten. Not yet.

"I don't think that's a good idea, Maddy." Settling in at her desk, Delia blew on the steaming coffee, then took a slow sip. "Oh, I needed that." She leaned back. "Okay, here's the thing. I tried to talk to Linda, but she was evasive."

"Evasive?"

"She really went out of her way to sidestep most of my questions. I wanted to get a feel for what was going on with the vampires and the coven. After all, the treaties were forged between Lena—the previous vampire queen—and Linda."

"Right. And?"

"Linda wouldn't talk about them. So I did a little digging. Now, I know you're going to discuss this with Sandy but please, don't let it reach any other ears. Especially anyone who might be involved in this mess."

By her tone, I knew she had discovered something disturbing. "I promise. So what did you find?"

She held up one finger. "Wait." Crossing to the door, she peeked out, then shut it carefully and came over to sit beside me. In low tones, she said, "We have a serious problem in town, Maddy. Since you're on the Inner Court Council of the coven, you need to know, especially since I think Linda knows, but she won't talk about it. But you can't tell Aegis—at least not now."

"Because he's a vampire?"

"Right. So here's what I managed to dig up. Essie has been chafing at the bit ever since she moved to town. As I said, the previous vampire queen of this region was named Lena. Apparently, she was dusted a few years back when her watch stopped on her and she didn't make it home in time. I know that vampires are supposed to have some sort of internal chronometer, but apparently

Lena's was on the fritz that day. She didn't realize it was near sunrise until it was too late."

"Where did Lena live?"

"She lived here in Bedlam. She was out on the water fishing—don't ask me, I gather it was a hobby of hers—when the sun started to rise. She tried to row to the docks, hoping to hide under it, but she didn't make it in time. *Whoosh*—so much dust and ashes. Even worse, a group of school kids from Neverfall were there. Their teacher had taken them there for a sunrise lesson on water sprites. They saw the entire episode."

Neverfall was a magical school for gifted students located on the other side of Bedlam Island. Children of all ages were sent to Neverfall from all over the country, and the academy had earned a stellar reputation among the elite magical circles.

I grimaced. "That must have been traumatic."

"Well, yes, it was. And the school ended up soothing a lot of parents of upset youngsters, even though it had nothing to do with them. On the other hand, there were enough witnesses that we knew exactly what happened. Except..."

"Except what? There wasn't anything suspicious, was there?"

"Maddy, think about it. Lena was in a boat. The motor gave out. Because she was out on running water, she couldn't dive in and swim for cover."

Vampires could travel over water, but they couldn't swim. They also had to remain in their corporeal forms and couldn't transform into mist or a bat or anything else until they were back on dry land. Which meant if Lena had gone out in a boat, then she couldn't have returned to shore any other way than via the boat. And if the motor conked out near sunrise, she was shit out of luck.

I suddenly realized what Delia was getting at. "Did you examine the motor?"

"Yes. Somebody had deliberately disabled it. Even a cursory examination showed evidence that it had been rigged to work for a short period, then burn out. So why would Lena go out on a boat that had been tampered with near sunrise?" Delia shook her head. "Somebody wanted her dusted. We'll never know why she was out there, but we can damned well bet that she was killed."

"When did Essie take over?"

"A few days after Lena died. Essie moved to Bedlam, took the crown, and instituted a number of changes. Lena had been working with your coven to establish good grounds. Essie has been far more resistant. As I said, when I tried to bring up the treaties and Essie, Linda clammed up. But from everything I've discovered, I now believe that Essie's doing her best to gain a foothold in Bedlam free from the coven's oversight."

"You mean the vampires want autonomy free from the treaty that Lena worked out."

Delia shrugged, then leaned her elbows on the desk. "I can't say for certain, but given what I know about Essie, I'm beginning to think so. And given the fact that we are pretty sure Lena was murdered and Essie swept in within days, I'm thinking she may have been behind it."

I thought about it for a moment. If we couldn't trust Essie, then we couldn't trust that she didn't know where Rachel was. But why would she warn me about Rachel if they were in cahoots? Then, a light bulb flashed. I snapped my fingers.

"Essie and Rachel seem to have some power control issues. My guess is that Rachel is after Essie's throne, like Essie was after Lena's throne. Essie wants to get rid of her so of course she's going to warn me that Rachel is dangerous."

"I was thinking over what you told me about your meeting with her. That's when I remembered Lena's death. When I told Linda everything I was thinking about, she seemed reluctant to go there. She briefly took Essie's side and insisted that Rachel's the real danger."

"Either way, the vamps are looking to make inroads on Bedlam." I shook my head. "Who do you put your bets on? Rachel or Essie being the main problem? Well, Rachel's a problem for me, but I mean for Bedlam?"

Delia paused, then blew out a long stream of air. "I don't know, but Rachel's rogue. She's not bound by the treaty. Though if she wrested control from Essie, she would ostensibly be, but I have a feeling she wouldn't abide by it. Essie's bound by a treaty she didn't create, but she's more subtle than Rachel."

"So, on one hand, if Rachel ousts Essie, she'll outright defy the treaty, while Essie may be working behind the scenes to dismantle it. No matter who's in charge, Bedlam is in danger."

With a nod, Delia added, "Remember, too—if the vamps are attempting to break the treaty, the only way to do that is to destroy your coven. Or at least, cripple it. The Moonrise Coven is the one group that was vested with controlling the vampires. Bedlam can make all the laws we want, but when a vampire doesn't want to follow the rules, there isn't much to force them to."

"But there aren't that many vamps on the island." I really didn't like the can of worms that we were opening.

"Essie is the vampire *queen* of the entire Pacific Northwest. Her nest—her court—may be *here*, but her reach extends throughout several states. Can you imagine the number of vamps that she can potentially call to her bidding?"

"And perhaps Rose's murder—whether or not they thought it was me—was the first attack against the coven. Ralph's feud with me was public. He was a convenient pawn." With another headache looming, I let out a long sigh. "I'll see if I can talk to Linda and get some answers. The Inner Court needs to prepare against more potential attacks. So, Rachel is after Aegis. She wants him back. But she may also be out for Essie's crown. And Rachel—or Essie—or both—may be out to destroy the entire coven."

With that lovely thought on my mind, I made my good-byes and headed out to finish my errands before meeting with Sandy. We had a lot to talk about, and I wasn't looking forward to any of it. As I crossed the snow-covered parking lot, the morning took on a silvery gloom, and for the first time, I wondered if spring would really come again.

Chapter 9

AFTER FINISHING UP some more of my Yule shopping—I found the perfect brandy flask for Sandy and a remote control mouse for Bubba—I stopped at the post office. The return address on the envelope in the box made me blink twice. My *mother* was writing to me? I hadn't heard from her in over a decade, since my wedding to Craig. But I'd sent her pictures of the Bewitching Bedlam, and a quick note about what I was up to, and I guess I should have expected her to respond. There was also a packet of papers from city hall, including several approved licenses and another short form to fill out.

As I slid back into my car, I stared at my mother's handwriting. The letter was postmarked from Dublin, so she must be on vacation because she usually stayed close to her home near Aughrusbeg Lough. She had moved there about thirty years ago, bored and—I think—lonely. She had friends who lived near there, and the change was a fresh start. Over the years, my mother had grown bored of so many of her hobbies. That was one of the troubles of having an incredibly long life span. The same-old, same-old year in and year out made it easy to grow weary and lose heart. I blew on my fingers—my gloves were fingerless for easy driving—and hesitantly edged open the letter.

My mother and I weren't on the best of terms and she had constantly been after me to find the right man and settle down. *Find yourself a nice quiet witch*, she had said over and over, someone who could handle the vagrancies of a wife with "too much go in her get-up-and-go." After a while, I quit protesting and just let her ramble on. Twenty minutes into any subject and she would start to wind down and I'd be able to shift the conversation. I had to face it. My mother was a golden-hearted ditz with a brain that was never going to win any races.

Dear Maudlin,

I read your letter as of late and I don't mind telling you, I think you're better off without Craig. He must have been an addle-brain to think he could keep you in the first place. You always were awfully smart, and he just didn't have what it took to keep you interested. I always, always said you shouldn't attempt to bond with a human. They just can't fathom our lifestyle and Craig was too arrogant. He couldn't handle his wife being better than he was. But darling, that certainly doesn't mean I meant you should take up with a vampire.

For the sake of the gods, think about this before you get in too deep. You've always been on the rebellious side, and I can't help but feel this is just another way for you to throw dirt in my face. I thought your wild side was firmly in check after that Mad Maudlin business. Granted, you had reason to be upset, but darling, really, turning into a vampire hunter because of a man? If I'd been upset over your father's desertion, do you think I'd be in the place I am now—

I tossed the letter on the seat beside me. That was as far as I could make it without seeing red. Not only was my mother a ditz, she was a tactless one and she had very little compassion for others. My father had almost died at the teeth of a vicious dog pack. Wild, they were out hunting for food when they found him. He was in the woods, gathering herbs for tinctures and salves when they attacked.

If a friend of his hadn't been near and heard the commotion, he would have died. After Jonathan brought him home, Father managed to heal up, even with my mother badgering him about how he had almost left us destitute, with "her being so helpless." After he was able to walk again, he took a job with the Society Magicka, a secret organization that watched over witches. With worldwide branches and a lot of casework, they kept Father away from home more often than not. Finally, he moved out altogether. I kept some contact with him, more than with my mother actually, but she had never forgiven him.

He moved out around the time I took up with Tom. My mother always blamed my father for being a bad influence on me. She still didn't know that I was in contact with him after all these years, but one of these days she was going to push me too far and it would come out. For now, though, she was safely on the other side of the ocean and I could set her letters down when they got too much to handle.

Shaking my head, I put the car in gear and headed for the Blue Jinn.

SANDY WAS WAITING for me. She jumped in the passenger seat as soon as I stopped.

"It's freaking cold out there," she said, clearing the mail off of the seat. As she fastened her seat belt, she smoothed out the pages of my mother's letter and began replacing them in the envelope when she caught sight of the return address. "You got a letter from *Zara*?"

"Um hmm. You can read it if you want." I didn't care. Sandy knew most all of my secrets, including how batshit crazy my mother was.

As she skimmed through it she snorted, then paused. "Um, have you read all of it?"

"No." I suddenly realized I didn't know where I was going. We had meant to go into the diner for lunch but apparently neither one of us had remembered that fact. "Where do you want to go? Piper's Chicken?"

"That sounds good," she said absently. "Maddy, you need to read the rest of this."

I turned left into the parking lot and edged into a spot near the door of the fast-food chicken joint. "Why? It's the same-old, same-old."

"Not quite. Near the end, she says, *'So I thought I'd come stay with you for a month in the summer. You'd like that, wouldn't you? It's been decades since I visited and I can meet this vampire of yours—if you're still together—and see what kind of business you're trying to run. If I like it, I might think about moving over there.'* That doesn't sound like the same-old you talk about."

Crap! My mother wanted to come visit. And maybe *move* here? The last time she flew over to hang out with me, we barely made it through my wedding before getting into a huge fight. I put her on a plane back to Ireland first thing the next morning. I loved Zara, but she made me want to tear my hair out.

"No. Just no. She's not coming here. I'll call her tonight and tell her to forget it. Last time was a disaster. You'd think she would have learned that we just don't get along in the same room."

"Your mother needs a crash course in reality. I hate to say it, but if there's any way you can waylay her, do it. She's not a good person for you to be around." Sandy tossed the letter over her shoulder into the back seat. "So, visit Rose's parents first?"

As much as I was dreading it, I nodded. "Let's do this thing. Remember, we can't say much about the case. Delia would have our hide."

"I know." Sandy stared at her hands. "If they act out, just remember, they're in mourning."

I nodded. They might very well blame me, since Rose died on my land. And with Rose's sister missing, they'd already be on edge. "Yeah. I'll be kind, no matter what they say."

I turned left on Wolfbane Street, then parked in front of a modest house. It looked like every other house of its generation, but the Williamses kept up the grounds, and the house was clean and tidy. Somehow, the sight of it made me feel sadder than before.

"Let's get this over with." I glanced at Sandy. "I'm not sure what the hell to say."

"Just say 'I'm sorry.' That's all we can offer."

We entered through the trellis-arched gate. A white picket fence cordoned off the yard. A tall maple shaded the right side of the house, and a couple of small firs stood guard to the left, but the overall impression was one of genteel poverty.

The Williamses kept their house looking neat—it was freshly painted—and the yard was manicured, but they probably had lived through some lean times. Usually magical families were fairly well off, gathering centuries of accumulated wealth. But nowadays, that wasn't quite so true. While there were magical ways to summon up wealth, prosperity spells didn't guarantee wealth beyond measure, and given the high cost of living of the current days, fewer witches found themselves in the filthy-rich category.

I stomped my feet on the top step to shake off

the snow as Sandy knocked at the door. I really had no idea what to expect. The Williamses were nice people, but their daughter had been murdered at my house. I wasn't sure how I'd feel about it if the situation was reversed.

The door opened. Mrs. Williams stood there, looking older than I remembered. Her hair was graying and her shoulders sloped, as if she were wearing the weight of the world on them.

"Maudlin, Sandy...won't you come in?" Her voice cracked as she took a step back, opening the door so we could enter.

The house was as tidy inside as it was out, although everything had a threadbare look to it. I had met too many families in this predicament. Everybody would be friendly and helpful, but when they insisted you stay for dinner, you knew it would come at a dear price for them.

"Thank you," I said uncertainly. "We wanted to come by and pay our respects. I'm so sorry, Mrs. Williams."

She led us into a parlor barely big enough for the love seat, sofa, and upright piano that it contained. The walls were papered in a faded hydrangea print, and the fireplace mantel looked like it could use refinishing. But there wasn't a speck of dust anywhere. Framed pictures lined the mantel, several of them I recognized as of Rose. Two were current, but in one, she had to have been four or five. She was standing knee-deep at the shore, laughing as she held up a starfish. There were pictures of another girl on the mantel too. She looked a lot like Rose, only she was a little older. In one photo, the girls were hugging.

"Rose always loved the water," Mrs. Williams said. "My girl, she was in tune with the Ocean Mother. If she'd been born one of the Fae, she would have been a siren, or an undine perhaps. She spent every moment she could near the water and loved living on an island."

"She was smart and talented, that's for sure." I glanced over at Sandy.

"We'll be sending out service notifications soon," her mother said. "When it's time for the actual Cord Cutting, we'll be in touch with your coven. We would like to ask if you would plan it for us, since she was a member."

"Of course." The service would be the first of three steps in our death rituals. It was a farewell to Rose, a look at her life—a tearful good-bye. The second step—the Cord Cutting—would be where we magically let her go and wished her well on her transition. That usually happened a year after the service. And shortly after the Cord Cutting would be the wake—the party to celebrate Rose's life and to close the cycle.

"I want to thank you for being her friend. Can we ask what she was doing at your house? The sheriff didn't really go into that. But whatever we can find out about our daughter's last hours, we'd like to know." Rose's mother fished a handkerchief out of her pocket and lowered herself to the love seat. "I'm sorry. I'm so tired, it seems."

As Sandy and I sat on the sofa, I realized there was something I needed to do. "Rose asked me for a Finding spell. To help locate her sister. I gather she's still missing?"

The expression on Mrs. Williams's face was painful. "Yes. Lavender vanished a couple weeks back. We know she's in danger."

"If you like, I'll come by in a few days, after you're over the worst of the shock. I can cast the spell I gave to Rose for you." I crossed the room and sat beside her on the love seat, taking her hand in mine. "Rose wanted so badly to help find her sister. I couldn't stop what happened to Rose, but maybe I can help you find Lavender, Mrs. Williams."

"Please call me Primrose." Rose's mother burst into tears as she squeezed my hand. "Thank you. Thank you. We're kitchen witches. We just don't have the knack for spells like that. My husband's been so angry. He thinks Lavender walked away from the family, but I know in my heart that she would never vanish on her own. Not without telling us. You'll have to work with me—he wouldn't like it, especially now with Rose...now that she's gone. But I know my daughters. Lavender loved her family."

I nodded, impulsively gathering her in my arms. She rested her head on my shoulder, weeping, and the sound of her crying was the sound of her heart breaking.

Sandy motioned for me to stay where I was and headed out into the hall.

A few minutes later, she was back, carrying a cup of steaming tea as Primrose's tears slowed. Primrose sat back and wiped her eyes with the handkerchief, then blew her nose. Sandy handed her the tea, cadging a grateful smile out of her.

"I can't thank you enough for your visit. My Oak, he's hurting so bad that he won't talk about it. So I've spent the past twenty-four hours keeping my mouth shut, but it's so hard. I felt like I was about to explode." She dabbed her eyes again, then took a sip of the tea. "Thank you. I feel so lost. I'm not sure what to do next."

Sandy scooched in on the other side. She picked up a shawl that was draped over the back of the love seat and draped it around Primrose's shoulders. "I'm going to send my assistant over. His name is Alex and he can help you sort out what to do next. He'll help you make arrangements for the service and so forth. Will that be all right?"

Primrose nodded, her eyes welling up again. "I can't thank you enough. Oak will come around. I think he feels he failed them both. If we can only find Lavender and make sure she's all right, that will help."

"I'll call you later this week and we'll talk over a time for the spell." I took down her number, storing it in my phone. Then Sandy and I left, after a round of hugs. Primrose waved at us from the door, a wistful look on her face.

As we slid back into the car, I gave one last look at the house. "I know what losing Tom was like for me. I can't imagine losing a child. Two, actually. I hope to hell we find Lavender alive and well, or the pain is going to be too much for that woman."

"I suspect Primrose is more resilient than you think. She just needs to be able to express her grief. It's keeping it bottled inside that does the damage. I hope for her sake, her husband comes around to facing his loss. Grief can turn into a mean bitterness when ignored." Sandy glanced at me. "We've done all we can here today, and I suspect we helped a lot more than you might think. Now, let's talk about Rachel. I told you I had an idea."

"Yeah, of finding her and staking her. If what Delia told me is true, then that would make Essie mighty happy."

"It would make you happy too, don't deny it."

I grinned. Then, sobering, I said, "How can I, though? What do you think? You've lived on Bedlam a lot longer than I have. Why do you think Linda wouldn't talk to Delia? Do you really think Essie might be looking at staging a coup and overthrowing the coven's rule? And, by the way, where are we going next?"

"Why don't we drive through the Bouncing Goats Espresso Shack and get a mocha while we talk?" She grinned at me. "Don't tell me you're going to pass up free caffeine?"

I snickered. "Of course not. Bouncing Goats it is."

As we pulled into line, I told Sandy about the text. "What's Durholm Hall? I don't think I remember it from when I lived here last."

Sandy stared at the screen. "Crap. That's where I suspect Rachel might be hanging out. Durholm Hall was a private estate at first. The Durholm family owned it—well, the last of the Durholm family. Sheila Durholm. She was a dryad. The house is like a massive ode to nature with a tree growing right through the center. The entire mansion was built around it. But Sheila developed root cancer and she willed the house to the Arborview Society."

The Arborview Society was a fraternal order of woodland-oriented Otherkin. Dryads, centaurs, nymphs, earth witches, anybody whose focus was on the preservation of nature and the practice of earth and water magic was welcome. They were a generally peaceful but powerful group who kept to themselves. Yet their lobbying powers in Congress were a silent, quiet force behind the scenes. They had affected a number of human measures regarding the forest industry, but managed to work so far under the covers that practically nobody outside of Bedlam—at least nobody in the human world—had heard of them.

"Why would she be there? A vampire? You think they'd hide her?"

"No, I don't. But the mansion has a number of tunnels beneath it. The perfect place for a vampire who's rogue to hang out. Nobody lives there. It's a day-use facility for their organization. Generally, they roll up the sidewalk at sunset and seldom start before sunrise from what I understand. Sheila died three years ago and I doubt if the Society has explored even half of what's hidden below that old mansion."

"What made you think of it? What made you think that Rachel might be hiding there?" I edged up toward the speaker. "What do you want?"

"Triple-shot large mocha with a dusting of cinnamon."

I ordered that, and a quad-shot white chocolate peppermint mocha for me. As we rounded the corner toward the service window, I started to pull out my card, but Sandy shoved a twenty my way.

"Let me pay today. Tell her to keep the change. It's the holiday season. She can't make all that much money."

"Okay, but I buy the next one." I eased into place at the window, handing the barista the twenty. As I accepted the drinks and handed them over to Sandy, she nestled them into the cup holders. Then I pulled into an open space in the parking lot next to the mini-mall adjacent to the coffee shop.

Sandy yelped as she burned her tongue on the hot drink, leaving a mustache of white foam on her lip. "Yowch. You'd think I'd learn to be patient one of these days."

"Yeah, well, you'd think we'd both learn that finding an unopened bottle of tequila doesn't mean we have to make a pitcher of margaritas and then drink them down in one sitting. But we know that's not going to happen. We're both unbalanced as hell and we probably always will be." I scrunched up my nose at her. "So now, tell me why you thought of Durholm Hall."

"Well, I was trying to think of all the best places on the island for a vampire to hide out. I realized there are far more than I could possibly come up with, so I began correlating what we knew. Rachel, as much as she's a vampire, doesn't seem the type to want to hide out with the worms and bugs in a cave. She probably wants to be near your house, given the object of her obsession is there. And did you forget? Aegis and the band are playing at a benefit for the Arborview Society for New Year's—they'll be right there in the hall."

I blinked. How had *that* slipped my mind? "I've been so focused on the bed and breakfast that I haven't paid much attention to his band schedule. If she's there, it means easy access."

"There's more. I decided to do a little digging, since I had some free time this morning. I searched for Rachel on Wyrdwix."

Wyrdwix was a Pretcom-oriented search engine. While it rivaled the other big ones, it also gave higher priority to the Pretcom and nature and focused on information not readily available to humans. Most of the humans hadn't even caught on that it existed, though a few diehard ghost-busting types had, and word was slowly leaking out.

"What did you find?"

"Rachel tried to buy Durholm Hall seven years ago. There was a scuffle between her and Sheila Durholm that resulted in Rachel being ousted from Bedlam. Apparently, Sheila threatened to stake her if she didn't leave well enough alone, and Lena ordered Rachel to leave the island. Rachel didn't belong to Lena's court, of course, but she acquiesced."

"Do you think Essie knows about that?"

"I don't know, but Rachel isn't supposed to even be here, given nobody lifted Lena's sanctions against her. I think Linda *has* to know this. She and Lena were actually friends."

"So, if Rachel wanted to buy Durholm Hall, there had to be a reason. I mean, there are a lot of estates on the island and some of them have been sitting empty for a few decades. Why not buy one of the other ones if she couldn't buy Durholm?"

Sandy consulted her notes. "I think I can answer that. Durholm Hall is built over a vortex—a land vortex. That's why the Arborview Society was so grateful that Sheila willed it to them. The earth energy there is strong. But it also acts as a gateway, from the bits and pieces of information that I found. There are rumors of something buried in the tunnels. A powerful artifact or gem, perhaps. I don't know. But there's something down there that amplifies power. Rachel is all about power."

That made sense to me. "Maybe it's something that would help her fight Essie for control. If Rachel is looking to oust the vampire queen and take her place, she's going to need help. Essie is too strong, otherwise. *And* Essie has a small army behind her. Not just the members of her nest here, but the members of her court."

"Do you think that they might be working together?" Sandy's question jolted me out of my thoughts.

"Why do you say that?"

"Consider this: Essie tells us that Rachel is out for control. The coven's concerned enough that we turn our attention in Rachel's direction. Rachel, of course, stirs up trouble and we take her out. That leaves Essie free to move, to start her revolt while everybody's focused on Rachel."

I thought about it for a moment, but it didn't track. "Unless Essie's the best damned actress there is, that doesn't track to me. But the idea that

Rachel could be searching for something buried below Durholm Hall makes sense. I wish I'd asked Aegis more about her last night."

"Well, do you want to go out to the hall?" Sandy's tone was on the verge of a dare.

I thought about it for a moment. "Don't you think that members of the Arborview Society are there right now? It's only 1:00 p.m."

"No, they're closed for the holidays except for a Solstice bash and a New Year's Eve party. We can sneak around the grounds and have a look, if nothing else."

Laughing, I capitulated. "Remember, we have an Esbat meeting tonight that we need to get ready for." I glanced at the clock. "We'll go, but we have to leave there by four o'clock at the latest. If Rachel *is* hiding out, I don't want to be around when she wakes up. Sunset falls at 4:18 today."

"You know to the exact moment, huh?" Sandy let out a snort.

"Hey, I like to keep tabs on my boyfriend's schedule."

"Let's get a move on, then. You dressed warm enough for this?"

I nodded. "Yeah, unfortunately I am. You know, the last time I went along with one of your bright ideas, I bought the house."

Sandy laughed as she leaned back in her seat. "See? I know what I'm doing. Besides, you know our pact."

"By heart. I still think we're a couple of fools." But I joined in as she started to sing. We had thought up the chant centuries before when we had sealed our friendship in a blood-bound oath, binding ourselves as sisters of the heart.

Out of the frying pan, into the fire.
To the adventure, we always aspire.
Though the flames may be harsh and the smoke may be thick,
Whatever may come, together we stick.

Still singing, I put the car into gear and we headed toward Durholm Hall. Probably to our deaths, I thought, but hey, at least we'd be together.

Chapter 10

BEDLAM ISLAND WAS heavily wooded. The town proper was centralized and most of the inhabitants lived on the outskirts. Durholm Hall was further out than my house, along Razor's Edge Road, a narrow two-lane road bordered on both sides by deep ravines filled with massive ferns, tall fir and cedar that reached for the sky, and birch and madrona trees. Brambles grew thick in the ravines and traversing through them could be an adventure in piercing all sorts of body parts you never considered piercing.

The road was of a fairly steep grade—a good seven to eight percent, uphill all the way. Though the two solitary snowplows the city of Bedlam owned got a good workout during the winter, Razor's Edge Road was one of the last to be plowed. It had been scraped clean a few days back, but the latest buildup of snow had left a thick covering of compacted ice and frozen snow on the asphalt, making the drive slick and dangerous.

"How on earth does the Arborview Society come out here every day to open up their offices? Or do they?" I gripped the steering wheel, leaning forward to make certain I could see clearly. The extra caffeine in my system wasn't hurting matters any, either. I had snow tires on my car, but it still felt like the tires weren't fully gripping the road.

"They don't. Except for a skeleton staff a couple days a week, they close down right before Thanksgiving and open up again in mid-January." Sandy stared out the side window. "You might want to pull toward the center a bit. You're getting awfully close to the edge of the ravine over here."

"That's because this damned road is a narrow-ass strip that should probably be one-way, but they decided to try to make two lanes out of it. I can scrunch over a little more but if anybody on the way down took one of these S-curves too quickly, we'd be toast if we get any farther toward the center line." I eased over another foot, but that was the best I could do. "I'm going twenty miles an hour right now."

"And you're doing just fine. At least we don't have that far to go. It's only about fifteen minutes away from your place."

"Makes me glad I didn't choose to buy farther out. My house is plenty rural, thank you." I let out a short breath. "So, do you happen to know anything about the layout of this place? How big is it? You said there are tunnels below it?"

"Tunnels, yes—they're sealed brick, I gather.

No dirt walls. I don't exactly know why but they're there. They can't be terribly extensive, though, or the house would cave in on top of them. The land up here isn't all that stable and one good quake could probably send a wall of mud and debris sliding down the ravines. Any house built near the edge of one would go right along with it."

"Is the land gated?"

"Gated, yes, but not to keep the public out. One of the purposes of the Arborview Society is to promote an understanding among the woodland Fae and others. They're working to protect the environment, so they make themselves as accessible as they can to humans and Pretcom alike. Because you know as well as I do that the werewolves and some of the other shifters aren't nearly as eco-conscious as witches and Fae."

She was right. The preternatural community had its problems, and one of them was an inborn tendency to cling to one's own kind. The werewolves and a few of the other shifters tended to be more human in nature than the rest of us. They had learned to walk among human society for years before we all just came out of the broom closet, so to speak.

When the clock turned over to the year 2000, the Otherkin slipped out of the shadows. The next couple years had been rocky, with a number of skirmishes, but society had finally quieted down. The hate groups were still around, but for the most part they were more afraid of us than we were of them. They kept their rhetoric on the verbal side rather than putting it into action. The few times the backlash reached violence, the Otherkin had made certain to exhibit exactly what we were capable of. There would be no repeat of the Spanish Inquisition, no government-sanctioned witch hunters. That was a given—not up for debate.

But a subset of humans preferred some of the Otherkin over the rest because they seemed most familiar. The good old boys tended to like the werewolves. The feminists liked the witches. Everybody both gravitated to—and feared—the Fae. And so on.

Sandy pulled out her phone and consulted her notes. "Durholm Hall is about the size of your place, in terms of the house. But it sits on fifteen acres, so there's a lot of land there and most of it is heavily wooded. There's a grove in the woods somewhere, about an acre in size, that they use for public rituals and ceremonies. I think they must have private areas that are cordoned off, too, but that's my own speculation."

"I doubt if we can cover the entire area—not thoroughly—before four o'clock, but we should be able to scope out at least part of it. What are we looking for?"

"Your guess is as good as mine. Anything that seems odd or out of the ordinary. Anything that seems misplaced." She glanced at me, then lifted her backpack that she had brought along. "I know you're going to yell at me, but I brought along a few things."

"You *didn't*." I had asked her time and again not to bring any wooden stakes to the house, in consideration of Aegis's feelings. Sandy tended to go around armed with whatever she could find that would fit in a tote bag. She owned a pearl-handled gun, though our magic was stronger than most bullets—stronger, though maybe not as lethal, usually. Bullets had one use: to shoot things and/or people. Magic could be targeted in a number of directions. Sandy also carried mace, pepper spray, brass knuckles, and a switchblade. I had to hand it to her—she lived by the motto, "Be prepared."

"Yes, I did. I brought four stakes in case we find more vampires than we bargained for. And given the text you received, that's a distinct possibility. We can't just sit back and wait, Maddy. The more we find out, the more it sounds like we're at the tip of the iceberg, the edge of a vampire war. If Essie or Rachel intend to take over Bedlam, it doesn't matter which one it is. We're all in trouble."

She had a point. I just didn't want to think about it, but since I had somehow been dropkicked squarely in the center of this altercation, I had better face it. "Fine. We're going vampire hunting. I just hope we find them before they realize we're tracking them down."

"Me too," Sandy said. "Me too."

THE GATE AT Durholm Hall was closed, but unlocked. I stopped while Sandy jumped out from the car and waded through the snow to open it up. She waited until I pulled through, then closed it behind us. No use in drawing attention to the fact that we were here. The drive to the house only took a couple of moments, but the snow was fresh and unmarked by tire tracks other than ours. We were the only ones who had come through today, as far as I could tell.

Trees on either side of the drive loomed tall and dark. The fir and cedar had kept their needles, of course, but the interspersed maple and oak were bare-limbed, their boughs lacing like a dark tangle overhead. The drive was narrow enough that, in places, trees from one side stretched wide across, tangling with their kin on the other side.

The estate came into view. Sandy was right. The mansion stood as large and imposing as the Bewitching Bedlam. Stately, it looked like it had been built yesterday, and the walls were a soft green against the white of the snow. Not quite mint, the green was the color of pale young buds at the beginning of spring. The driveway encircled the house and I followed it, parking in back where nobody would see the car from the road. We had left tire tracks, but chances were, nobody would bother to check them out, given the drive to the house had curved through forest, but I wanted to make certain.

As I turned off the ignition a soft hush fell around us. I closed my eyes, reaching out. The steady throb of earth magic ran deep, pulsing like a heartbeat through the land, through the house, through the very air surrounding the estate. It was firm and alive, vibrant and powerful and protective.

"This land is old," I said, feeling the need to

whisper. Spirits lived in these woods and I didn't want to waken them.

"Yes, Bedlam Island is old, but so very awake and aware."

That much, most people sensed when they came to visit. But living on Bedlam was like living in a battery charger that was set to "High."

The San Juan Islands had been created by the march of the glaciers as they traveled down through the northwestern states, and then again as they receded. The tectonic plates had moved and shifted, causing massive upheavals in the earth, as their quaking drove the land upward. The ice from the glaciers carved channels through the land, bringing the islands to life.

Most of the islands existed in a rain shadow of sorts, protected from the rain that the Puget Sound area usually received. But Bedlam was at the northernmost edge of the archipelago, jogging out at just the right angle so that it received the brunt of the storms. Add to that the fact that storms tended to follow magic. They were attracted by the powers of the ley lines that ran through the island, the power radiated out by the inhabitants called stormy weather to it like a lightning rod attracted lightning.

What it came down to was that Bedlam received weather anomalous to the rest of the San Juan Islands, thanks to both its positioning and the magical energy that permeated the island.

I gazed up at the darkened house. "We can't just break in, so what do you suggest?"

"I doubt that Rachel would be hiding out inside. I think we should start with the outskirts of the house—look for anything out of the ordinary around the estate. You've got a really good nose for trouble, Maddy. Time to put it to use."

Sandy was right. My inner alarms were always on hyperdrive. I might not always act on them—my bad—but they usually were spot-on. I pulled my coat tighter and wrapped a scarf around my neck to protect both my throat and ears from the chill. As I slid out of the car, the chill hit like a freight train.

"Damn, it's cold."

I crossed my arms, jamming my be-gloved hands under my armpits, as I scanned the area, not quite sure what I was looking for. But Sandy was right. I'd know what it was when I saw it.

She trudged through the snow around the car to stand beside me, huddling as best as she could away from the blowing snow. "I think back that way is the public ritual area."

"There probably won't be anything there. A vampire who wants to hide isn't going to stick her coffin in plain sight in an area that a number of people are likely to frequent. Besides, she's not going to be aboveground. Or at least not out in the open. She needs to hide from the sunlight—daylight—whatever."

As I probed the ether, I became aware of whispering on the wind. It didn't sound human, or even like the Otherkin. Instead, I heard a faint singing drift past and I closed my eyes to listen. A ballad, it sounded like, a tale of lost love and frozen hearts from a time long lost. The song was melancholy and muffling, as though it were pressing my joy deep down to a place that was difficult to find. The song was a death dirge, a maiden left to early widowhood singing on the cliffs above a thrashing sea.

"Maddy? Maddy? Are you all right?"

As Sandy's words penetrated my brain, I realized I was crying. I dashed away the tears, which were almost frozen on my face, feeling and lost. "I think I picked up on a kelpie's song, or a naiad's lament. So many of the bog and water spirits have haunting voices."

Some of them were very good at using their melancholy songs to lure humans into their traps, too. The naiads weren't quite so dangerous, but the kelpie and will-o'-the-wisps were just two of the deadly Fae who liked to dine on a good-size morsel of flesh whenever they could. And the Fae didn't hesitate to mesmerize witches.

"Just don't go prancing off in search of whoever the singer is. Jenny Greenteeth eats whoever she can catch. And there are other dangerous Fae around." Sandy frowned. "Is that all you're picking up?"

"Let me search again. If you notice me drifting off, stop me before I do something stupid." I closed my eyes again, trying to ignore the cold that was seeping through my coat. "I wish we were immune to cold," I muttered.

"You and me both. But wait till we hit the hot-flash stage. We'll dive into the snowbanks and melt them."

I laughed, breaking out of my trance. "We have a ways to go before then. I'm just glad that vampires are sterile."

Sandy stopped, slowly turning. "Where did you hear that?"

I frowned. "They're dead. They don't...*surely* they don't still produce sperm?"

"I dunno. They can still eat and shit and piss, can't they? I don't know whether the notion that they're sterile is an old-wives' tale or not." She arched an eyebrow. "Haven't been using protection with Aegis, have you?"

I stared at her, hoping to hell she was wrong. "I think maybe I'd better find out before we... Crap. I *can't* get pregnant, especially from a vampire. What the hell would happen then?"

"I have no clue. Come on, back to our quest here. We can look up the facts when we get home. Linda has to know. We can ask at the Esbat tonight." She grinned, watching the horror spread over my face as I envisioned casually dropping that question in Circle.

Oh by the way, do you know if I can get pregnant from banging my boyfriend? He's dead, and a vampire, but can he still become a babydaddy? Oh, hell no.

I refocused my attention on the energy surrounding Durholm Hall. As I forced myself to move beyond the ballads and laments that beckoned me into the woodland, I discovered another layer of energy. A deep, sweeping reverberation. The heartbeat of the earth. It buoyed me up, swept me in like nothing else. I understood this sound and the cadence shifted, matching my own heartbeat. The earth elementals were strong here, and they were alive and awake. But there was a blip in the pattern—something that didn't belong there.

A disturbance in the force, Luke.

Frowning, I tried to analyze it. The energy was unnatural. It was the fly in the ointment, the even number in a field of primes. And then, I began to understand what was wrong. The rhythm was the heartbeat of life—of the living earth. The blip? It was something that should not be alive. I tried to trace it, to follow it back, but there was too much static. I lost my focus.

My eyes flying open, I whirled to face Sandy. "She's here. Well, *some* vampire. I don't know if there are more around. I was able to key in on something that's unnaturally alive. But when I tried to trace it, everything vanished." I looked up at the house. "So, the tunnels that are below this place?"

Sandy nodded. "It would make the most sense. The trouble is we have to find the entrance, and then make our way through the labyrinth to where she's hiding." She didn't sound nearly as confident as she had before.

I glanced at the sky. "We don't have that long. I sure as hell don't want to be caught belowground with a vampire who would like to see me turned into yesterday's news. Besides, if she's not alone, we'll be in deep shit. Remember, our blood is like candy to them. We don't want to tempt fate."

Sandy pulled out her pocket watch. Witches usually had trouble wearing watches. Our energy fields put a stop to all sorts of electronics. Though as long as we didn't sit right next to them, we managed just fine with TVs and stereos. But watches were another matter. Sandy, however, had managed to find a pocket watch that didn't stop around her. One of the Tinker Fae had made it for her, and had enchanted it to work even around her magical field.

"It's already three-fifteen. We have forty-five minutes. I think you're right, we'd better call it quits for the day. Or at least, we can hunt for an entrance but come four o'clock, we get back to the car. And if we find the entrance, we mark it so that we can come back at sunrise, after they're asleep, and have all day to hunt around for them."

"Good idea. Where do we start? It makes sense that there's an entrance inside the estate, but I don't want to get caught breaking and entering. You know that they're going to have wards and alarms set up. Given that, there should be at least one outside entrance. Otherwise, Rachel and her cronies wouldn't have found it."

I cast a glance around, looking for any obvious entrances. "Maybe there's a small Barrow around here? Wherever the Fae tend to congregate, chances are you're going to find a Barrow."

"Yeah, or a portal on a tree. Let's have a look at the trees closest to the estate." Sandy waded through the snow over to one of the large firs that shadowed the hall. As I watched her go, I realized that we were leaving tracks.

"You realize that even if it snows all night, we're leaving breadcrumbs behind? The snow won't fall fast enough to cover our trail."

Sandy shrugged. "Well, we'll just have to hope

they don't look too hard. Or don't care. After all, we could just be visitors interested in the Arborview Society who didn't know that Durholm Hall was closed today. Right?"

I didn't share her optimistic outlook, but decided to play along. There wasn't much else we could do. I followed her over to the fir and we examined the trunk of the tree. Nothing. Five trees later, I was beginning to think this was a stupid idea and that we were wasting our time.

"You know, there are hundreds of trees. By the time we examine them all, the snow will be gone and we'll be staring summer in the face." I wiped my forehead with one of my gloves. The exertion of tromping through the snow had worked up a sweat, and the chill from the air had turned that perspiration into a clammy, cold trickle of water that was dripping down my face.

"Then what do you suggest?" Exasperated, Sandy rested her hands on her hips. "You don't want to break into the house, so this is the next best thing I can think of."

I snorted. "*Really?* You *seriously* think we could waltz into that place without any repercussions?"

She squeezed her eyes shut, then blurted out, "*No.* I'm sorry, I'm just frightened for you. I think Rachel's out to kill you and I want to find her first. This is bringing up flashbacks of the Burning Times. I remember when the witch hunters were chasing you. I managed to stay undercover most of the time, but I remember what it was like, wondering if they were going to trip you up and if I was going to lose my best friend. My blood-bound sister." She lowered her voice. "Maddy, vampires scare me. I admit it. I stood by you when you ran as Mad Maudlin. I've tried to be supportive because Aegis seems like a pretty good guy, but vampires scare the fuck out of me."

I waded through the snow over to her side and wrapped my arm around her waist. "Most of them scare me too. I'm being careful with Aegis, but I promise you, he's different from the majority. But tromping around in the woods looking for a secret entrance to an underground lair, and doing it in three feet of snow? This just isn't feasible. We have to think of a better way. Come on, let's head back to my place and get ready for the Esbat."

A thought struck me as we made our way back to the car. "Maybe Aegis knows about the tunnels. We can ask him."

"You really think he'll tell you if he thinks you're going after Rachel?" Sandy frowned. "I think he's scared enough of what she might do to you that he might lie. You can ask him, but I'm not betting on the truth there. However, there's another possibility."

As we got into the car and I started up the heater, grateful to be out of the falling snow, Sandy fastened her seat belt and then let out a long, slow breath.

"Lihi? I need you." She grinned at me as we waited. "She's got a wealth of knowledge and is very astute about finding out things I need to know."

A moment later, the homunculus appeared. Lihi yawned, stretching as she fluttered up, her wings gently flapping, and then sat on the dashboard of my car.

"You rang?"

"Lihi, you see that mansion?"

Lihi nodded. "It's rather hard to miss, considering we're parked right in back of it."

"It's called Durholm Hall. Maddy and I need to know about a set of secret tunnels running beneath it. We need to know where the outside entrances are. I'd like you to check into it, but be cautious. Vampires are involved." Sandy fumbled through her purse, then pulled out an especially beautiful Herkimer diamond about the size of my thumbnail. The double-terminated quartz crystal shimmered, prisms reflecting within it. "If you find out before the end of the week, you can have this as a bonus."

Lihi's eyes widened as she reached out to run one perfectly formed, tiny hand along it. "Oooo, that's so pretty. On the job, boss!" And without another word, she disappeared.

"She does love her crystals," Sandy said. "I'm not sure what the homunculi do with them, but they're a prized commodity in their community."

"Are they demons of some sort?" I wasn't clear on what the homunculi were. "They aren't like golems, are they?"

"No, they're not artificially created. They bear their young live. That much I do know. But I don't think they're demons, either. I believe they inhabit the same realm as the djinn. Bubba might know. Or I can ask Lihi. I don't think she'll be offended."

"You mean, she's never mentioned her home before?" I found it odd, but then again a vast number of the Pretcom kept to themselves. The Otherkin were cagey, and spreading around knowledge about one's nature led to vulnerability.

Sandy shook her head. "No, she never has. I just know that one day when I decided I needed a magical assistant and cast a Summoning spell, she was one of the ones who appeared to apply for the job. I got along with her best, so we made a pact."

"How many did you interview?" I started the ignition and eased out of the parking lot. It was close to three-forty-five and I wanted to be long gone by the time the vampires rose. We'd be safely back in my house by sunset.

"I talked to three homunculi, one brownie, and a couple of house sprites. But Lihi and I hit it off from the beginning." Sandy frowned. "Rachel can't get in your house, can she?"

"I've never invited her in. Hell, I've never even met her." But something nagged at the back of my thoughts. "Wait. Franny said she saw her in the house talking to Aegis. So yes, Rachel has been in my house. The house was standing empty so she didn't need an invitation. And since she was there at least one time—more by the sound of it—she can still gain entrance until I officially revoke her invitation. I'll do that first thing when we get home."

That led to all sorts of thoughts. Had she been in my house while I'd been asleep? Had she left the rose outside on my balcony? While Aegis and I had been making love? The thought that she might have snuck around, peeking in on us like some undead voyeur squicked me out in all sorts of ways.

"I'm glad I asked." Sandy glanced out the window. "Why do you think she approached Ralph? The Greyhoof boys aren't the most generous of souls but they aren't really a bad lot, either. They've done a lot of charity work around the island over the years, even if they did grump about it."

I cautiously maneuvered onto the road and tried not to clench my teeth as we began the harrowing drive down the steep and winding hill. The fresh snow over black ice made for dangerous driving conditions and the thick wall of flakes coming down made it difficult to see. I turned on my brights, not wanting to blind anybody else, but it made it easier to see the road.

"I'm not sure. Maybe because they have the Heart's Desire Inn. I suppose her choice was calculated to put them into the spotlight instead of herself. What she didn't count on was that Ralph runs off his mouth more than an old fishwife. He's not shy about talking to save his own skin. When I caught him in my bathroom, he was more than anxious to avoid being turned into some nasty beetle or a worm." I snorted. "I don't think he realizes I can't do that, and I intend to keep that misconception alive."

"Always leave them thinking you're more powerful than you really are." She searched through her purse. "Want a mint?"

"Sure." I held out my hand, then slapped the wintergreen lozenge into my mouth, biting into the creamy explosion of sugar and mint. "You do realize that we have to press Linda on the vampire issue tonight? If the coven is in danger, then we can't keep quiet about all that's been happening. Linda's going to have to talk about it."

"Why do you think she wouldn't talk to Delia?" Sandy popped another mint in her mouth, then closed her purse.

"I don't know. But we have to keep this quiet from the public for now. What do you think would happen if Bedlam finds out that the vampires are looking at staging a coup on the island? I'm worried about Aegis." Visions of dozens of wanna-be vampire slayers ran through my head.

"You think people will be out with pitchforks and torches? Bedlam's more advanced than that, don't you think?"

"More like wooden stakes and silver chains. The werewolves don't like the vampires to begin with. And if they've got a reason to go vampire hunting, you know they will. And witches—the ones not aligned with the coven? Remember, our blood is an aphrodisiac to vampires. Witches aren't likely to stop and think, 'Let's give them the benefit of the doubt.' "

"Well, you have a point there. So what do you want to do about it?" Sandy worried her lip. "What concerns me is this: if the vamps are planning this here, are they also targeting other communities? Maybe in human-centric towns? Humans are far less capable of fighting them than we are. We have magic and strength and an understanding of the Otherkin nature that a human just doesn't have."

I didn't want to think about it. I remembered all too well running cross-country, staking vampire after vampire because they were dead set on feeding on the humans, even as a number of those humans would have happily burned me at the stake.

But times had changed. During the Revealing, a good share of the human world had managed to adapt. There were pockets that feared us, and some smaller nations that had driven out the Pretcom, but overall, we were as much a part of the world now as they were.

"You're right. We have to discuss this. But we also have to reinforce the idea that not all vampires are in on this. Not all of them are out to climb to the top of the food chain."

We were nearing the bottom of the hill and I began to breathe easier. As I swung a left, heading back to my place, I glanced at the clock. Four on the dot.

"Maddy, I hate to remind you of this, but they *are* at the top of the food chain. There isn't any more room for them to climb. It's all a matter of whether they want to enforce their power, or whether they're willing to live and let live. To work with us rather than against us. I'm afraid that if Essie and those of her mindset decide to make a move for control, not only will it set everybody against all vampires, but it will lead to a civil war among their own kind. And that thought is a bloody terrifying one."

I eased into the driveway, grimacing. "You come up with the most delightful thoughts, you know." As I gathered my things from the backseat, I picked up my mother's letter. "And to think, a few hours ago the most worrisome thing on my mind was the fact that my mother wants to come visit."

Sandy laughed then. "You know, I still think that tops the list in frightening events of the day. Come on, let's get inside and get ready for tonight. This Esbat promises to be a doozy, all right."

As we headed into the house, I glanced up at the darkening sky. We were approaching the longest night of the year, and it certainly felt like the darkness was crowding in.

Chapter 11

AS I GATHERED my things for the meeting, I felt nervous. Not only was I unsure of just what we were facing, but I wasn't looking forward to talking to Aegis about all of this.

"I have to get back to my car. My things for the meeting are in the trunk," Sandy said.

"We'll stop on the way and you can drive from the Blue Jinn parking lot. I need to officially un-invite Rachel from entering the house tonight. But if we don't find her, it won't do any good after next week. A bed and breakfast isn't a private residence. She'll be able to enter whenever she wants, unless I use garlic as an air freshener and silver-leaf every surface."

That was one of the problems with barring vampires. A private residence could be protected by simply refusing them entrance. A *public* place? Not quite so easy, although it could be done. But the magic involved in the warding was energy-intensive, and it had to be shored up on a regular basis. I could do it, but then it would prevent Aegis from living with me.

In my bedroom, I stripped off my clothes. "I need a shower. If you want to shower before the meeting, feel free. You can wear one of my gowns back to your car to pick up your ritual regalia, so you don't have to dress in those wet things again."

We were both soaked from tromping around in the woods. As I tossed my jeans and top in the laundry basket, Sandy gratefully began shedding her own clothes.

"Aegis will probably be up before I'm out of the shower, so when you come back to the room, I'd be wearing something."

She laughed. "The last thing he needs is to see me naked. I don't want to scare the shit out of him or make him think I'm interested in a threesome."

"I thought we left those days long behind," I said with a snort. "But I doubt he'd say no."

"Don't be so sure. It's obvious that fangy boyfriend of yours has eyes only for you, Maddy. Which is one reason I feel so bad talking trash about vamps. I know he cares about you. I'm just worried about his essential nature." She waved me on. "Go on. Get wet. I want a hot shower and I can't have one till you do."

"Yes you can, doofus. Use one of the showers in one of the other guest rooms. We have four guest rooms." I tossed her a towel. "Go on, don't be shy."

"Thanks, don't mind if I do." Wrapping the towel around her, she sauntered out the door.

I headed into the bathroom, frowning as Bubba followed me. "You going to keep watch for me again, Bub?"

"Mrow." He rubbed against my leg, his tail pluming out to tickle my knee.

"I'll pet you when I'm done. Go hop on the bed and wait."

With a mild huff, he turned and bounced over to the bed, stretching out. I blew him a kiss and shut the door behind me. After I turned on the water, I pulled my hair back into a ponytail so it wouldn't get wet.

Staring at myself in the mirror, I ran my hand over my stomach. My abs weren't flat and toned. My hips and tummy had a layer of extra padding on them, and my breasts made it hard for me to see my feet, but I loved my body. It had stood the test of time for me, and I remembered the centuries when lean bodies usually meant poverty. Extra padding meant a person had enough food to avoid starving. Witches weren't as affected by the economy as humans—we had other ways of finding food—but I'd known too many people who died from starvation. I never complained about a bit of extra weight.

The water was warm and steamy and I stepped beneath it, keeping my hair from getting wet. As I lathered up, the spicy scent of foaming winterberry soap clouding my senses, I visualized the stress of the day washing away, spiraling down the drain. The fragrance of pomegranate and cinnamon, of clove and cranberry enveloped me in a pleasant haze and I finally began to relax for the first time since waking up. I lingered under the water for a while, not wanting to step out of the spray, but finally I was about as clean as I was going to get. Any longer and I'd start to prune up. Reluctantly, I turned off the taps and emerged from the shower. I wrapped the towel around me and opened the door to my bedroom, grimacing as the chill hit me.

"Good evening." Aegis was waiting on the bed next to Bubba.

I slipped into my robe as he crossed the room to kiss me hello. "Hello, love."

"Who's in the shower down the hall? I decided it would be rude to look, so thought I'd ask first and attack later."

I stroked his face. "Sandy's here. She's taking a shower here so she can just change into her robes before our Esbat meeting tonight. We had a long and rather interesting day." I padded over to my closet and held up my own Esbat robe. It was a rich, deep purple halter-top gown, ankle length with a plunging neckline that left very little to the imagination, and silver crystals beaded onto the front. The back was low and I ended up wearing a nude strapless bra for support.

As I dressed, Aegis watched, sitting cross-legged on the bed. "What did you do today?"

I adjusted my dress, then fastened a lilac shawl around my shoulders with a crystal brooch. I usually used a silver pin, but I'd save that until we were out of the house so that I wouldn't accidentally brush against Aegis.

"We went to visit Rose's parents. Talked to her mother. It was so sad. I promised to help them cast the Finding spell Rose came to me about, to seek out her sister."

"What if the girl doesn't want to be found?"

"She's not the type to run off without telling anybody. She's in trouble of some sort or another. I have no doubt about that." I paused, wondering how to approach the next point of conversation, but was saved by Sandy's entrance. She was wearing one of my maxi-dresses. It was a little short on her, but far too big. Sandy was about a size two compared to my size eight. I handed her a sash and she belted it around her waist. The dress was still too large but at least she wasn't swimming in it.

"I don't know if I have anything smaller," I said, assessing her.

"Doesn't matter. I'm only going to be changing again for Circle. So don't sweat it." She paused, waggling her fingers at Aegis. "What's shaking, glam boy?"

He snorted. "I'm about as glam as a glamour photo."

"Dude, you really are. Don't be self-deprecatory. It doesn't become you." She paused. "So, has Maddy told you our thoughts about Rachel yet?"

He frowned, glancing at me. "No. What are those thoughts?"

I rolled my eyes at her. "See? I was about to dive into that conversation, but now it feels even more awkward because...well...never mind." I climbed on the bed and began to pet Bubba, like I had promised. He preened, tilting his head back so I could scritch the good spots, right behind his ears. Purring, he began to knead the covers.

"Here's the thing," I finally said. "Aegis, the sheriff has evidence that Essie may be staging a coup on the island. And Rachel's vying for the throne. If she manages to dethrone Essie, things could get very ugly."

He blinked. "What? One thing at a time, please."

"Essie's rumored to be attempting to stage a coup. She might be working against our coven, actually. That possibility has come up more than once today."

As the words soaked in, Aegis's expression darkened. "This isn't the news I had hoped to hear. And you say that Rachel might be looking to dethrone Essie?"

"Yes, and she'd be worse than Essie. At least Essie has some inkling of the importance of working with people—humans and Otherkin alike—but we don't think Rachel has that sense of integrity. Not to mention, it looks like she might be hanging out in the tunnels below Durholm Hall. We went out there but weren't able to find any tangible proof yet. It's important the island not be caught off guard if this is really something Essie is planning."

Looking perplexed, Aegis began to sputter. "But how does Ralph fit into all this? How does—I'm getting confused."

Sandy cleared her throat. "We think that Ralph is in thrall to Rachel. That she's using him against Maddy because she's out for revenge against you, and what better way than destroy the livelihood of her ex-boyfriend's girlfriend?"

"And if she's trying to destroy the coven, might as well start with the member she hates the most.

Whatever the case, it also occurred to us that you've had her in this house before. She's been here and there's nothing to keep her out until I revoke the invocation. But once the Bewitching Bedlam opens, it won't be so easy. If I do a general keep-away spell toward vampires, that will catch you in its net." I stopped, out of breath.

"Rock and a hard place, dude," Sandy said. "But we need to know anything we can about Rachel's weaknesses. Whether you like it or not, we're going to have to stake her to keep her from coming after Maddy here. It's a bad situation, no matter which way you turn it."

Aegis deflated, slowly lowering himself to the bench next to my vanity. "You're right. This is a nasty mess. You're absolutely correct in that she's been in this house and can still get in. I didn't even think about that until now. I can't very well revoke my invitation—it won't work vampire-to-vampire. But you can seal her out until the grand opening. Maddy, do that before you leave tonight. Do that now, in fact."

He sounded so grave that I headed over to my French doors. The spell would work housewide when cast from any door, and this seemed as good a place as any. I raised my arms to my sides, breathing deeply, then envisioned Rachel in my mind. Creating a barrier against her, I focused on the doors, representing all doors to my home, all entrances—windows, grates, and ducts, including Aegis's secret door.

"Rachel, I revoke your passage into my home. I revoke your ability to enter through any opening.

You are barred from my house, by the power of the gods, by the power of my will, So Mote It Be." As my will rang out, there was a sudden swish, as if doors slammed shut all around us. Then, silence and a feeling of protection. I opened my eyes. "The spell took."

"I felt it settle in. Until you open to the public, you're safe enough in here from her. But remember—her allies can enter. So don't invite strangers over," Sandy said.

Aegis dropped to the bed, hanging his head. "I feel so responsible for this. I'm so sorry."

"There's no reason to blame yourself. You didn't know she was going to turn out to be a stalker. But before we have to leave, can you tell us anything that makes her vulnerable?" Sandy motioned to my heavy black cloak in the closet. "You're going to need that."

I slid it around my shoulders, fastening the Celtic knotwork pin.

Aegis rubbed his hands through his hair and cleared his throat. "All right. What I know about Rachel is she's stronger than most vampires. She's also smart."

"Not feeling so positive about this," I said, touching up my lip gloss. "We're looking for weaknesses, not reasons to fear her. We've got enough of those."

He laughed, but it was a broken laugh. "Well, I can tell you she's so vain that she's susceptible to flattery. She actually tripped up once before because she believed a couple who were praising her strength when she was threatening them. They almost manage to stake her before she realized that they weren't all that impressed with her beauty and wit. That threw her for a loop, but I don't think she learned a lesson from it."

Sandy frowned. "Is that all you have?"

"Well, there's one other thing. If it were anybody else, I'd hate to use this against her, but..."

"Tell us. We need every ounce of weaponry we can get." I turned, ready to go.

"Rachel had a child once, before she was turned. She suffers an incredible amount of guilt that she channels into rage because when she was turned, she killed her daughter. It was horrible, I gather. She went home after rising. Before she realized what she was doing, she drained her daughter dry. The girl's name was Rebecca, and she was only six years old." He rubbed his chin. "You can see what that might do to someone."

I stared at him. "Yeah, I do. It could push you a couple of ways. She chose to go all hell-on-heels. I understand how things like that can threaten to destroy you." I paused, trying to dial back my judgment. Maybe she hadn't had a Cassandra or a Fata Morgana to force her to look in the mirror. Maybe she had no one except a voice in her head reminding her over and over of what she had done. "I suppose I see how she could become what she is. But that doesn't change what we need to do."

"I know, but maybe it helps explain why she's the way she is." Aegis shrugged. "We all have our hair shirts." He glanced at the clock. "Are you sure you have to go tonight? I'd feel safer if you weren't out there on the road. I know what she's capable of, Maddy. I don't want you to pay for my mistakes." He wrapped his arms around me, kissing the top of my head. He smelled like leather and musk and all things hot and sexy. "I couldn't bear it if something happened to you."

I nuzzled into his arms. "Be safe yourself, love. You know she's out to hurt you. I'll be careful but yes, I have to go. We have to talk to Linda tonight and there's magic that must be done." Carefully disentangling from his embrace, I pulled back and sucked in a long breath. "I'll call you when we get there safe. And I'll call you when I leave the temple."

"Please do. Or I'll be over there hunting you down." He glanced out the doors. "At least she can't get in here."

"M-row?" Bubba rubbed around my legs, leaving a trail of orange and white fur on my cloak. Par for the course.

I leaned down and petted him. "I'm sorry but yes, we all have to go out. You should be safe here, though. Rachel can't get in, and Ralph's in jail. You know how to hide if you need to, Bub." He licked my hand, then rubbed the side of his cheek against it. "Yes, I belong to you. Be good, Bubba. I'll be home as soon as I can."

As we all headed out, I glanced back at the mansion. At the beginning, I had bought it to spite Craig and for something different to do. Now, I loved the place, and I wanted to feel safe here. I wanted to create a long-term home that nobody could ever take away from me.

THE SKY HAD cleared and the night was icy cold. Our breath came in puffs as we headed toward our cars. At least, Sandy's and mine did. Aegis didn't breathe. He waited until we were safe in my car and pulling out of the drive before getting into his. As we headed toward the Blue Jinn, where we had left Sandy's car, I thought about what Aegis had said.

"That must have been horrible, what Rachel went through." I kept my eyes on the road, watching for ice.

"True, but it doesn't follow that she had to turn into a monster. We all have losses, some far worse than hers, and not everybody turns into a vicious killer because of it. You remember what Aegis said about her."

"Oh, I know she's deadly, but now I feel a little sorry for her. At least she didn't turn her daughter as well as kill her. That much, you have to credit her with." I pressed my lips shut. I didn't like feeling sorry for someone who was out to get me, but I did.

"Maddy, you did what you had to do. They were vicious killers and you saved countless people burning down that village." Sandy let out a soft breath.

"There were children in that village." I swerved to miss a dog that was crossing the road. "I was so angry, so furious. I burned them like the witch hunters burned our own kind."

"Those children were ruthless hunters. Vampires, Maddy. All of them. I was there. Your memory is tinged with guilt. But I was there. The flames were necessary. And Fata and I, we're just as responsible. But we knew what we were doing was right—what you led us to do was the right thing. We saved innocent lives."

I eased into the Blue Jinn's parking lot and turned off the engine. "I suppose so."

Sandy glanced at me. "You *know* so."

I bit my lip. "I think the Erris excommunicated me from the coven because of what I did. She didn't think I was right."

"The Erris was out of touch. She didn't see the victims. She didn't see the fear in the streets when the vampires were starting to rise. Besides, you grew so popular that she was afraid you were going to take her spot. That's why she excommunicated you. The other Elders didn't agree with her, but her word was law in the coven."

"What? She turned me out, named me pariah because she thought I was going to steal her thunder? Why didn't you tell me this before? All this time, I thought that the entire council censured me, when it was her own hunger for power? She's been dead for a century. You could have told me any time during the past hundred years. What the fuck were you thinking?"

Relief swept over me. I hadn't actually been cast out for what I had done, so much as for how much people had both feared and cheered me. I gripped the steering wheel.

"Maddy?"

"I don't think I can talk now. I'll see you at the temple." I stared straight ahead, waiting for her to get out of the car. Part of me wanted to scream for her to get the hell out, the other part was frantically trying to calm myself down.

"I'm sorry, Maddy. I should have told you sooner." Sandy fell silent. Then, with tears streaming down her cheeks, she silently got out of the car. As soon as she was safely in her own, I pulled out of the parking lot and headed toward the temple.

THE TEMPLE ARIANRHOD where the Moonrise Coven met sat on five acres. With a private grove where we held rituals on the High Holy days, and our Esbats during the summer and early autumn, the temple itself was dedicated to the goddess Arianrhod, the Lady of the Silver Wheel. I had been brought up in a family dedicated to her, so it made sense for me to enter a coven that was pledged to work with her.

For a temple, it looked a lot like an old brick schoolhouse—probably because that's what it had originally been: a small schoolhouse that had housed students of a particularly magical system that no longer existed in Bedlam.

Three families had practiced the tradition, but it was obscure and esoteric, and when the last of the children left the island, the trad died out. The coven had bought the building from the city thirty years before we had decked it out to our needs, transforming the land it sat on into a lush grove, complete with fire pit, ritual circle, and celebratory meadow for community events.

The building itself was three stories, including the basement. We kept the largest room for community-wide rituals, usually held on the High Holy days during winter and the rainy season. The smaller rooms were divided into administrative rooms, private practice rooms, and one member of the coven—Jonquil—lived here. She cleaned the school and kept an eye on the temple in exchange for rent.

The parking lot was full. It looked like everybody was here tonight. Which made sense, given we had to discuss Rose's death. I eased into one of the spots as close to the temple as possible. Still angry at Sandy's revelation, I also realized that we had to talk before ritual. Never enter sacred space without clearing out anger. If two members of the coven were angry at one another, they were required to either make peace before entering ritual space, or they were barred from participating.

Stray anger all too often took on form and manifested in scary-assed ways. Like the time I was pissed at Rodger—who had been glomming all over me—and forgot to clear it up before ritual. He had developed a raging erection that wouldn't go away, and he had ended up in the hospital for priapism. It had been embarrassing to admit that I had been at fault, but I confessed because one thing that was continually driven home among magical families was the necessity to accept responsibility for our actions.

As I stepped out of the car, Sandy eased into the spot next to me. She slammed her door and marched over to me, hands on her hips. "I have something to say and you're going to listen to me, Maudlin Gallowglass."

I glanced up at the gathering clouds. "Make it quick because it looks like we're in for another round of snow and it's coming on quick."

She licked her lips. "I should have told you. I know that. I screwed up big time, but after all these years, I wasn't sure how to approach it. I was scared, Maddy, that you'd think I was in on it with the Erris. But she threatened me. She told me if I ever mentioned what I had found out that she would strip our powers if Fata and I told you anything."

I stared at her. The Erris had been more than capable of carrying out her threats. And we had bent our will to hers without question. We trusted her, even though we seldom got to see her. Tom had adored her like a mother. When he was turned, it hit her almost as hard as it had hit me. But where I ran wild, she focused on gathering more power.

"What? She actually did that?"

Sandy shrugged. "Yeah. She did. After she died, I thought about telling you a thousand times. Every time I'd start, something would still my tongue. Until tonight. Tonight, it felt like the right time."

Still in shock, but no longer furious, I let out a long, slow breath. "Then I guess it's the right time for me to know. All right. I trust that you wouldn't deliberately keep something this important from me without good reason. And truth is, I don't know how it would have changed me. It would have been nice to live without the shame she piled on me. But it's too late to know what changes it would have made."

Sandy held out her hand just as the snow began to fall. The flakes melted against her skin. "Friends? I can't stand it when we're mad at each other."

I pressed my lips together. We had been through thick and thin. Through centuries. And always, Sandy had been there for me. My best friend. My blood-oath sister.

I slowly took her hand. "Friends. Always."

After all the years, that was all we needed to say. I took her hand and we ran toward the building, trying not to slip on the ice and snow.

Chapter 12

LINDA AND THE others were gathered in the preparation room, sitting in a semi circle. The Moonrise Coven consisted of twenty-one members. Thirteen of us were in the Inner Court, seven were Outer Court. Only now that number stood at six with Rose's death.

Among the Inner Court, five of us—Linda, Sandy, Terrance, Angus, and me—formed the council. We were responsible for the final decisions of the coven. Everybody was present, except for Rose, of course. And by the looks on their faces, they had all heard the news.

"Sorry we're late." I slid into my place, with the other council members. Sandy sat next to me. I glanced over at Linda who shot me a puzzled look, but when I shook my head, she turned back to the rest of the coven.

She held up her wand. "If we're all here, then, I

declare the December Esbat meeting of the Moonrise Coven under way. Before we go any further, I have made a decision that tonight we will forgo ritual. With all that's happened this week, the energy would be far too volatile to practice any magic. But we have several issues to discuss."

Shauna, a member of the Inner Court, raised her hand. "What happened? We know Rose is dead but I've been out of town and have no clue what went on."

Linda let out a long breath, then glanced over at me. "Are you comfortable taking questions? I don't have the answers to a lot of them and, considering the circumstances, you might."

I wasn't, but sometimes we all had to step up and take on uncomfortable roles.

"I'll tell you all that I can, but with the case under investigation, it's limited. I found Rose in my backyard. She was murdered. Ralph Greyhoof is in jail for questioning on the matter. As to anything else, I can't discuss it, so please don't ask any other questions about it." I turned to Linda. "Sandy and I *really* need to talk to you in private."

Looking confused, she led us into her office while the others broke out the post-ritual snacks. Given we weren't working magic, the food promised an early comfort.

As she shut the door behind her, Linda cast a quick Silence spell to keep what we said within the confines of the room. Nobody would be able to listen at the door to hear what we were saying. While theoretically that shouldn't even be a worry, the others were curious and it was better to avoid the possibility.

Linda motioned to the sofa near her desk and we sat. I leaned forward, elbows resting on my knees as I entwined my fingers together.

"Linda, we need to talk about Rachel and Essie. You do know who Rachel is, don't you?"

She slowly nodded. "Yeah, I remember Lena having issues with her."

"Then we need to know if you're aware that the vamps may be trying for a coup."

She pinched the top of her nose, between her brows, and let out a sigh. After a long while, she nodded. "A coup? What are you talking about?"

Linda was lying—it rang in her voice. I glanced at Sandy, who shot me a "WTF" look. "Surely you know or heard what Delia had to say? She and I talked today."

Linda's shoulders sank. "All right. Yes, I know that Essie and Rachel are vying for control of the throne. And yes, Essie assassinated Lena, although nobody will ever be able to prove it."

"And you never said a word to us *because*—?" Sandy's eyes narrowed.

"Because it's ancient history. Lena's dust. Essie agreed to abide by the treaty. End of story." Linda frowned. "As High Priestess of this coven, it's up to me what information to disseminate to the group."

"The full coven, yes, but the Inner Court Council? No." Sandy scowled. "What gives you the right to keep an assassination silent? I remember when that happened. You never said a word about Essie being responsible for Lena's death."

"You're questioning my authority?"

I broke in before Sandy could respond. "Enough. Linda, this is personal. Delia thinks that Rose was killed by mistake. That whoever murdered her was after me instead."

Linda paused, breathing deeply as she straightened her shoulders. "I'm sorry about that, Maddy."

"So, you know they're vying for the throne. That means you knew Rachel was back in town even though Lena had barred her from returning?" I asked, trying to piece together the puzzle. There were still several gaping holes and Linda seemed to know some of the answers, but she was resisting and that made me terribly suspicious.

Linda inclined her head, but said nothing. The pinched look on her face was growing stronger.

Sandy suddenly snapped her fingers. "I think I've figured something out. What if Essie's behind Rose's death? What if she enthralled Ralph and made him believe she was Rachel. That way she could take out one of the members of the Inner Court *and* her rival for the throne at the same time and Rose was the unintended victim."

I cocked my head, trying to follow her reasoning. "How do you figure?"

Sandy sounded excited as she laid it out for me. "What if Essie thought, why not kill you and make it look like Rachel's fault? Ralph was quick about giving you info on who put him up to sneaking into your bathroom, wasn't he?"

I nodded. "Too quick. I see your point. When a vampire enthralls someone, they usually put a gag order on them to protect themselves. But he told me right off, full description, and that he thought she was a vampire."

"Then you get the text telling you where Rachel is hiding. Not overly obvious but enough for you to put two and two together. Essie had to know that Aegis would go after Rachel if you were hurt, and he could easily win. He's stronger than Rachel by a long shot."

I was beginning to see where she was going with this. "And if somehow Essie's plan didn't work, then I would assume Rachel was after me and take care of her myself. Which would leave Essie in the clear, her rival out of the picture, and there would be one fewer member of the coven to worry about."

Sandy reached over and laid a light hand on my arm. "Maddy...you were Mad Maudlin, one of the scariest vampire hunters in history. Essie's bound to know that. While you were living in Seattle you weren't such a threat, but you moved to Bedlam. If she's out to stage a takeover, then you are a serious threat to her and her people."

I felt a shiver race over my back. "Damn. I never thought of that, but it makes sense."

"Are you sure about this? Rachel sounds like the most likely suspect. Plus, she has a grudge against you." Linda's voice was shaky.

I turned to her. "Linda, what aren't you telling us? You know full well we're on the right track, so why are you clamming up? What do you know about Essie?"

Linda paused and I thought she wasn't going to answer, but then she finally crossed to her bookshelf where she withdrew a thin volume.

"Here." She handed me the book. "Page fifty-two."

I opened the journal to find that it was hand written rather than actual print. "It feels old."

"It *is* old. It's five hundred years old and the only way it's managed to make it this far is because it's been magically enchanted to stand through time." Linda reached over to lovingly stroke the leather. "Whoever takes over as coven leader will inherit this and be responsible for its upkeep."

I opened it to page fifty-two and glanced at the writing. In clear, concise cursive was a description of Essie, along with a careful drawing of her. I recognized her right off, even though the style of dress had changed and her hair was different.

Essie Vanderbilt: Essie Vanderbilt was born in New Orleans in 1844. She was part of the Voudou community, and studied with Marie Laveau, the Queen of Voodoo, and later with Marie's daughter—also named Marie—who was also a practitioner. Essie was considered one of the most powerful Voudou priestesses ever, and people far and wide feared her as well as flocked to her for help with their problems. At the height of her career, when she was 33, Essie made the mistake of walking down a back alley. Where no human in the area would dare harm her, vampires didn't have the same qualms.

A vampire named Philippe, originally over from Paris, ruled as the Vampire King of the Southern States. He had fallen for Essie and also saw her a potential business partner, decided it was time to stop taking "No" for an answer. He dragged Essie into the shadows and forced her to drink from his veins, then drained her dry. When she rose, he expected her to succumb to his will, but he had no clue how powerful Essie was. She had managed to retain some of her powers, though she would never again be accepted in her Voudou House, and she set out to destroy Philippe for what he did to her. The two waged war, dividing both the vampire community and the Otherkin community, and in the end, she threw him down, staking him in front of his court, and took his crown. When she later decided to move north, she forged an alliance with her successor and moved up in the hierarchy of the Vampire Nation, a loose alliance of regents.

She later moved to the Pacific Northwest, and supplanted Lena Verda as queen.

I silently handed the book to Sandy, who quickly skimmed the passage.

"Crap." She set the book on the coffee table. "So, Essie would certainly know what to do with your hair, all right, if Ralph got away without you finding him. Rachel doesn't have a magical background, does she?"

I shook my head. "I don't think so. Aegis certainly didn't mention anything of the sort. So, we have Essie, a Voudou vampire who apparently enjoys her power. Given her reaction when Philippe tried to assert his authority over her, it's clear she doesn't play well with others." Turning to Linda, I added, "All right. You knew Essie's a Voudou priestess. Why on earth did you allow her to stay on the island?"

Linda stared at her feet. She began to rock back and forth, biting her lip. I had the strange feeling that we were about to enter territory that would shift everything.

"Linda, Rose was murdered. I'm a target and—apparently—so is our entire coven. If you know anything, you owe us an explanation. I know you've been our High Priestess for decades, but you *can't* hide something that might put us all at risk."

"I know that!" A shower of sparks sizzled around her. Linda ran heavy fire energy and it flared when she was upset.

Sandy tapped the coffee table. "So, out with it."

"*All right*. I guess I can't hide it anymore. Essie has something on me. She's holding some information over my head and I'm terrified to cross her." Linda looked so miserable that I wanted to reach over and give her a hug, but I refrained.

"What is it? You can tell us."

"Apparently, I have no choice." Sounding bitter, Linda crossed to her desk and retrieved a picture frame from a locked drawer. She returned, handing it to us. We found ourselves staring at a lovely young woman with an innocent look on her face. "This is Patricia. She's my daughter."

That was odd. Linda had never mentioned a daughter before, or a husband. "You're married?"

"No, I've never been married. But I used to live with a man named Ryan. I got pregnant and he left. Patty is the result of that union. He was human, so she's mixed blood. But Patty is a special-needs child...woman now. She's developmentally disabled. She has the emotional age of about a ten-year-old, even though she's seventy-two. She inherited my longevity, but few of my other powers. I realized early on that she would be a target for my enemies, and I have more of them than you want to think. So I took her to Kali, my best friend at the time. Kali always wanted children but couldn't have any. She welcomed Patty in as her own and has raised her from the first month." Her voice was wistful, and I could see both regret and relief in her eyes.

"Essie found out about Patty?"

Linda nodded. "She's threatened to turn Patty. She also somehow convinced Kali to keep Patty prisoner in the house. I don't know what she promised her, but my best friend has been cooperating with the vampires to keep my daughter confined, away from me. Essie has enough threads in her network to kill Patty if I make a move against her or Kali. I'd never make it down there in time."

Heartsick, I rubbed my forehead. "Why don't you just take out Essie?" But even as I said it, I knew the answer.

Linda shrugged. "Because she left instructions that if she's staked by any person, Patty's to be attacked without question. And Essie's allies are widespread enough that there's no chance I could save my daughter before they got to her. So you see, Maddy, I have to protect Essie in order to save Patty's life."

"Holy fuck on a hand grenade." Sandy's irritation vanished, as did mine. "What can we do to help?"

"Nothing. No one can help me." Tears trickling out of the corners of her eyes, Linda hung her head. "I'm so embarrassed. I've broken my oath to the coven. I'm as good as a warlock. I've put you all in danger, and I know I should resign, but Essie wants me in power. I'm her pawn. And now, she'll find out that you know, and my daughter will die."

I glanced over at Sandy. This complicated matters in an entirely jacked-up way. But it explained why Linda had tried to sidestep the discussion.

"So that's why she's targeting me instead of you. I'm a threat. I'm a known enemy to vampires, even though I may be canoodling with one."

Linda sighed, and the sound settled around us. "Maddy, you're so well-known for your past. You thought you could walk away from it, but memories run long and deep among Otherkin. Add to that you've taken up with Aegis, an unaligned vampire who's refused to join Essie's court. He's too powerful for her to destroy, and you're under his protection."

"So Essie doesn't intend to wipe out the coven. If she has you under her thumb, she has control because nobody questions your authority. Once she gets rid of the members of the coven who might make waves, nobody will know what's going on until she takes control."

The thought that the Moonrise Coven had become a sock-puppet for the vampires was sobering. But I realized that the drive to protect one's young was primary among most beings. Now what the hell were we going to do? We couldn't leave things alone. On the other hand, if we made any sort of move, it would endanger an innocent girl.

Sandy appeared to be thinking along the same

lines. She flashed me a warning look, her gaze darting from me to the door. Linda was a powerful witch—stronger than Sandy and me put together. She could probably destroy us and then spin some lie about what happened.

"So what are you going to do?" I finally asked her.

Linda closed her eyes and we tensed.

Then, she slowly opened them again and gazed at us with resignation. "I don't care about what happens to me. You're asking me to choose between my daughter and your own lives. How can I sacrifice an entire coven of people who depend on me? I'm so lost right now."

I bit my lip. "What if we can smuggle Patty out of where she's being held captive and then make sure you two reach a sanctuary? You could go to the mother temple, perhaps? You and Patty could live there until Essie is long gone."

"I'd willingly give up everything to make sure my daughter is safe. But how can you manage it? Kali and her family are threatened, as well."

"Let Sandy and me find a way. We've got resources and I have the beginnings of an idea. We won't do anything to put you or your daughter in danger without consulting you."

With a whisper, she agreed. "I suppose I have no choice. At least you know the truth."

"What do we tell them?" I nodded toward the door. "We've been in here a long time."

Sandy stood, brushing the wrinkles out of her robes. "We tell them that we were discussing how best to help Rose's parents through this. And that we were discussing matters concerning Ralph Greyhoof."

"That sounds like a plan." I turned to Linda. "I want you to be ready to leave. We won't do anything without your permission, but in case the opportunity arises, you need to be ready to go." That was the first time I had ever lied to my High Priestess, but I had no choice. If I told her what I was planning she'd freak and put a stop to it.

She gave me a long look. "I'm holding you to your word."

I nodded. I'd deal with the aftermath later.

"All right. Let's go." She led the way.

We returned to the others, who looked at us expectantly. I kept my expression neutral, as did Sandy. Linda quietly explained that, with so much going on, we were going to meet later in the month. That tonight was just not the best time. Within ten minutes, the room had emptied and Sandy and I were standing outside by our cars. I let out a long breath, realizing that I had been afraid that we wouldn't be allowed to leave the temple.

"Speaking of Ralph, if he's in thrall to Essie, how do we break it?" Sandy asked.

"First step: find out if he is. I asked Delia to check Ralph for fang marks but she hasn't gotten back to me yet."

"Give her a call."

I pulled out my cell. "Good thought."

Delia answered on the first ring. "Maddy, I was going to call you but I knew tonight was an Esbat night. Ralph's definitely in thrall to somebody. We found the marks. I've got an APB out on Rachel right now. Hold on."

I heard the rustle of papers, then she said something to someone and came back on the line.

"Sorry. We've got an incident over at Benjar's Tavern. The Shalof boys are roughing it up again and they've broken out into the street. It's become a street brawl."

The Shalof boys usually spent at least one night a week cooling it off in jail. They were a couple of happy-go-lucky centaurs until they got drunk and then they took to jousting in the streets, usually with a couple of their goblin friends. Goblins weren't officially welcome in Bedlam, but somehow they always managed to show up and cause havoc before Delia rousted them out.

"All right. I've sent a couple of units over to deal with them. Now, about Ralph."

"Delia, you said you think he's in thrall. Do you think he actually killed Rose? Because I don't. I think somebody else did it and set him up. He was in the wrong place at the wrong time."

"Well, there's one way to find out for certain. We can draw some of his blood and run it by the Oracle. She can tell whether or not it's Rachel holding him in thrall."

I thought for a moment. If Essie found out and she suspected she might be exposed, then Ralph was a dead man. But there was another way to cope with someone caught in thrall.

"No! Don't do that. Ask Andy McGee for one of his Tochlan potions. It will cost a small fortune but I'll pay for it if the department can't. Give it to Ralph and it will break the thrall. It might also destroy his memories of the incident, but please—I guarantee you, he didn't do it."

"You know who did." Delia lowered her voice. "And for some reason you can't tell me who or why right now."

"Right."

"All right, we'll play it your way. I'll get the potion. I have to keep him locked up for now, but he'll be out of thrall and no longer subject to control."

"Keep a watch on him. Don't leave him alone for a moment. I'll talk to you in a little while. Meanwhile, I've got a few things to arrange."

As I hung up, I turned to Sandy. "I need to go home and talk to Bubba."

Sandy gave me a long look. "You aren't—"

"Can you come back home with me?" I asked. "And ask Lihi to come over."

"All right, but if you're thinking what I think you are, heaven help us."

"Right now, we could use a little help from the gods. I'm going to call Aegis. We have to trust him. We're walking on shaky ground right now and I really don't want to topple over the edge." As I started the engine, I made sure Sandy was safe in her car before easing out of the parking lot and heading back to my house.

"Call Aegis." I activated the voice control on my phone.

"Maddy?" He answered quickly. "Are you all right?"

"Heading home. Can you meet us there? I've got

a lot to tell you, and the sooner the better. Sandy's coming with me. Tell the band it's important if they complain." I could hear the strumming of Jorge's guitar in the background.

"I'm on my way." He didn't ask questions, didn't try to make any excuses. Just those four words. Before he hung up, he added, "Be careful, Maddy. Especially on your way into the house. I'll try to be there before you arrive."

Bedlam had always seemed such a happy place to me, but now it felt fraught with danger in all directions. The realization that Essie had Linda over a barrel had hit me like a sledgehammer. Not only did it mean that a woman I cared for deeply was being manipulated and blackmailed, but it felt like the entire base on which I had built my current foundation was crumbling. I had devoted myself to the coven and to the Inner Court. And now, to find out that our High Priestess had sold us out shook me to the core.

By the time we arrived at the house, easing into the driveway, Aegis was waiting for us. He opened my door, then escorted me to Sandy's car where he did the same. We said nothing as we silently passed through the backyard until we were through the sliding door and safely inside. Aegis shut the slider and locked the door, then moved to the kitchen island where a pot of tea was steeping, the fragrant scent of raspberry and lemon rising through the air. He had also made sandwiches and soup—grilled cheese and tomato soup, and a batch of gingerbread cookies.

"You work fast." I stared at the homey scene,

feeling my eyes cloud over.

Craig, my ex, had never done anything like this. He had been so threatened by the fact that I was a witch that I had turned into Suzy Homemaker trying to make him happy. In the end, I had lost myself. I thought I had left most of the baggage behind. But when I saw Aegis, wearing an apron over leather pants and bare chest, making soup and sandwiches for me and my best friend, I burst out into tears.

"Are you all right?" Concerned, he reached out for me, but I held up my hand.

"Stop. Yes, I'm okay." But I wasn't. I looked at him and he set down the teapot. With a gentle smile, he opened his arms. I buried myself in his embrace as he wrapped me in his love.

"I love you. I do, Maddy. I will do anything to keep you safe."

"I love you too. It never ceases to amaze me how supportive you are, and how caring. You changed the entire paradigm of my world." I was talking into his chest, muffled by my tears, but somehow he heard me.

"Don't lose your suspicion, Maddy. I'm not typical of my kind. Outside of this house, away from me, you'll find most vampires are deadly predators who wouldn't think twice about using you as a tasty witchy juice box."

"He's right. Maddy, we need to talk about tonight." Sandy carried over the pot of soup and ladled it into our bowls. "You know, I thought you were nuts, but if Bubba can help, then we need to go that route. Otherwise, everyone in town is in danger."

That put a stop to the hugging. Aegis let go. "What are you talking about?"

"We found out that Rachel isn't our biggest problem in the vampire world. And frankly, if we don't put a stop to this, it could easily destroy Bedlam and everybody who has made a life here." And with that, I called Bubba in, and we told both of them everything we had discovered.

Chapter 13

AFTER WE FINISHED, Aegis leaned back and set down the cookie he was eating. He rubbed his chin, his dark eyes flashing. “So it’s true. Essie and Rachel are having a pissing contest over Bedlam. I didn’t expect Linda to be caught up in this, but it’s easy to see how Essie engineered it. If you want control over somebody, find their vulnerability, especially if it threatens someone or something they love. People will do anything they can to protect their loved ones, more than they will to protect themselves.”

“We need to figure out how to safely smuggle Patty away from her prison. Neither one of us knows anything like a teleportation spell—only the most powerful among witches and magicians know those.” I looked over at Bubba, who was stretched out on the table, listening.

“Maddy, are you sure about this?” Sandy petted

Bubba's head. "You know what can happen."

I contemplated Bubba carefully. He stared back at me, just as intently. "I know. I also know that Bubba can be incredibly understanding. When a life hangs in the balance, he's not likely to mess around."

"M'rrow." Bubba rolled over and crouched, his belly low to the table.

Aegis winced but said nothing.

"We can't let Essie take over Bedlam. Nobody would be safe." I stared into Bubba's eyes. "Oh, Bubba. I wish that Patty would be safely reunited with her mother, and that the pair of them make it to a safe haven without endangering anybody who's innocent in the process."

Bubba flopped on his back, exposing his belly. Hesitantly, I rubbed the thick orange fur. He let out a trill, purring loudly, then gently licked my hand and sat up. Holding my breath, I looked around. Nothing. A moment later, I shrugged and sat back in my chair as Bubba meandered off to have himself a nosh.

"I guess we wait now. If he decides to help us, we'll know soon enough." Turning back to Aegis, I added, "Delia's watching Ralph."

Sandy toyed with her sandwich. "Things are a mess. What do we do next?"

"We finish our dinner." I dipped my sandwich in my soup, then sat back and let out a soft breath. "Relax as much as you can. Eating while stressed isn't good for you."

"All right." Sandy concentrated on her meal, holding out her soup bowl for seconds. As Aegis refilled it for her, she said, "Before I forget, I think we should set some ground rules for the position of High Priestess. No kids. We can't chance having this happen again."

"I don't know if we can make that a requirement." Talk of children jogged my memory. Blushing, I licked my lips. "Aegis, that reminds me. Vampires can't sire children, can they?"

He looked confused. "We can turn just about anybody."

"No, I don't mean *that* kind of sire."

Once again, the blank look.

Sandy let out a laugh. "She means, can you get her pregnant? I heard some rumor that a vampire can spawn a kid, but I'm not sure how accurate that was. Is your sperm up and jumping, or did they die with you?"

Mortified, I covered my face, peeking between my fingers. "Put it any more bluntly, why don't you?"

With a snort, Sandy leaned across and patted my arm. "He doesn't mind, do you, Aegis? After all, you weren't getting anywhere asking your way."

Aegis placed her soup bowl in front of her. "I don't mind. I wasn't expecting that question. I guess it's not a subject that comes up every day, is it?" He refilled my bowl next, then took his place again. "After all, vampires can eat and drink, even though the food passes through with minimal processing, so to speak. We don't absorb nutrients from it."

"Yet another visual I never want to think about again. Brain bleach time." I tried to shake off the image of what "minimal processing" meant.

"As for getting you pregnant, I never thought about it. I do know that a vampire can father a child, if he rises from being turned before thirty-six hours. Other than that, I'm not sure. I've never heard of a child engendered from a union with a vampire, but that doesn't mean it hasn't happened. Now, I'm wondering." He looked so freaked that his mood transferred to me.

"So the only way to know at this point is if I get pregnant." I frowned. "I'll start using a fertility blocker, because the last thing we need is a vampire-witch baby." I wasn't interested in being a mother, and the thought of what such a mix might turn out to be terrified me.

With that settled for the moment, I turned back to my food. We ate in silence for a while, trying to enjoy the downtime, until the doorbell rang. I frowned, wondering who it could be. Aegis went to answer.

"Do you really think Essie would turn Linda's daughter? It seems like such a cruel thing to do." Sandy pushed back her dishes. "I know vampires can be nasty. I'm the first to caution people about them. But that's downright ruthless."

"I think Essie's about as ruthless as they come. Sandy, what the hell are we going to do about Linda? Not only is she our High Priestess, she's also the mayor. I understand her reasoning, but the fact is, she turned traitor to the coven and to Bedlam. This is a lot more complicated than I ever expected it to be."

I was struggling to sort out my feelings on the

subject. We couldn't just leave things alone. Sure, if we went after Rachel as the main culprit, it would appease Essie, and remove the worry that she might strike out at Linda's daughter. But that wasn't an answer. The vampires would increase their control over Bedlam. Being a party to that was as good as actively working with them to destroy the town. Once they got their fangs hooked into running this island, it meant that all the Otherkin would be at their beck and call.

"We can't let it go," I said, making up my mind. "I don't know if Bubba will help us, but one way or another, we have to drive them back. Linda has to resign. She can't ever approach this objectively. Not with Patty's life at stake."

"Accept collateral damage?" Sandy asked. When I gave her a scathing look, she added, "I'm not judging your decision. I agree. But you know as well as I do that we're going to be blamed for any fallout."

"We've been blamed for far worse in the past." I quieted down as Aegis returned, Delia following him. "Delia, I'm glad you're here. We need to talk."

She glanced at Aegis, who motioned to a chair. He looked about as happy as I felt.

"We have a problem," she said, sitting down and resting one elbow on the table. "Did either of you know that Linda has a daughter?"

"Yeah, we just found out tonight, in fact. Why?" I shifted, suddenly chilled. Had Essie already gotten to Patty? Was the girl already dead?

"I got the strangest call twenty minutes ago from a police station down in Georgia. They told me that

Linda's daughter is in jail. They tried to contact Linda, but when they dialed the phone number the girl gave them, it rang my private line."

Bubba meandered by, stopping to stare at us and let out a loud *"'Row?"*

"Yeah, I see, Bub. Thank you, buddy." I bent down to rub his ears. "Is she safe? Patty?"

"Pa—oh, the girl. Patricia. Yes, actually. I don't know why, but I felt compelled to tell them to keep a watch out for vampires."

"I know why, but I'll explain in a moment. What happened then?"

"First, I had no idea that Linda had a daughter. But when I went over to her house to tell her about the phone call, she was tossing clothes into a carry-on. She told me she already knew that Patty was in trouble. It seems somebody contacted her shortly before I arrived. Linda is heading to Georgia immediately. When I asked how she was going to get to the airport—I was planning on offering her a ride—she said she didn't need a plane." Delia tapped her fingers on the table. "She can't *fly*, can she?"

I shook my head. "No witch I know can. Spells like that? Along with teleportation? Those are abilities only the most ancient and powerful witches have. Invisibility is a different matter. I don't know how she's planning to get there, but you can bet that she'll find a way."

"Did the Georgia police say why Patty was in jail?" Sandy broke in.

"Yes. Somehow the girl managed to get away from her caretaker. Patricia was picked up on the street after a man called the police to report that he was with a confused woman who kept telling him she had been kidnapped and needed to call her mother. But when she gave the cops Linda's name and phone number, the phone number was mine. I have no idea how the mix up occurred, but I told the cops I'd contact Linda."

Bubba jumped up on the table and flopped on his side next to one of the empty plates. He started to purr so loudly that the rumble echoed through the air. I reached over to give him another ear rub. Sandy let out a muffled snort.

"I wonder how Linda found out. Do you know?" Aegis began to clear the table.

Delia caught my attention and held it for a moment, her dark eyes flashing. "Actually, yes. She told me that Rachel called her and told her. Now, how would Rachel know about that?"

How indeed, unless Essie had gotten a call from Kali, and Rachel had managed to listen in somehow. As in possibly a bug planted in Essie's lair? That was my best guess.

I turned to Sandy. "I wonder if Linda can make it before Essie's goons can get there?"

Sandy rubbed her chin. "Who in Bedlam is capable of casting a teleportation spell? That's the only way Linda can make it down there that fast. If she can manage that, she can get there faster than Essie can send her hit squad."

" 'Essie's hit squad'? What's Essie got to do with this?" Delia cleared her throat. "If you know something about this, I'd appreciate it if you would enlighten me."

"We'll tell you in a minute." I turned to Sandy. "So who in Bedlam is capable of casting that potent a spell? Nobody in our coven, for sure."

Sandy jumped up. "I know who. You've never met her. She moved to Bedlam a few years back and she keeps to herself. I doubt if hardly anybody on the island knows who she is." She grabbed her coat. "She refuses to even have a telephone in the house, so we're going to have to drive out there."

"You're talking about Auntie Tautau, aren't you?" Delia asked.

I stared at them. "*Auntie?* We have an *Auntie* living in the town?"

Aunties were incredibly powerful witches. In fact, we weren't even sure if they belonged to our kind. But they were all extremely old, and extremely irreverent, and they belonged to no coven or circle or any other group.

"Right." Sandy motioned to Aegis and me. "Come on, we need to head over there. Aegis, you come with us. We'll want the protection in case Essie's on the prowl tonight. Or Rachel, for that matter."

"We really need to change clothes first. Aegis, you run out to Sandy's car and get her other things while we head upstairs to change. Delia, we'll tell you everything, I promise. But we have to make certain Linda's safely away first."

Delia looked ready to grumble, but finally just shrugged. "Hurry up, then."

Sandy and I dashed upstairs. I was halfway through changing when Aegis peeked in the door and tossed Sandy her tote bag with her regular clothes in it. He vanished again before we could say anything.

"How come you never told me about Auntie Tautau? Since when did an Auntie move to Bedlam?"

Sandy shimmied into her jeans and shirt. "Oh, some time ago. She's so old that she could have easily known Merlin. I don't know where she's originally from, but she's lived all over. She moved into a cottage on the outskirts of Bedlam and though she makes regular trips into town, she cloaks up. She's one of those people nobody seems to see unless she's got a good reason. I'm not sure Essie even knows she exists."

I had never met an Auntie before, but I had known other people like that during my life. They glided through life, making massive impressions on select groups of people, but to the rest of the world, they remained unknown and uncounted.

"If anybody on the island could cast a teleportation spell, it would be her. And Linda spent a lot of time out at Auntie Tautau's place." Sandy buckled her belt and we headed downstairs.

Aegis was waiting, leather jacket on, holding our coats for us.

Delia held up her keys. "We can all fit in the squad car, so let's take that. I don't know what's going on, but there's safety in numbers and if Essie has anything to do with this—it's dark, and there are vampires roaming." Delia paused. "No offense, Aegis. It's just not all of your kind wish us as much good fortune as you do."

He shrugged it off. "Not a problem. I'm certainly not going to argue the point with you. Not with

Rachel and Essie on the loose."

When we were in the car and on the way, Sandy and I filled Delia in on everything we had learned about Linda and her daughter.

Delia slammed her hand against the wheel, the car lurching on the ice a moment before she regained control. "Sorry. It's just that Linda's our mayor and she's been selling us out to Essie and her court? Whatever else happens, that needs to stop."

"Oh, we agree. Linda's *our* High Priestess, but she's compromised the coven. At the same time, any mother worth her salt is going to fight to protect her child. But you see how this makes a difference in the case of Rose's death? If Essie could pin it on Ralph and Rachel, then Rachel would be up for staking, and Ralph, simply collateral damage. His part was to divert our focus to Rachel, away from the little war that she and Essie have going on."

"So, Ralph takes the fall, and because we assumed Rachel was behind it, we stake her. And Essie stays queen and goes on controlling Linda and filtering her influence into the island." Delia let out a sound of disgust. "I can't believe Linda was playing into this."

"Sadly, word will spread, and the main temple may vote to strip Linda of her powers."

"Yeah. I wouldn't want to be her when the Society Magicka catches up with her. Don't forget, Maddy, the plan was also aimed at taking you out. Linda probably didn't intend to set you up, but Essie put two and two together when she figured out you were the Mad Maudlin of history. Your skill in hunting both witch finders and vampires makes your presence doubly dangerous."

Delia shook her head, turning a cautious left onto Blackberry Avenue. The flakes were falling lightly, and the sheen of fresh snow over the ice made the roads slick and dangerous. "I'm just glad all this came to light before Essie got her fangs fully into this island. There's not much I can do against her, unless she deliberately makes a grab for control, but we stay on alert from now on."

"There—up ahead, Auntie Tautau's house." Sandy pointed at a small cottage to the right, which was partially hidden behind a tangle of vegetation and shrubbery. We eased into the driveway. I didn't see any cars, but that didn't mean squat. Not everybody drove.

The lights in the cottage were on. The moment we stepped out of the car, the porch light went on. Obviously, Auntie Tautau knew we were there. As we approached the wraparound porch, the front door opened and a squat, sturdy woman bustled out. She was dressed in a Hawaiian floral muumuu with a very stiff, very wide straw hat that had a bright pink ribbon wrapped around it. Perched on the side, above the bow, was a crow. Auntie Tautau's gray hair hung down to her waist, pulled back in a thick, expertly plaited braid.

"Come in, come in. I've been waiting for you," she said, opening her front door wide and shooing us all inside off the porch. "It's a desperately cold night and you'll be wanting some hot cocoa, I expect. I have shortbread, too. You may cross my threshold too, Aegis, vampire though you may be. You'll not be able to harm me."

I blinked at the Irish accent. For some reason, given her dress, I had expected to hear an inflection straight out of the Hawaiian islands. But nope, everything in the house except for Auntie Tautau's dress said, "Irish." Including the picture that hung on the hallway wall of a leprechaun dancing beside a rainbow. It was a photograph—not a painting. Leprechauns were rare, but it was possible to hunt one down if you tried. Something told me that Auntie Tautau wouldn't have any problem scaring one up.

She scooted us into a living room that was jammed with curios, yet felt neat as a pin. "Sit down. I'll call for the cocoa and you can ask your questions."

"You knew we were coming?"

"Linda said you would be here. So yes, I anticipated your visit. Now, sit and I'll strengthen the fire. The chill outside is a nasty one, cuts to the bone. You don't want to catch your death. Or anybody else's death, either." With that curious statement, she waggled her fingers toward the fireplace and the sputtering flames roared to life, the heat emanating off them to fill the room.

"So Linda was here?" I asked, feeling rather sad. I looked around, realizing we had missed her.

"Yes, indeed. She was. She's gone now, you know. I sent her off to reunite with her daughter. Sad bit of business, that is. But there's nothing for you to do now. She won't be back. I vested her and her young one with a safe passage ticket to a private place. But there's no coming back from the WPP."

Delia cleared her throat. "You're part of the WPP?"

Auntie Tautau nodded. "I am indeed."

"What's the WPP?" Aegis asked.

"The Witches' Protection Program," Sandy said. "We—that is, witches like Auntie Tautau—can make people disappear safely who have a bounty on their head, or who are in trouble like Linda."

"It's not invoked very often, because it requires tremendous power and a complete reconstruction of their life web," Auntie Tautau said. "And there must be extenuating circumstances. The Aunties are very clear about this. None of you know the good Linda has done in her past. She helped thousands of people over the centuries, and has gone uncredited. But the Society Magicka keeps an eye out for those on a slippery slope. Her name was bandied around more than most."

I pressed my lips together, trying to sort out my feelings. She had compromised the island, but still the Society Magicka had seen fit to overlook that. Yet, I couldn't help but breathe a sigh of relief that Linda and her daughter were safely out of the way.

"That leaves the matter of Essie and the island, though. We have a very delicate situation on our hands and somebody better take the reins of power now because if Essie's going to make a move, you can bet she'll do so soon. With Linda gone, it's the ideal time for her and her crew to swoop in." Sandy turned to Delia. "Can you take over as interim mayor until a new election can be held?"

She paled. "I just had a horrible thought. What's to prevent Essie from running for the position and scaring her way into the vote?"

"Yes, I can, and vampires can't hold public office. She can't run for mayor because that would be breaking the rules governing public servants." Delia chewed on her lip. "I suppose I can call an emergency meeting of the town council for tomorrow morning. We'll need a representative from Moonrise Coven. Usually, that would be Linda. Who's second in command in your coven?"

I shook my head. "It will have to be a member of the Inner Court. So Sandy, Terrance, Angus, or me."

Sandy pulled out her phone. "I'm calling Angus and Terrance right now."

While she was setting up the conference call, I turned back to Auntie Tautau. "Are you sure Linda and her daughter are safe?"

She smiled softly, pushed a stray wisp of gray hair behind her ear. "Child, they are safer than anybody in this room. Don't fret. I sent them to a happy space where they can be together. A mother should not be parted from her daughter. Linda will miss her life here for a while, but she'll blossom into the new one I've provided."

As Auntie Tautau spoke, her voice took on the tone of absolute certainty. My doubt faded and I thought back to Bubba. Somehow, he had helped make this happen, and Auntie Tautau had done the rest.

"So, you confirm Linda's safely out of Bedlam, with her daughter?" Delia opened her notebook to make a note, then stopped. "Why is my pen not working? It was a few seconds ago."

"Because anything you write about someone in the WPP won't translate to the page. We're *that* good. And yes, Linda and her daughter are safe. Auntie Sagewind down in Georgia contacted me."

The room was silent for a moment as we digested the information.

Aegis cleared his throat. "Can you do anything about Essie?"

Auntie Tautau shook her head. "No, I cannot. I can't directly intervene with regards to the troublemakers. The Aunties protect and guard. We aren't like the Society Magicka. They have no control over us, although we sometimes work together. But we are only here to help and not harm." She pressed mugs of hot cocoa in our hands, along with shortbread.

I didn't have the heart to tell her I wasn't hungry, so I nibbled on my cookie. The Witches' Protection Program had been born out of the mists. I wasn't sure where it started, but they moved when they would—not at anybody else's bidding. During my time on the run from the witch hunters, I had prayed they would take me in, but they never had and I knew better than to complain. I wouldn't have known who to petition, anyway.

"I've got Angus and Terrance on the line." Sandy returned, setting her phone down and putting it on speaker so we could all hear them. "I've explained to them that Linda's gone, though I didn't tell them why, but they know she's not coming back."

"Can someone confirm that?" Angus's voice

echoed out from the phone.

With a frown, Auntie Tautau leaned forward, glaring at the cell phone. "Bah. Technology. I don't like it, for the most part. You listen to me, young witch. I am Auntie Tautau. Cassandra speaks the truth. Don't question the will of the gods."

There was a brief pause.

"Right." Angus cleared his throat. "So we need to pick a leader for the coven?"

"Right. We have to call an emergency town council meeting and I need a representative from the coven there. This is vital, Angus. Lives may depend on it. So you four better get in gear and decide who's taking Linda's place as High Priestess right now." Delia leaned back, closing her eyes. She looked tired.

"That's easy." Terrance laughed. "Maddy, don't you think?"

I jerked, my shoulders stiffening. "What? You want me to take over being the High Priestess? Are you kidding? I haven't lived here long—"

Sandy laughed. "Too late. I just briefed them on the basics. All three of us agree that you're the one for the job. You don't have a choice, Maddy. You're the new High Priestess."

I stared at her. "You're in on this?"

"You're the best choice. I'm too busy and I don't have the reputation you do. Terrance and Angus are men, so they can't assume the title. Ergo—you." She shrugged, then leaned in toward the phone. "You guys good on that?"

"We are," Terrance said.

"Aye. Maddy's for the job," Angus said. They

both hung up before I could say another word.

"That's settled then," Delia said. "The meeting will be at nine tomorrow morning. Meanwhile, we better make certain Ralph's safe. I've set a watch on him, but when he came out of the thrall state, he was in a bad way. He doesn't have many memories of what happened, but when he found out that he's been under control of a vampire, it set him off good. He's been howling up a storm, threatening to stake any vamp that gets in his way. He also feels horrible about what he did to you, Maddy. And he's terrified that he might have actually killed Rose."

"Let's go. You do realize that once you assume the title of mayor, Essie's going to make you a target."

Delia shrugged. "We'll cross that bridge when we come to it. Auntie Tautau, thank you. You've been more helpful than you know."

And with that, we headed for the squad car. Auntie Tautau waved from her porch. I started to warn her to be careful but then the realization hit that she probably had more power in her little finger than I had in my whole body, and I dropped the thought.

As we headed toward city hall, it occurred to me that Bedlam was proving to be a lot more complicated than I had expected it to be. Quiet little town, my ass.

Chapter 14

THE CITY HALL was dark and silent when we arrived. A couple of deputies were headed toward their squad car as we jogged up the steps to the main plaza, and they waved at Delia.

"Sheriff, we've got a five-two down at the Star-hopper's Mini-Mall."

"Be careful. You never know what else might be waiting." She waved them on. "Damn kids. There's been a rash of break-ins at some of the smaller stores. You'd think around here they'd realize that magical alarms are cheap to come by. But there's always some idiot kid who thinks they can beat the system and break in."

We hurried through the silent hallway, passing the city hall and the courthouse. As we swept through the doors to the sheriff's office, the flurry of busyness startled me. At times I forgot that some careers never had a lull.

"Ralph's in one of the main holding cells." Delia wove us through the cluster of desks till we came to a door on the other side of the room. There, she brushed a keycard against the scanner on the wall and an audible click sounded as the door opened.

Once through that door, the hall was concrete, and I could sense a thick muffling wave that made my magic settle into a slow pulse. A magical reduction ward, I guessed. They'd have to have that, as well as other safeguards, in place, given the nature of Bedlam's inhabitants.

The hall stretched on for a ways, several doors along each side. It ended in a T-junction. We followed Delia to the end of the hall, turning left behind her. About fifteen feet later we came to a large gate that barred the path with a door in the center. Ten feet beyond the door was another iron gateway stretching across the hall. Beyond that, I could make out a row of cells.

The officer inside scanned Delia's keycard and then looked at us. "Any weapons to declare?"

Sandy handed him her bag. "You might as well keep that till I come back. Gun, brass knuckles, pepper spray, switchblade...a few other things."

The guard suppressed a smirk as he locked it away in a cabinet, then proceeded to run a scanner over the three of us. I wasn't sure what he was scanning for, but apparently none of us had any hidden contraband that showed up, so he locked the door through which we had just entered, then opened the one leading into the cell block.

Delia led us down the hall. We passed a couple large, barred windows that let in the light from the storm outside. Huge floodlights illuminated the grounds outside, and in their light we could see that the snow had picked up again. The Winter Fae must be partying hard, I thought.

The walls were taupe. The color was bland, draining the brightness out of everything. The hall also felt like it muffled energy, as well. Nothing to trigger tempers or sadness. Just a soft smoosh of bland, bland, bland.

We came to the end of the hall, and the cell block ran to the left and right of the archway. The cell in front of us was empty, but to the left sat Ralph Greyhoof, staring quietly at the television that was playing a football game. Ralph was a Seahawks fan, and he often threw huge football and tailgate parties.

The cells to either side of his were empty as well, and I could see cameras aimed on him from all directions. He really was under surveillance.

The moment he saw us, he turned off the television, slowly standing. "Sheriff, what's going on?" He did a double take when he saw me. "Maddy..." Flustered, he stopped and lowered his head, staring at his hooves. "I don't know what to say."

"I know you were in thrall, Ralph. We may have a healthy competition between us, but I know you wouldn't deliberately try to kill me. Or anybody else." I tried to keep from wrinkling my nose as the scent of his discomfort hit me square in the face. One thing about satyrs: they couldn't keep their moods hidden. Their scents gave them away every time, which was why so many of their first dates went bad. When you can smell a guy's erection, it tends to put you off your dinner.

"Yeah, but we don't actually know that I didn't hurt that girl." His voice was raw and he looked up, his gaze locking with mine. In his eyes I could see the whirl of guilt and fear and concern roiling up one hell of a storm.

"We're going to try to find out for sure. If you didn't, then you deserve to be free. If you did..."

"Then it's better all the way around for everybody to know."

"Ralph, we're worried that you might be in danger. Don't ask me why or who, but I'm going to move you to premises that are more secure." Delia pulled out a large hoop filled with keys. She glanced through, finding the right key. "Stand back from the door, please."

Ralph obliged, moving to the back of the cell. As I watched him, I knew I had been right. Ralph was no killer. This wasn't someone who could easily cast aside someone's life. He might be lascivious, but he wasn't vicious.

Delia opened the cell and motioned for him to move forward. He held his hands behind his back, turning around so she could cuff him. Wincing at the iron in the cuffs—satyrs could handle silver, but iron roughed them up—he followed her as she led him out of the cell.

We quickly walked the other way, to the opposite side of the juncture. There, we came to a heavy steel door painted red. Delia glanced back at us. "This is a safer area."

"What's going on?" Ralph asked.

"We're just trying to protect you in case the vampire who enthralled you comes back to—" Delia paused, glancing up at the satyr, who stood head and shoulders above her.

"To kill me?" Beads of sweat broke out on his forehead and he began to fidget. "You really think I'm in danger?"

"We aren't certain, but we'd rather be safe than sorry," Sandy broke in.

"Sandy's right. And behind this door, you'll be in a vampire-free zone. They can't get beyond the magical wards we have set up. And neither can anybody else." Delia wasn't quite being truthful. I could sense a discrepancy, but Ralph couldn't.

He calmed down as she opened the door and led him through, motioning for us to wait. A moment later she returned and once again locked the heavy door. "He'll be okay for now. Truth is one of the Aunties could get through, or someone like them. But I doubt that's going to happen. Come on, let's go talk to forensics and see what they've found."

We returned to the main office, where she led us through another door. We stopped at a small cubicle toward the back of a narrow hall. With a quick knock, she opened the door.

We followed her through into a room that was larger than I had expected. On one side of a room was a row of lockers labeled "Evidence." To the left were long workbenches, with magnifying glasses, microscopes, and all sorts of equipment. Straight ahead was some sort of a testing ring, where large white boards were covered with splatters mimicking blood. Several mannequins had taken a bad turn and were lying on the floor, ragged blood bags strapped to their chests and backs. We followed Delia over to one of the desks, where an officer was poring through a sheath of papers.

"Darren? What have you got for me on the Rose Williams case? Anything?" Delia leaned over his desk.

Darren—who I could tell at first glance was a werewolf, he had that lupine look to his eyes—glanced up at her. "I think we do, actually. We tried out several scenarios as to how she was stabbed. Sheriff, the person who killed—" He paused, glancing behind her as we all crowded around.

"Go ahead. They're all right."

"Okay, then. Williams was killed by somebody who had to be under five-eight. The angles of the wound are all wrong for anybody taller than that. I'd actually place the assailant at between five-five to five-eight. So that's a fairly narrow range."

Delia glanced at me. "Ralph's six-three."

"That occurred to me," I said.

Darren held up another paper. "However, the killer was incredibly strong. The coroner just sent his report over and the wound to her stomach was so forceful that it chipped her spine. So the knife had to be strong and the assailant had to possess a massive amount of strength. Given there's only one stab wound and no signs of struggle, I would say that she either knew the killer, or was taken by surprise."

"Anything else?" Delia asked, glancing over the forms he handed her.

"Yes, actually. We found two partial prints on

the panpipes. The pipes were wiped clean, otherwise. Neither print matches the satyr's. Even though he verified they belong to him it looks like they were planted at the scene. Whoever left them there wiped them clean, but wasn't quite thorough enough."

"This is all good news for Ralph. Anything else that we can use to exonerate him?" Delia blew a thin stream of breath through her teeth.

"Actually, yes. Greyhoof is left handed. If you look at this picture, you'll notice the angle of the injury. When we recreated it, the killing blow came in on a right-handed angle. Also, and perhaps most important, when satyrs are highly excited—be it arousal or adrenaline—they give off a strong odor."

"We knew that already."

"Perhaps what you didn't know is that their scent markers contain particles that cling to anybody near them. We can test to see if someone's been within arm's reach of a satyr within the past few hours and be reasonably sure of our answer."

This was news to me and it made me wonder what any number of suspicious husbands—and a few wives—would do if a home satyr-scent test was invented.

Aegis spoke up. "You mean, because we were close to Ralph just a few minutes ago, we'd show positive for satyr dust?"

"*Particulates*, not dust. But yes. If he's in any way aroused or excited or frightened, you'll test positive. And the tests on Williams's body were negative. Not a speck." The deputy shrugged. "I'm going to say that we have no circumstantial evidence to place him there."

Delia took one last look through all the forms and handed them back to him. "Then that clears him. We're looking for a shorter killer who's incredibly strong, and who definitely isn't a satyr."

"There's nothing that can mask those particulates?" Sandy said.

Darren shook his head. "Not really. Oh, there are some magical charms that might be able to do it, but given everything else, no."

I stared at the papers in Delia's hand. "If Rachel was behind it, Ralph would probably have been the triggerman. But why wouldn't Essie do the same if she's the one responsible? Why get blood on her own hands?"

"You say Ralph isn't capable of killing, right?" Aegis was frowning.

I nodded. "Right."

"I'll tell you something not many people know. Thrall won't turn the victim into an automaton. If Ralph really doesn't have a killer's nature, he'd resist and it would be a mess of trouble. Whoever tried to set him up didn't count on Ralph being more blowhard than bite. If you resist an order while under thrall, and you resist hard enough, it can break the connection."

"So the vampire—be it Rachel or Essie—had to do the actual dirty work. Ralph couldn't, so she did," I said.

"There's one other possibility," Sandy said. "Essie likes control. Maybe she didn't believe Ralph would actually manage it without fucking it up. So she set everything to look like he did it, but made certain that Rose—whom she thought was you—actually ended up dead."

Delia frowned. "I'm not sure where to go from here. First, there's Essie. And then, Rachel. Because of her obsession with Aegis, she's likely to be more off kilter than Essie and therefore, more dangerous."

I frowned. "Do you think that Rachel *knows* Essie set her up as the one behind Rose's murder?"

"That's a good question. I suggest we use that to our advantage." Aegis cocked his eyebrows. "I have an idea, but it's going to take a little while for me to implement. Until then, we sit tight. Let's talk in a private place, shall we?"

And with that, Delia led us back to her office.

BY THE TIME we left the station, it was nearly 3:00 a.m. All of us were tired, so Delia had one of her deputies drive us back to my place.

"It's so late. I'd rather not worry about you driving, even with that spell on your car. Stay the night. What good are four guest rooms if I don't have somebody in there?" I wrapped my arm around Sandy's waist as we hurried from car to kitchen. Aegis kept a watch until we reached the back patio and had entered the house.

"I guess you can talk me into it, if you give me plenty of coffee in the morning. But if you don't mind, I'm going to crash now. I'm so freaking sleepy." Sandy yawned. "I can sleep in the room where I took the shower. That looked comfortable."

"Oh, the Garden Room? Yeah, go ahead. I specifically infused that room with earth energy to give it that nurturing, growing sensation. I'll head up in a few. Aegis will keep watch over the house till morning. Won't you, sweetheart?" I turned to him as he reached out to rub my back.

"Of course. There should be a few snacks in the mini-bar, Sandy. Don't worry about messing up anything. It will be a quick cleanup tomorrow." Aegis waved as Sandy heaved a sigh and began to drag herself up to the second story.

When she was out of sight, I let out a slow breath and dropped into the rocking chair in the kitchen, pulling Drofur into my lap. The stuffed unicorn said nothing, but he smelled like cotton candy and bubblegum. "This has been one hell of a day."

"And night. You've been up too long. You look beat, Maddy. Why don't you go to bed and sleep now?"

"I will in a moment," I said. "My brain's churning so much that I'm not sure I'll be able to sleep." I glanced at the clock. "I wonder where Linda and Patty are by now? I hate to think of them alone in the world, but I guess they're beyond our reach now." And then it hit me: I was the new High Priestess of the Moonrise Coven. I felt totally unprepared for the job, like a deer caught in the headlights.

Aegis pulled one of the kitchen chairs over to

my side and took my hand. "Maddy? Are you all right?"

"I just realized that I'm going to have to take over the coven and be responsible for it, starting tomorrow morning. Its failure or success will depend on me. It all comes down to the High Priestess, and I'm not at all certain I have the expertise that's needed."

"You most definitely do. You just lack the confidence. I hope you don't sell yourself short. Sandy will be there to help you."

I straightened, turning to him. "But what am I going to tell them? I can't tell them that Linda was turning on them, handing them over to the vampires."

"They have to know. You have to be transparent with them, or they'll sense you're hiding something and become suspicious. Linda hid her secrets and look what happened to her. That put her at the mercy of Essie and her ilk. I may be a vampire, but this is why I do not get involved in the politics of Fangdom. It's a dangerous, murky area. We're fighting for our rights, but so many of my kind make that difficult by being exactly the type of creature that makes others run in fear. Go to bed, Maddy. Sleep. Everything will look clearer in the morning."

Deciding there was nothing else I could do for the night, I agreed. But it was a long time before I could sleep, and I tossed and turned all night, running from shadows in my dreams, and from a dark figure wearing a bright crown of sparkling blood, frozen into crystal form.

I GROANED AS the alarm clock went off at 8:00 a.m. I really didn't want to get up, but then I remembered the meeting at the Town Hall and grimaced, slipping out from beneath the covers. Bubba was staring out the window, but when I stirred, he merely glanced at me and let out a *"Murp?"*

"Yes, I'm getting up. Good morning, you little tosser. By the way, thank you for helping Linda and her daughter. I know you had something to do with it and that nothing got twisted around. You're a sweetie, you know that?" I reached down to run my hand over his tail as I stared out the window. The morning was starting off with a pale shimmer of sunlight breaking through the clouds, but even the sun looked cold at this point. Given the amount of snow and storms we had had, magic use must be up.

Bubba just flicked his tail and haughtily strutted over to the door. *"Mrow."*

"I know you're hungry. I'll be down in a few minutes. Go wake up Sandy, if she's not already up." I waved him off and he darted out the door.

A quick shower later, I dressed in my best indigo wash jeans, a mauve V-neck sweater, and a silver belt. I slipped on my big old Fugly-Boots, my favorite brand. Knee-high, they were leather and laced up the front. They had thick wedge heels, non-skid. They were stiff enough to keep my ankles from turning, and easily navigated the snow.

By the time I made it downstairs, I smelled espresso brewing. Sure enough, Sandy was at the helm and a frothy hot latte was waiting for me, along with toast and jam.

"I don't think we have time for much more before the meeting, but at least this will get us through an hour or so of the shockwaves about to hit the community."

"What should we tell them? Aegis thinks we should tell them the truth. But won't that make people paranoid against the vampires?"

"Well, maybe they should be. I think he's correct. But if you phrase it right, it won't sound like we're under siege." She shifted her shoulders, then lifted her shirt to adjust her bra. "This is the last time I ever buy a Naomi Varjhas bra. The damned band won't lay flat."

Bubba leaped up on the table and stared at her.

"You little perv. Quit watching me."

I laughed. "Bubba's just waiting for you to ignore your toast. He likes toast and tries to steal mine whenever he gets the chance. I doubt if he's entranced by your boobs."

She snorted. "Neither am I. I accidentally caught my right one in the door yesterday when I leaned too close while shutting it. Mother-freaking son of a bitch, but that hurt."

I snorted latte out my nose. "Thank you for that. I needed a sinus irrigation, yes indeed. Okay then, so we head out to this meeting in a few minutes. I don't care if you think you're not invited, I'm dragging you along." Sobering, I set down my cup. "I don't know about all this, Sandy. I'm not sure how to be the High Priestess. Am I serious enough for it? You know as well as I do, I don't take things as reverently as I should. Won't Temple HQ decide that I'm unfit for the job?"

She frowned. "Maybe it's time we had somebody who wasn't exactly a model-fit for it. Look at what happened with Linda. You'd think she'd be perfect but the vamps found a way to exploit her and turn her to their own use. I don't know where the Aunties transported her to, but I can tell you this: if someone as strong and as serious as she was can be so easy to blackmail, maybe it takes somebody with a sense of humor and an alternative view on life to run things properly."

"I'm glad you have faith in me, because without it, I'd probably just pack up and move." I glanced around the kitchen, realizing how much I had come to love the mansion. "Or maybe not. Whatever the case, let's get this show on the road. Delia will be waiting."

WE HEADED OUT to the Town Hall. Bedlam during the day looked quite a bit different than Bedlam did during the night. Both times the town was magical, but during the day Bedlam was a cheerful, bright spot. At night, she was a mysterious, moody town.

"The snowfall this year is ridiculous," Sandy said as we maneuvered through the freshly plowed streets. "We have to have close to three feet. None of the other islands have that."

"The Winter Fae are having one hell of a party this season."

"True that. The summers have been warmer, winters colder, and we have definite rainy seasons during the autumn and spring now."

I eased through the town, waving at old Mrs. Pennyhessy as we passed her ice cream parlor. She was one of the few avian shifters we had in town. In her younger days, she had flown many a mile in her hawk form. Now, she mostly shifted when she was feeling poorly and stayed in hawk form till the spell passed. She seldom took wing anymore, though. Nobody knew how old she was, but she claimed to be at least three hundred years, which was getting up there for a bird shifter. She did a lot of babysitting for young mothers, thrilling the kids with her stories of the old days.

She waved back, then vanished inside to the soda fountain. I had the sudden craving for an ice cream float, but decided it would have to wait until after the meeting.

"Well, there's the Town Hall." I finally found a parking spot—the lot was crowded during the day with all the government workers—and stared at the building. "So you really think I can do this? Because once I walk through those doors and officially announce myself as the new High Priestess of the Moonrise Coven, that's it. There won't be any going back, not unless I do something as stupid as Linda did. Or unless Rachel manages to find me and slay me."

"No going back and don't worry it. I called Angus and Terrance this morning and they still think you're the best choice for the job. We'll need to convene a special meeting as soon as possible to vest you with the circlet and sword, and pick another member for the coven council. I'm leaning toward Tanith, if you want my opinion."

I nodded. Tanith would be a good choice. She was experienced, level headed, and best of all, she liked me, so I wouldn't get a lot of static from her.

"We also should add someone to the Inner Court from the Outer, and then open the Outer Court to applications. I am thinking Kyle. He's grown so much over the past couple of years."

"Well, we have our game plan. Let's get you in there and make it official." Sandy swung out of the car. I followed suit, more slowly.

As we passed one of the city workers who was shoveling snow and sprinkling rock salt over the steps, I realized that nothing would ever be the same. I had moved to Bedlam on a lark. Within two months I not only was deeply immersed in a relationship, but I was now High Priestess of my coven. The responsibilities of both hit home, pointing out to me just how much I had been drifting for years.

Oh, I had been a member of the coven for a long, long time, but even though I was on the Inner Court Council, there hadn't been many decisions for me to make. And I had played with relationships—all of them failing. The last failed due to his emotional abuse and my lack of will to disentangle myself from it, but none of them had worked out for long. I realized that I didn't want that to happen with Aegis. As scared as it made me, he meant more to me than any man in a long time. Vampire or not, he had a heart. I didn't want to hurt him. And I didn't want to be hurt again.

"What are you thinking about?" Sandy asked as we passed through the doors.

"Life. The Universe."

"Forty-two?"

I laughed. "Not quite. No, I'm thinking about relationships and Aegis and how I've managed to sabotage myself over the years. I don't want to do that anymore."

"When was the last time you were seriously involved with someone where it worked out?" She consulted her phone. "We're looking for room 432. Down this hall and to the left, I think."

We wove through the bustle of clerks hurrying about their work. The smell of business was in the air, a crisp, get-things-done scent that burned into my brain.

"Honestly? Tom. After he was turned I guess I never fully had the heart to make things work. You know I've drifted in and out of relationships but none ever stuck. I'm just starting to realize how lonely I've been." I froze, turning to her. "Sandy, I'm falling in love with Aegis and it scares the hell out of me. Not just because he's a vampire."

"You're afraid of being hurt again."

"Tom—he was a part of my soul. When I lost him, I lost a part of myself. I'm afraid to chance that again, but the more time I spend around Aegis, the more I realize he's everything I've missed.

He's everything Tom was, without that little spark of crazypants that Tom had. And that scares me too. What if it doesn't work out? What if some wanna-be vampire hunter goes full-Buffy on him and stakes him?"

"What if you get everything you want and live happily ever after?" She put her hand on mine. "Maddy, you deserve so much more than you've allowed yourself to have. You deserve love and happiness. I know there's more there blocking you—I can tell that some part of you is holding yourself back from fully committing. What's going on?"

I shook my head. I had an idea of what my block was, but truth was, I didn't know if I was ready to explore those feelings yet. When I ripped the bandage off, it was going to open an old, old wound and the prospect of revisiting that pain was more than I could think about now.

"We'll talk about it later. I need to focus on the present. We have too much to worry about without me diving into all those old feelings right now."

"You're going to have to face whatever it is soon or it will interfere with your relationship with Aegis." Sandy motioned to the next door to the right. "We're here. Are you ready?"

I wasn't ready to face my fears about love, and I wasn't ready to face my fears about taking on the responsibility of the entire coven. But the fact was, I didn't have much of a choice. I could either cut and run, which had been my modus operandi for most of my life, or I could finally plant my feet on the ground, dig in, and fight for what was right. And the thought of Essie reaching out her bony, clammy hand to grab the throat of Bedlam and hold it hostage was about as wrong as it could get.

I summoned up my courage and straightened my shoulders. "I'm ready."

Sandy opened the door, standing back to allow me to enter first. Head held high, I let out a long, slow breath and entered the room. There, the leaders of the city council were waiting. They looked up expectantly. I met Delia's gaze and realized she was as scared as I was. She was about to step into Linda's shoes as mayor of the city. I just had to lead the coven. And with that thought, I felt more secure.

Delia motioned for me to sit down. "Maudlin, I'm so glad you could make it. Members of the council, meet the new High Priestess of the Moonrise Coven—Maudlin Gallowglass."

And with that, I committed myself to Bedlam, to my bed and breakfast, and to growing up after years of running wild through the world. As I took my chair, I felt something shift inside, and realized that I no longer felt afraid. Even though we were facing a threat that I wasn't sure we could win against, I was feeling relieved. I had made my choice.

Chapter 15

I WAITED FOR Delia to take the lead, but got one hell of a surprise when she turned to me and said, "Linda was mayor of Bedlam for twenty-six years. Because the Moonrise Coven has been around for almost seventy years, your organization has had an active role in shaping the nature of this community as Bedlam has evolved. The question is, are you interested in taking on the role of mayor as well as that of High Priestess? I'm acting in that capacity in the interim, but it isn't my intention to continue as such."

I stared at her. "Me? Mayor? Oh, *hell* no!" Clapping my hand over my mouth, I winced as everybody broke out into laughter. But the laughs were strained and I realized that nobody really knew what was going on yet. "Don't you think we'd better bring everybody up to speed before we discuss the position of mayor?"

Delia gave me a satisfied nod. "I think you're right. This is new to us both. I think I speak for both Maudlin and me when I ask the council to be patient with us. We've got a lot to sort through and so much of this is still a tangle of confusion."

"Then we untangle it one knot at a time," Leonard Wolfbrane said. He was leader of the AlphaPack and represented the werewolves who lived on Bedlam. Each of the major shifter groups had a member on the town council. Two members belonged to the Fae world—one from the Summer Court, one from the Winter Court. Ralph Greyhoof, who represented the satyrs and centaurs, was noticeably absent. I was the representative of the magical community—the witches.

Goblins, ogres, and their ilk weren't allowed to sit on the council. Technically, they weren't allowed to live in Bedlam but more than once, a grungy little nest of goblins had been found and ousted, and the occasional ogre or troll ended up hiding out on the island and had to be deported the hard way.

Delia cleared her throat. "By now, you all know Linda Realmwood has left her post as mayor and vacated the leadership of the Moonrise Coven. The coven has voted Maddy in as their new High Priestess. Therefore, she's takes her place on the town council. I'm acting as the interim mayor until we figure out what to do about the position."

"Can you elucidate as to what's brought on these changes?" Elsa Liftwing, the Avian shifter representative, asked.

"Yes. Over the last couple of days we have discovered that Linda was being blackmailed by Essie, Pacific Northwest Queen of the Vampires. Essie had been threatening a daughter whom no one knew about to tighten her hold over Bedlam. We have reason to believe that Essie has been making a power play for control over the town."

The room erupted then, everybody talking at once. Delia glanced at me and I shook my head. We knew this was going to happen. Sandy jumped up and, two fingers in her mouth, let loose with a whistle that almost pierced my ears. As the room fell silent, she stood on her chair, hands on her hips.

"Yo! Hold it down. Let Delia and Maddy talk."

"Thank you, Sandy." Delia shuffled some papers and I realized she was trying to figure out where to go with this.

"We'll be launching an investigation as to how far this goes. I strongly suggest that if any of you have made similar deals, you stand up now and walk out of here before we find out. Because we aren't going to be lenient on anybody who's been selling Bedlam over to the vamps." I sounded more confident than I was, but the first rule is always: *fake it till you make it.*

Delia picked up the thread immediately. "Maudlin is correct. We will be starting our investigation as soon as this meeting is adjourned. Leave now if you have something to hide. Essie's going to know the jig is up by tonight, if she doesn't already know, so you have one day to figure out what to do."

I glanced around. Blackthorn, a werebear, was

shifting uncomfortably in his seat, tugging at his collar. "Anything you want to tell us?" I asked.

He slid down in his chair a little, then gave an impatient shrug. "No. I—I've got nothing to say." But then, he jumped out of his chair and headed for the door, the scent of his anger filling the room. As he slammed the door behind him, more chatter broke out.

Delia slammed her gavel on the table. "Come to order! Now!"

One by one, people quieted down.

"Anybody else need to leave?" She looked around the room, her eyes narrow. "We will discuss what to do about the vampires in a bit, but if anybody else has been colluding with Essie, then let them leave now."

"What about Ralph?" Ateria, the representative from the Winter Fae Court, spoke up. "Is he off the council, considering he's being held for murder?"

Delia shook her head. "No, we've found evidence that Ralph is innocent. He's being held right now for his own protection until we can sort out exactly what happened."

"Who's responsible for Rose Williams's murder, then?" Brentwood, a rabbit shifter, asked.

I jumped on that one. "We're not sure, but it wasn't Ralph. We are fairly certain that I was the target, and that the killer mistook Rose for me."

"Will Linda ever be coming back?" Ateria asked. It struck me that I needed to make some contact with the Fae courts if I was going to be the coven's new High Priestess. There was a long-standing tradition of the Fae and witches uniting for various magical purposes, but Linda had kept relatively clear of them. I wasn't ever sure why, but I decided that isolation would come to an end.

"No." I debated on how much to tell them, then finally added, "The Aunties smuggled her and her daughter to safety. Linda sold us out, but you have to understand the predicament she was in. Her daughter's life was being held forfeit. Now, they're together and safe. While I totally disagree with the choices Linda made, I do understand the stress under which she was working, and why she made the choices she did. I may not have children, but I'll bet any one of you who do can see that she was between a rock and a hard place."

"That's probably why Blackthorn left. His family has been under a lot of economic stress the past few years. Want to make a bet that Essie bought him off? I do know his business recently made a drastic turnaround and he was making money hand over fist." Brentwood shrugged. "I have a huge family. I can see the appeal if things aren't going well. It would be easy at first to say—Oh, I'll just give in a little. And then a little more."

"What does Blackthorn do?" I couldn't help but wonder just what Essie had found useful in a werebear.

Brentwood leaned forward, frowning. He shoved his coffee cup back on the table. "Blackthorn trained as a general contractor and structural engineer. But there hasn't been a lot of building going on here on the island, and we're too far away from the mainland and Seattle area for him to commute down there. He's been focusing on odd jobs for the past year or so, and I know that he was trying to take out a second mortgage on his house so they could pay off some sort of medical debt they incurred when their eldest was in a car wreck and needed surgery."

That would do it, all right. Medical bills? Fear of losing one's home? Not knowing how to get out from under a mountain of debt? Those were all grim prospects facing too many people and when a parent was desperate to protect their family, options that seemed unthinkable suddenly became viable.

"I empathize, but we can't have anybody on this council sneaking around with the vampires. If we deal with Essie, we do it aboveboard and in general agreement."

"What about your boyfriend?" Ateria asked.

"I'm very open about Aegis. He's not in collusion with Essie and she's been trying to lure him into joining her court, but he wants nothing to do with her. He'll come talk to the council if that makes you more comfortable, though obviously it will have to be a meeting called after sunset." I knew this was going to come up.

Apparently, Delia was thinking along the same route because she suddenly stood and clapped for attention. "As the interim mayor, I'm going to make a suggestion that we include two representatives on this council from the vampires. One unaligned—Aegis would be a good choice for that. And the other from Essie's court. Then they couldn't argue that they weren't being fairly represented and we could keep an eye on what they were up to."

Even I hadn't been prepared for that one. I stared at Delia, open-mouthed, along with everybody else.

"But don't you think they'd just go right along working against us? It would be so much easier to lull us into a false sense of security by pretending that everything was all peachy while behind the scenes they were making plans for taking control of the island." I wasn't sure of where Delia's head was, but the idea seemed ludicrous to me.

"Listen, one of the problems is that vampires have no real rights. They're still not included under the Pretcom Equal Rights Treaty, and they are always shunted to the side."

"That's because they kill people!" Ateria snorted, as did her Summer counterpart.

"Not all vampires are like that. Aegis isn't." I hadn't intended to defend the idea, but Delia's comment made a lot of sense. "If we start the movement here, maybe then vampire–human interactions will mellow out some. Granted, we can't give rights to those who go out foraging for victims, but if we allow bloodwhores here—make them legal—then maybe the vamps will stop preying on the rest of the community. And once the movement begins, it can spread."

Visions danced in my head. What if we could loosen up the yoke of fear that ran rampant between vampire–Pretcom–human relations? Perhaps my visions weren't sugarplums, but the concept seemed seductively simple. "Sometimes you have to start with the outer branches and prune your way into the tree before you can make any significant changes."

Delia shuffled her files. "At least we can talk to Essie about it. I do not suggest we confront her about her attempted coup. That could backfire on us. I think her plans depended so much on secrecy that they'll collapse. Now, we can discuss how to go forward."

Enough of the others were nodding that I felt confident about calling for a vote. "All in favor of summoning Essie to a détente meeting, raise your hands."

It was seven in favor, four against.

"Motion carried and passed." Delia consulted her agenda. "Next on the list, we have humans who live on the island—not many but enough—and we should look toward including one of them as a representative. Arguments for and against?"

As another squabble erupted, I was suddenly very grateful that I had chosen to forgo vying for the position of mayor. My temper was already swirling, given how much whining was going on. Finally, the motion was passed. The council would choose another member for the werebear community, and a representative from the humans as well.

"Finally, we need to vote on what to do about the position of mayor," Delia started to say.

I jumped to my feet. "Madam Mayor, I vote to keep you in the interim position until the next election comes around. Then you can decide what to do. We need someone who is familiar with the situation that's just occurred, and who has the authority to make arrests, should we need to." I was referring to Blackthorn but by the outbursts that followed, I realized I had just implied that there were other people on the council who might end up in trouble.

When we finally got everybody under control again, I explained myself. "I just think that it's a good thing for the mayor to understand law enforcement and have some authority in the field. We run differently here in Bedlam than other places. You know Delia isn't going to use unfair advantage of her position as sheriff—"

"We thought Linda had our best interests at heart, too." Naia, the Summer Fae representative, shook her head. "But I agree. For now, let's vote to keep Delia in as interim mayor. We can revisit this at our Spring Equinox meeting and make more definitive plans then. That will give us a little over three months to see how the council sorts itself out. We can also use that time to find out what information has been compromised. For example, I'm wondering just how much personal information of ours Linda might have divulged to Essie."

We took a vote and it passed.

"Then it's official," Delia said. "I'll serve as interim mayor. Come March twentieth, we'll revisit this issue. Until then, Naia, will you chair a committee to check into information leaks? I doubt anybody but Linda and Essie know the full extent. Linda's long gone and Essie...well...I doubt if we can trust her to give us a clear answer, but find out what you can."

Naia jotted down her notes. "All right. Elsa,

would you like to help me?"

Elsa agreed, along with Brentwood, and the committee was put to a nomination, voted on, and approved.

"Excuse me, Ms. Mayor, but I have a luncheon to attend." Trix, an elk shifter, stood. "Can we wrap this up before much longer?"

I glanced at the clock over the door. We had been hashing out things for over two hours. It was going on eleven-thirty. "I second the motion, actually."

"Vote?" Delia called. She counted hands. "All right, we have a unanimous vote to wrap up this meeting. I know that we have our monthly meeting next Monday, but given the reason for this emergency meeting, I think we ought to keep it on the schedule."

Although everybody groaned, including me, it was generally agreed on. As people began to file out the door, I walked over to Delia.

"Well, that was...an experience."

"You took the words out of my mouth. I think I'll let Ralph out today. I can't very well hold him now that we have evidence he didn't do it, even if it is for his own protection." She shrugged. "You want to walk over with me and talk to him?"

I really didn't feel like talking to Ralph, but I couldn't think of much else to do. Everything seemed so convoluted and nothing had been solved. But I wrapped my arm through Sandy's and we moseyed over to the sheriff's department. Delia asked us to wait in a small room, and within ten minutes, she was back with Ralph, who was no longer wearing handcuffs.

When he saw me, he ducked his head, a frown on his face.

"Maddy, I'm sorry." He awkwardly took the seat opposite me. "I don't blame you if you don't want to talk to me. Even though I'm grateful that we know now I didn't kill Rose, I still was in your house uninvited, trying to steal your hair. And I did write those things about you on Flitterbug." His gravelly voice was morose, and the happy-go-lucky look had drained from his face. Even when they were being serious, most satyrs couldn't help but look seductive and cocky, but Ralph seemed the opposite.

"Ralph, I know you were in thrall. We may never know exactly who managed it, but people do the stupidest things when they're under the influence." I wasn't quite ready to forgive him for trying to ruin my business, but the fact that he apologized and seemed to mean it went a long way.

"Delia told me it might not have been Rachel who put me in thrall. That I might have implanted memories due to another vampire's suggestion. I wish I could help you. I wish I could remember but I can't. I'm almost afraid to go home, to be honest. I have no idea when it happened. I don't remember any point where I suddenly went, 'Oh, vampire!' I remember meeting Rachel, but if that memory is false, then I'm not sure what to think." He looked as confused as he sounded.

"I think we're all a little confused. But you have to shake it off. You should just go home and watch your step." I wondered if he realized that once enthralled, the ability to resist a second attempt diminished. But it seemed cruel to say anything—like rubbing salt in a wound.

"I'd be glad to help you around your bed and breakfast. If I can do anything, just let me know. And I'll get my brothers to stop dissing your business online. We'll take our bad reviews off Blisty, and I'll send some business your way."

Boy, Ralph really must have been scared straight, I thought. He was never usually this helpful. But then again, he had spent a few days in jail under the suspicion of murder, and that tended to change a body. Or so I had been told.

"You want a ride home? Sandy and I are heading that way."

"Nope. My brothers are coming to pick me up." He stood, looking uncertain. Then, finally he said, "Well, I guess that's it for now. I'll talk to you later."

As we watched him go, I realized how tired I was of this whole mess, and how ready I was to just have it over with. Except there was still somebody out there gunning for me. Even if Essie backed off, Rachel still had a target painted on my ass.

"Do you think he means it?" Sandy asked as we headed back to my car.

"I think so. I really do. The Greyhoof boys aren't a bad bunch. They can get rowdy and crude, and they have the manners of an ox, but when you get down to it, they're actually pretty nice. Come on, let's go."

"We could go back up to Durholm Hall and look for Rachel." Sandy looked so serious that I began to sputter, then she laughed. "I'm kidding. We wouldn't have time today, anyway. So, what do you want to do?"

I thought about it. "I really need to buy furniture. I've been saying that for weeks. Come with me while I pick out what I still need for the Bewitching Bedlam?"

We spent the afternoon shopping. Finally, Sandy took me to a boutique store that I hadn't noticed before and there, I found the perfect furniture for the rest of the mansion. It was a mix of styles—part Mediterranean, part island-style, but by the time I finished, I had new sofas, several new chairs, the nightstands to complement the beds in the guest rooms, and a few other assorted pieces. I also was about fourteen thousand dollars poorer, but my bank account could handle it. Aegis had offered to help defray costs, but I didn't wanted to be in debt to him. Now, as I flashed my credit card and watched the balance climb, I felt reassured I was doing the right thing.

We arrived back at my place at around four-fifteen. "I have to take off," Sandy said. "I really need to get some stuff done around my place. Will you be all right?"

"I should be fine. Neither Essie nor Rachel can get in the house. Aegis will be awake soon and I've got Bubba here for company. I don't have to go out anywhere for anything. You run on home and text me when you get there so I know you're okay."

I gave her a hug, then dashed inside as the afternoon clouds threatened to sock in again. Bubba was sitting on the table. He knew that I didn't like him there, but he ignored me as I settled at the table and pulled the bowl of fruit over to nibble on a few grapes.

"You okay, Bub?"

"Mur." He lazily meandered over to me, rubbing his head against my arm.

I reached up and scratched behind his ears. "Bubba, how long have we been together? Seventy-five years or so?"

"Purp."

"I thought about that. So tell me, during that time have you ever seen me participate in a functional relationship? Have I ever made the right choice?" I rested my head on his side and his purr threatened to lull me to sleep.

"M-row?" He turned, pressing his nose against mine, looking concerned.

"I'm all right, Bub. I'm just thinking that I found a keeper in Aegis, and I don't want to screw this up. You know how I am. If there's a way to sabotage a relationship, I usually manage to find it and exploit it." As I leaned back, contemplating the fruit bowl, I began to let my mind wander. "Damn Sandy, the woman makes me think. And sometimes, I just don't want to."

I pushed to my feet, shoving the chair back under the table. As I stomped upstairs to my room, I realized that I was going to have to have this out with myself. I threw myself across my bed, face-down, burying my face in the covers.

Bubba came running up, landing on the bed beside me. He nudged my arm and finally, I rolled to a sitting position and let him crawl into my lap.

"I know this is wrong. I really do. I know I'm being silly, but here's the thing, Bubba. I'm afraid..." My throat felt phlegmy and I realized I was tearing up. "I'm afraid that if I love somebody new, it means I'm betraying Tom. It's so much easier when you know somebody died. At least, died for good. At least then, you can't think, 'Maybe they'll come back. Maybe he'll return to me someday.' There's always been a piece of my heart that's believed he'll come back to me. That maybe he's decided to make amends. That he's not still out there, hunting down victims. If I give into my love, if I commit to Aegis, it means that I've lost my hope for Tom. That I've given up on him."

As I burst into tears, burying my face in Bubba's fur, there was a soft swish behind me.

"Oh, Maddy. I didn't know you were struggling that way." Aegis's voice was gentle, soft against my ragged nerves.

I turned. "I'm sorry—I'm so sorry. I feel like I'm letting you down and that I'm letting Tom down. I don't know what to do. I have to let go of the past to embrace my future, but I'm so afraid. I feel like I'm the worst person ever."

I threw my arms around him as he lowered himself to my side, and he held me, murmuring softly as his lips brushed my ear. Aegis let me cry it out for a while before he grabbed a tissue and began to dry my tears.

"I know you miss him still. I know he was the love of your life, but wherever he is, do you think he'd want you like this? Crying and afraid to love again? Do you think he'd be cruel enough to expect you to pine away for him, forever?" Aegis placed two fingers beneath my chin and tipped my head up so I was looking at him.

"If I love you, will I forget about him?" For all my magic, for all my powers and long life, my heart was like anybody else's heart—easily broken, and easily scarred.

"Maddy, do you really think you'll ever forget him? He's part of you. His love helped make you the person you are. You can no more forget about him than you can about your mother or Sandy or Bubba. Every person we meet who touches our heart stays with us. Do you think I'll ever forget about Astra? I loved her so much, and I don't know what happened to her, but even if I never see her again and never find out, I carry that love inside me. Not to blot out new love, but to remind me of the person I was around her."

He placed his hand on my heart. "You carry Tom's love inside your heart. And that's okay. We move on. We love many people in a lifetime. But the ones who truly touch our hearts, we keep them with us forever."

His fingers were cool against my chest, and I softly reached up to clasp his hand, to press it between my breasts. "I never expected to fall for a vampire."

"I never expected to fall for a witch, so we're even." He leaned forward. "Maddy, when I say I love you, I'm not just spouting off the top of my head. I mean it. I don't say those words easily, and the few times I've fallen in love, it's been that *head-over-heels-meant-to-be-with-each-other* type of love. The kind *we* have."

I shivered, wanting to be free to love him, wanting to quit carrying around the dying hope that Tom would return to me. My emotions churning, I closed my eyes and found myself standing in a gray mist, and there was my Tom, staring at me from across a chasm.

"TOM, TOM! I miss you." I wanted to go to him, but the chasm was deep and filled with mist, and I couldn't see a way across. "Tom, come back to me."

He reached out, holding out his hands. "There's only one way for us to be together again, my love. And that's for you to come to me. For you to become like me."

"Are you still alive? Are you trapped somewhere?" I hung my head, weeping, but then yanked my gaze back to slake over him hungrily. It had been so long since we had seen one another. So many years since I had felt his touch.

"Yes, I'm trapped, but you can be with me, if you make the choice. You can walk into the chasm and then, when it's done, we'll be together." His voice ached against my ears, and I felt myself moving to the edge of the cliff, stopping only when my toes were against the edge. One step and I'd fall into the crevice. One step and I'd be with my Mad Tom.

"Come to me, love. Maddy, me girl, you take that step and we can be together again. Take one more step and we'll never be apart."

But something off-putting about his voice struck me. I opened my eyes. There he was, reaching for me, but there was something wrong. He looked misshapen, oddly bent and twisted. And behind him, I saw another shape rise—this, too, was Tom, but he raced over to shove his broken doppelganger to the side.

"Maddy, don't. Go back. Don't—it's deadly. It's a trap. There's no way for us to be together. You go back. I love you, but I'm letting you go because I don't want you here. Go away and never look for me again." He was screaming now, waving for me to turn and run.

My stomach clenching, I began to weep. "I don't know what to do."

"Go. Go! Live, Maddy. Don't give up everything because of a dream long gone." And then, Tom shoved his doppelganger toward the edge. The creature roared up, dark and frightening, made of bones and blood, and it turned on him, looming over the Tom I knew in a terrible fury.

I stumbled back. "Tom! No!"

"Maddy, I love you. Now get the hell out of here. Never come back. You can't save me, but you can save yourself." Running, he took off away from the edge, back the way he had come, with that horrible creature thundering after him.

Weeping, I stared into the mist, down deep in the chasm. One step and I knew I'd be on the other side, with Tom, wherever he might be.

"Maddy? Maddy? Come back to me." A voice broke into my thoughts and I turned around. Aegis stood there in the twinkle of dusk and starlight, holding out his arms. He was real and substantial, vibrant with love and energy. I glanced over my shoulder, across the chasm where my Tom was screaming. Aching, horrified by what I had seen, I forced myself to slowly turn back, to face Aegis.

"Aegis, take me away from this pain. From this madness. Take me away from the loss and the ache and the memories." I ran to him then, and he caught me up and spun me around, kissing my cheeks and my nose and my forehead and, finally, my lips.

"Come back with me, Maddy. Come back and be my love. Tom begged you to leave this place. He loved you enough to let you go. Let me love you enough to enter your life."

Weeping, I wrapped my arm around Aegis's neck as he carried me out of my memories, into the present, and into his heart.

Chapter 16

"SO, GO WITH me to rehearsal?" Aegis asked. We had made love, and showered together, and now I was eating a bowl of clam chowder, along with a handful of crackers. Aegis had declined to join me—he wanted to change out the strings on a new guitar he had bought.

"I wish I could go." Franny appeared, startling us both. "I never get to do anything." Great, she was on another one of her jags.

"When things settle down, I promise to look into what's keeping you tied to the house." I didn't have the strength—or the heart—to yell at her.

She smiled at me, which was a little ghoulish, and then let out a mournful sigh that would have rivaled any melodrama on the stage.

"Laying it on a little thick, aren't you, Franny?" Aegis grinned at her.

"How rude can you get?" She glared at him for

a moment, then flounced away, vanishing into the wall through the refrigerator.

"That always gives me the creeps when she does that," I said. "Since when do you play guitar in the band?" My heart felt lighter than in decades. Tom had let me go and that had allowed me to let go of him.

"I can play. I can play a number of instruments. I just happen to be the singer. But Jorge may have to take a trip to visit his mother and I'd like to be able to fill in for him if we can't find a guitarist to take over while he's gone. We're holding tryouts next week, but it never hurts to have a backup." He grinned at me. "You're my groupie, you know that?"

I snorted. "You have a lot of groupies, dude. Do you even realize how gorgeous you are?"

"Yeah, I do. But we make a good pair that way. You're pretty fucking gorgeous yourself. I love your boobs and your ass...and your eyes and your neck and your mind." He set down the guitar and moved behind me, wrapping his arms around my shoulders as I tried to balance the clam and potato on the spoon. Whispering, he began to nuzzle my ear. "I love your ears and your toes and your fingers and your—"

Laughing, I shook my head. "You're tickling me now. Stop!" But I didn't protest too loudly, and I ended up wearing some of my soup as he continued to tease me. Finally, he returned to his guitar.

"Yes, I'll come to rehearsal. I haven't been down there in a while and with everything that's gone on lately, I need a break."

"Good. Can you be ready in fifteen minutes? I promised the guys we'd start at eight-thirty pronto, and that we'd end by eleven. Sid's wife really needs him to be home at a decent hour except for performance nights."

I raised the bowl to my lips and drank the last drops of my soup, then grabbed my coat and stuffed my feet into a soft pair of fuzzy boots. Bubba yowled in protest—he didn't want me going out—but I ruffled his hair.

"We'll be home in a few hours, Bub. You're safe here. Be good." To Aegis, I said, "I'm going to take my own car just in case I need to leave early for some reason. With everything that's gone on lately, who knows what the fuck will happen next?"

"Hopefully, a peaceful rehearsal and then we can come home and work on some of the details for the opening next week. Have you received any more bookings yet?" Aegis held the door for me, then locked it behind him as we exited the house.

"Actually, there were two online bookings today. I think my Prosperity spell is helping. But I still need to cleanse and ward the yard, given Rose's death. I don't know why I didn't think about that earlier."

"I'd say it's because you've been busy with other things, maybe?" Aegis waited until I was safely inside my car and locked tight before heading toward his.

I eased out of the driveway with him following, and headed into the cloudy night. The skies were overcast but at least the snow was holding off. Given how much had fallen so far, come spring we'd best watch for flooding once all the white stuff started to melt.

By the time we got to Utopia where the band practiced during the weeknights when the club was closed, I was already regretting my choice to come. Not only had the temperature dropped to a balmy twenty-three—Fahrenheit—but I realized just how much energy the past few days had leeched out of me. I just wanted to go home, climb into jammies, and curl up under the covers with a good book. But I had promised Aegis and didn't want to go back on my word.

I hauled ass into the club with Aegis behind me. The band members were setting up, and they waved when they saw me. I found the most comfortable chair in the club, and the row of bottles that Jack-Az allowed the boys to plunder, pouring myself a large glass of wine. As I sank into the overstuffed beanbag and stretched out my legs, it occurred to me this might not be so bad after all. If I fell asleep, Aegis could drive me home, then bring me back to get my car before dawn broke.

As they warmed up, I realized how much better they were sounding than even a few weeks ago. There were still some rough spots—Keth kept a good beat with the drums, but once in a while he would trip over a particularly grueling part. And Jorge's fingers were fire on the guitar, but every now and then a riff would send him stumbling. But all in all, the more I heard, the more I had faith that they would actually land a record deal or make it big on their own. I wasn't sure what their end goal was, I hadn't thought to ask, but if they wanted to go big, there was a good chance they could make it.

They launched into a weaving medieval piece they had sexed up but then Sid suddenly stopped, shaking his head. “This is all wrong. To get the sounds we want, we need somebody who can play didgeridoos, shawms, and bagpipes.”

“Where are we going to find someone like that here on the island?” Aegis asked. “I’m not being facetious—I seriously want to know.”

“We won’t find anybody if we don’t look. We’re holding tryouts for a substitute guitarist, why not for the others?” Keth frowned. “I can play a little on the didgeridoo but not the extent we could use. And if I were playing on that, we wouldn’t have percussion in the piece. Unless it’s a track we lay down ahead of time and play in the background.”

I cleared my throat. “If you want a suggestion from the peanut gallery, I vote you take Keth’s suggestion and open up tryouts. You guys sound great, but you can take your music to a whole new level by adding in a few of those sounds. I’m serious—you have what it takes to become another Corvus Corax or Faun.” Two of my favorite bands were pretty much the role model for what the Boys of Bedlam wanted to become.

“Peanut gallery suggestions welcome, considering the comparison you just made.” Sid grinned down at me. “We can talk about that next time we get together to write some new material. Until then, let’s get started on rehearsing Saturday’s set. We had a few clunkers last time during the gig and don’t think that Jack-Az didn’t notice.”

I watched as they plugged in, turned on, and got down, but my heart wasn't in it. I was just too tired and the wine was going to make me even sleepier. I set the glass down after a few sips and—once they finished the first song—stood.

"Aegis, I'm sorry, but I'm going home. I'm too tired to tough it out."

"I'll come with you." He glanced at his band mates. "Sorry, guys, I'll be back in half an hour." They didn't grumble but I could tell they weren't thrilled.

"No, you just stay here and I'll text you when I get there. I'll be fine," I added as he started to protest. "I'm just too tired to manage tonight. It's not that far of a drive and I'll be careful. Traffic's light, anyway. Most of the people who are out and about are downtown, shopping for Solstice."

"Are you sure?"

"Yeah, now get back to work. If I'm asleep when you get home, just leave me a note, okay?"

He jumped off the stage, gracefully landing in front of me, and swung me in for a long kiss. Laughing, I patted him on the arm and disentangled myself.

"I love you. Play good. Become famous. Make me the happiest groupie around." With that, I waved at the guys, who waved back, and headed for the door. Aegis was still looking doubtful, but he hopped back on the stage and, as the door swung shut behind me, I heard them start up another song.

I kept my guard up, but the sidewalks were deserted and I made it to my car without seeing a single person. As I fastened my seat belt and started the engine, I let out a breath of relief. So much stress over so many days had left me a nervous goose.

I was halfway home before I realized that the energy felt off. I couldn't pinpoint it, but something was out of kilter. Given it would be stupid to lower myself into trance while driving, I tried to brush away the feelings but they kept up. Finally, half a mile from home, I eased into the parking lot of a city park and idled the engine, listening quietly to the silence around me.

Going into trance here might not be the best idea either, but at least I wasn't driving. The hairs on the back of my neck were standing up and I wanted to know what the hell was going on. Finally, I turned off the ignition after making sure all the doors were locked, and leaned back in the driver's seat, closing my eyes as I lowered myself into the soft fog that beckoned.

I tested the space around me, looking for anything that stood out of place. The car felt normal, except there was a heaviness that didn't belong. A sense of being latched on to, like a bungie cord attached to the fender. Yet, there was no sense that it had been tampered with.

You're tired, Maddy. Pay attention. Get your ass out of trance because you're in danger.

The voice echoed in my head, and I wasn't sure who was talking, but a fear rose as I realized that there was a magical binding connected to my car and it was putting me in danger. I shot up in my seat, suddenly all too aware that I wasn't alone in the parking lot. Figures were emerging from behind the trees. Five of them, they were coming in from all sides. I couldn't see who they were from here, especially since we weren't near the streetlights, but they were intent on my car.

I grabbed my phone and frantically texted Aegis. HELP. HONEYSUCKLE PARK IN PARKING LOT. SOMEBODY'S HERE AND I DON'T THINK THEY'RE FRIENDLY.

I managed to copy and paste the text over to Delia before the figures suddenly sped up. They had surrounded the car before I could turn on the ignition. As I stared out the driver's window, I saw Rachel, leaning down looking in at me.

Crap. And she had brought friends. No doubt lured in by the promise of witch's blood for dinner. My doors were locked, but that was no guarantee to keeping out a determined vampire, especially someone who was as old and powerful as Rachel.

"Open the door, Maddy. You don't mind if I call you Maddy even though we've never officially been introduced, do you?" Rachel's voice was melodic and hard to ignore, even through the closed window. She knew she couldn't get me with her gaze, but she could still win me over with her glamour. "Just accept that I win. Aegis will return to me, and you can't stop him. It's been a fun romp, though, hasn't it?" She sounded almost wistful, as though she were remembering her own time with him.

I jumped as one of the other vamps slammed his hands against the passenger window, peeking in. "She's a pretty one, Rachel. Can I play with her? For just a little bit?"

Rachel laughed. "Oh, Cane. I know you like big boobs and a fat ass, but honestly, isn't it enough that her blood's going to taste like ambrosia? Do you need to nail her, too?"

"I fancy me some jiggly butt," the vampire she called Cane said.

I realized I still had hold of my phone and frantically texted, CANE. RACHEL'S GOT A VAMPIRE NAMED CANE WITH HER. I DON'T KNOW WHO THE OTHERS ARE. GOING TO TRY TO GET OUT OF HERE.

Suddenly, texts began to flood in.

MADDY, I'M COMING. I JUST GOT THIS. HOLD ON. That was from Aegis.

And the next, from Delia. ON MY WAY.

I fumbled for the key, but in my fear, I knocked it out of the ignition and onto the floor. As I scrambled, trying to scoop it up, my mind was racing.

How long it would take Aegis to get here? And then, of course, we had vampires to deal with. Could I hold out? That would depend on whether Rachel and her cronies could get into my car. Some vampires could turn into—

Oh shit. As I came up with the key again, I saw Cane dissolve into a black mist. Shaking, I managed to get the key back into the ignition as he formed inside the passenger seat, coming through the vents.

"Don't you drink her down before I get my share." Rachel pressed her face against the window, her fangs gleaming in the shimmering light of the clouds.

I flipped the key, gunning the gas, and jammed the gearshift into drive as Cane grabbed my right wrist. The car lurched forward as I tried to pull away from him and steer with my left hand. The vampire to the front got hit and went down, under the car, but unless I managed to puncture his heart, being run over wasn't going to stop him.

Cane laughed, yanking me halfway across the gearshift panel. I cursed as the steering wheel spun wild and the car began to spin on the ice, skidding against one of the concrete stops. The back right wheel jammed against it and the car idled as the vampire managed to pull me into his lap. He planted a hand on my breast, squeezing hard enough to make me scream, and his fangs were gleaming in the light of the lamppost beneath which we were stalled.

The next moment, Rachel yanked open the driver's door. But when she saw how Cane had hold of me, she hissed at him, low and threatening.

"She's mine. You can play, but she's mine to drink and to kill. Get her out of the car. She's my trump card in the next hand of the game." In a blur, she sped around to the passenger's side and tried to open the door, which was still locked. Frustrated, she ripped it off its hinges as well and tossed it to the side. My blood ran cold as I realized that—one way or another—this wasn't going to be a win-win situation. I was on the losing end and the loss I was facing wasn't exactly one I could rebound from.

"Stop! Aegis is on the way and if you kill me, he'll just attack you. If you let me live, he might thank you and go with you." I had no clue how to approach this situation, but it seemed like playing to her ego might help me.

Rachel leaned into the car and grabbed my arm, pulling me away from Cane, who held on a moment too long. I heard a bone snap in my wrist, and then the pain hit. As I let out a shriek, they both laughed.

"My bad, I broke your toy," he said.

Rachel snorted. "Oh, no problem. You can play with the parts that aren't broken in a few minutes, but I need to use her first. Aegis is going to understand just what it means to have his heart broken. And then he'll realize that I'm the only woman in the world for him."

I focused on my wrist, sending a Muting spell down my arm to numb the pain. It wouldn't heal broken bones, but it would allow me to function without the pain interfering. At least for a while. But I was over any attempt to play nice.

"Bitch, you're fucking insane. You think that killing me is going to make him come back to you? What have you been smoking?" What was it they said? Don't look away? Don't show fear?

That's for mountain lions, you idiot. Again, that annoying inner voice, which I highly suspected was my inner, smarter, self.

Rachel ran her fingers down my cheek, using one of her incredibly sharp nails to raise a weal. I wasn't sure if it was bleeding but by the gleam in her eye, I suspected maybe it was, just a little. She leaned in and slowly drew her tongue across the wound, letting out a trill.

"Yummy," she said, her voice low and sultry. "At least Aegis gave us dessert instead of an appetizer."

Cane was holding me by my elbows, but Rachel was close enough for me to give her one hell of a good head butt. She wasn't expecting it, and so the blow sent her back a couple of steps. Cane growled, adjusting his grip on my arms and I had the feeling that once my spell wore off, I was going to regret doing that because I was pretty sure he had just managed to break another bone in my wrist. But for now, the fact that I had startled Ms. Bloodsucker made me smile.

"Feisty, isn't she?" Cane piped up as the other vampires gathered 'round. They all looked hungry and I had the feeling that I was one second away from being the honored guest in a five-way vampire fang-bang.

"Too feisty." Rachel's cloying tone was gone. She stared at me. "So, when Aegis gets here, we'll see just how much he wants you safe and sound."

One of her toadies leaned in to sniff my neck and Rachel went from being five feet away to knocking him across the car. All within one quick blur.

"Nobody feeds till I say so!" She suddenly turned as the lights of a car hit the parking lot.

I recognized Aegis's Corvette. I stiffened, not sure exactly how this was going to play out, but then I saw Delia's squad car pull in right after. Worried about her—she might be a werewolf, but vamps were freaking strong and there were five of them—I regretted having texted her.

Aegis leaped out of the car and came running over, a blur himself. He stopped out of reach, hands on his hips. In his leather jacket and dark shades, he looked so fucking bad-ass that for a second, I forgot how much danger I was in.

"Let her go, Rachel. It's over." His voice carried through the night.

"What makes you think it's done? It's not over till *I* say it's over, babe." Rachel sauntered toward him. "You want her alive? You want little Miss Twitch to come out of this in one piece?"

Aegis stared at her. "Rachel, you have to move on. I don't want you. I'll never take you back. And no matter how many people you threaten, you can't command me." His voice was so rich, so compelling, that I found myself mesmerized. I could float in that voice, I could bathe in it, live on it. A sudden parting of the clouds brought out the moon and it shone down, bathing us in the crystal white starkness of the snow.

He held up his hand, turning so that the moonbeam caught his ring. "You know what this is. I told you long ago."

Rachel suddenly froze. "You *wouldn't*. You wouldn't *dare*."

"Try me. Let her go and we'll have ourselves a fair fight. Touch one fang to her throat, and I unleash your death."

I was starting to get a very bad feeling about that ring. It was glowing faintly with a golden light. The ring was the symbol of the time when he had belonged to Apollo. It marked him as the Sun God's chosen. And then, it began to dawn on me.

"If you do that, you unleash your own death." Rachel cocked her head ever so slightly as though she were testing him, but she motioned to Cane, who let go of me with a clueless "Huh?"

"I've lived a long life. If I have to, I'm willing to sacrifice myself." He let out a mirthless laugh. "Do you think that I chose this state willingly? I embrace being one of the Fallen because I have no choice. But there are other paths and other lives."

"A fair fight, you say? We win, we get the witch. And you come back to me."

"You win, I won't have any say. Because you're going to have to kill me to end it. If I win...well... then I win."

She laughed. "Well, if you consider five against one fair, far be it from me to dissuade you. But no help from the werewolf. Or the witch." She reached over and shoved me hard toward Aegis. "Get your ass over there. Try to leave and you're dead, regardless of his rules."

I hurried past Aegis, giving him a desperate look, but he kept his eyes on Rachel. "Touch her before we're done and I won't hesitate to bring on the sun. But trust me, it will be a fair game. I brought my own backups."

At that, I saw three figures exit Delia's car. Vampires all. And Essie emerged with them. She passed by me, stopping to say, "I've loaned Aegis three of my men. I'll stay out of the fight, but I couldn't help but take a piece of the action, given you've been after my throne, you little upstart." Essie sat on the hood of Delia's car, glancing over at me. "Get in the car, girl."

I scrambled, diving into the front seat beside Delia. "Fucking hell."

"What does Aegis mean, he'll unleash the sun?" Delia slammed the door locks and kept the engine idling. "Don't worry, we aren't leaving. I promised Essie we'd stay in return for bringing her and her men over. Aegis set this up while he was on the way here."

"Aegis has a ring—it's from when he was a servant of Apollo. I didn't think much about it, though he wears it constantly. But now I think it contains the power of the sun. If he unleashes it, we'll get a blast of sunlight."

"And that will kill every vampire in the area who happens to be within range of the light."

"Right. Talk about deterrents. I had no clue what he was carrying around." I watched as Essie's men moved up to back Aegis. They poised, waiting, and then with the barest flutter of movement, the nine vampires engaged. Aegis went straight for Rachel, and the others gave the pair a wide berth.

I leaned forward, straining to get a better look. "I wish I could be out there, helping." My heart in my throat, all I could think about was Aegis and whether he could survive.

"All you'd do is get yourself drained. Putting yourself in the thick of that fight is suicide." She pressed her lips together. "I didn't like having to pick up Essie and her crew, but Aegis insisted and I trust him enough to pay attention."

Quickly running through the spells I had on tap, I suddenly realized I *could* do something. I had fire at my disposal. And even though I seldom tapped its power, I knew that if I was going to, now would be the time. I looked down at my broken wrist. Still numb, but that didn't mean it wasn't functioning.

"I need something for a splint to hold my hand

straight." I lifted my arm so she could see the swelling.

"Crap! That's—"

"Broken. Yeah. But right now, I'm playing without pain. Help me strap it up. I can do something out there." Regardless of Aegis promising he wouldn't use my help, I was determined to be part of this battle. And if I didn't ask, he couldn't stop me.

Without a word, Delia leaned down and pulled a first-aid kit from beneath the front seat of her SUV. She opened it up and poked around. "The best I can do is strap it with an elastic bandage."

"Then do it." I held out the wrist, watching as she wrapped the bandage tightly around and over the wrist and fingers. It wasn't as good as a splint, but it would do the trick for now.

As soon as she finished, I hopped out of the car and stepped over to Essie's side. Ahead of us, Aegis and Rachel were rolling in the snow, snarling like wild animals. Aegis was trying to throttle Rachel as she aimed a well-placed kick to his balls. He groaned, but kept hold of her throat. Apparently, a kick in the nads wasn't nearly as painful once you were turned.

The others were into the thick of it. Nobody was toast yet, but it wouldn't be long before somebody struck a lucky blow and dusted their opponent.

Essie glanced at me. "What are you doing?"

"What I would have done earlier if I hadn't been so startled." I closed my eyes and reached deep inside. There it was—the tiny flame, flickering with a pale ghostly light. I coaxed it brighter, feeding it my frustration, feeding my anger at Rachel, feeding it the pain of losing Tom and every other angst I could summon up. The fire grew quickly and I readied my hands, holding them out in front of me.

"Fire, attend me." The whisper was almost so soft I wasn't sure if I had actually spoken or if it had been my thoughts, but then a brilliant ball of orange roared to life, hovering over my palms. I focused on Rachel, on the trajectory between her and me, and with a soft puff, blew the fireball off my hand. It sailed, gaining momentum as it grew to the size of a bowling ball.

Rachel turned, staring at the fire that was on a collision course with her. She darted to one side. But the fireball shifted course with her. She raced off, blurring her speed, but the flame sped up and—like a missile tracking its target—it enveloped her, setting her dress alight.

She fell face first in the snow, screaming as the flames licked at her body. Aegis took one look at me, then darted toward her and for a moment I was afraid he was going to try to save her—the look in his eye had been frightening and feral. But as he loomed over her, she turned, dousing the flames in the snow, screaming for him to help her. He watched her for a moment, then brought out a thin sliver of wood about a foot long.

Rachel must have seen it because she scrambled to her feet, her skin blackened and charred. Aegis paused for one brief second, and then plunged the stake into her chest. There was silence as all the vamps stopped to watch, and then in a puff of smoke and ash, Rachel vanished into a cloud of charcoal and bone. The wind rose at that moment, and howling, it blew her away as it raced through the meadow.

Chapter 17

AFTER THAT, THE fight was as good as over. Rachel's goons tried to vanish into the trees but Essie waved her hand and her men were on them without another word. I said nothing, watching as the vampires staked their own with all too much glee. They returned to her side, eyes sparkling with the hunt.

Essie turned to us. "Thank you. My reign is secure for the moment."

I tried to think of what to say, given Essie was most likely the one responsible for Rose's death. A death that had been targeted at me. Our eyes met and her lips tipped in a faint smile.

"Détente?" She held out her hand.

I stared at it, but was smart enough not to make a show. As I took her fingers—cold to the bone—I inclined my head.

"You do realize that I'm now the head of the

Moonrise Coven. We will have to meet and discuss new terms. Things are going to change around Bedlam now that I'm in power. I'm not Linda, and I don't have a daughter." I spoke softly, so that only Essie could hear me, but my words were firm. "However, there's room on Bedlam for everyone, if we all cooperate. And if nobody develops any delusions of grandeur." I figured she might as well know that I understood what she had been up to.

Essie held my fingers in hers, tightening her grip. Then, slowly, she relinquished them. "The future's always a wildcard, Maudlin. That's one thing you can count on. Nothing is ever set in stone." Then, with a throaty laugh, she added, "I think we could be friends of a sort. You and I are much alike, even though you don't know it yet. So, Mad Maudlin has come to rule Bedlam. I suppose it's only fitting." She pointed to my broken wrist. "You'd best go have that set, and have the rest of your bruises and bumps tended to. You can't put off the pain forever, you know. Sometimes, it hits when you least expect it. Both pains from the present and from long, long past."

I started to say something but she turned away, motioning to her men. Before I could say another word, they vanished into a blur, back toward Delia's car, where they climbed in. Looking terrified, Delia edged out of the parking lot. As they vanished from sight, my stomach knotted. We hadn't seen the last of Essie. In fact, I had the feeling that our power struggle had only just begun.

AEGIS CARRIED OUT another bowl of potato chips. We were rocking the Winter Solstice, celebrating that the longest night was about to begin. In the cold frozen north, the Holly King and the Oak King were gearing up for their biennial battle. Over on the mainland, Christmas and Hanukkah and Kwanzaa were being celebrated. And here, we were lighting every candle in the Bewitching Bedlam. The band members and their families were chowing down on a spread that had filled every tabletop around. Tonight their music was all for us.

"So, tell me again why didn't you call me when you were in trouble?" Sandy looped her arm through mine, taking care to avoid my splint. My wrist was broken in two places, but they were clean breaks and I would be fully up and running in a few weeks.

"Because I had thought...*hoped*...that chapter of our lives was done and over." I motioned for her to follow me up the stairs into one of the back rooms. "I have something to show you."

As we climbed the steps, Sandy said, "Oh, by the way, I gave Lihi the Herkimer, even though we didn't need her to find the tunnels."

"That's sweet."

"Eh, it's the holidays." But she smiled as she said it. "What are you going to do about your mother's visit?"

I groaned. "I'm not even thinking about it till

after the holidays are over. Then, I guess I'll either capitulate or write and tell her that I don't want her here. I haven't decided which yet. Here we are."

There were several small storage rooms on the top floor that were no bigger than large walk-in closets. And in one of them, I had hidden a trunk. I knelt beside it and opened the lid. Inside was a silver dagger sitting on top of a silver stake. I stared at them, then slowly lifted the dagger and held it up.

"I haven't seen those since in a long, long time." Sandy drifted off, her eyes widening. "I thought you swore never to touch them again."

I swallowed. Hard. "Essie isn't going to make it easy on me. And you'd better watch your back too. She knows who I am, so she's going to figure out that you were Cassandra."

"Yeah, it's not that big of a leap from Sandy to Cassandra, I guess."

"No, and I don't trust her. I don't trust her. She's going to keep working to take control of this island and everybody in it. I know it. And more than that—Sandy, I think this is just the tip of the iceberg. So far, the vamps have been living in a truce with humans, but I think..." I fell silent. I didn't want to say what I was thinking. But the look in Essie's eyes when she had spoken about the future being a wildcard had chilled me.

"You think that there's going to be an uprising among the vampires," Franny said, popping in beside us. "You think they'll start a mass attack on people?"

I grimaced. “Franny, you have to keep quiet about this. We can’t have it getting out.”

Closing my eyes, I remembered that last day, standing atop the hill in Romania as we watched a village burn to the ground. Fata Morgana and Cassandra and I had tracked them down. After my fires destroyed them, we walked away, becoming the party girls of the century. I had tucked away the blade and stake that had tasted so much blood, swearing never again to use them.

Flesh to fire, fire to flesh. Time to weave the silver mesh.

Time to hunt the bloody fiends, time to stake and burn amends.

“Do you think we’ll have to do it again? The world is so different now.” Sandy bit her lip.

“The world is vastly different, which means there are so many more people to hunt. So many more ways to vie for control. Aegis will fight with us.” I paused. “You know, when sailors committed mutiny, they were left on an island with a gun with one bullet in it. I have the feeling that’s what Aegis’s ring is. Apollo’s gift to him. A way out.”

Aegis and I still hadn’t talked about his ring. Every time I started to ask about it, he changed the subject. Some things were better left until it was the right time.

Standing, I slid the dagger into a sheath, and the stake into a matching one. Slipping both into my bag of magical tools, I closed the lid and turned to Sandy.

"Do you really want to do this?" she asked.

I stared at the trunk. "No. Not really. I didn't think I'd have to ever revisit this path. But I guess we don't always get what we want, do we?"

"No, Mick, we don't." Sandy gave me a quick hug. "But I'll be there. Cassandra and Mad Maudlin back in action." She paused for a moment. "Do you think we could find *her*?"

A shiver raced down my spine. "The question is, do we *want* to?"

"I miss her, even though..." Sandy shook her head. "I can't help but wonder where she is. We'd know if she was dead."

"Yeah, I know. She was the crazy one, you know. Not me. I *ran* wild. She *was* wildness incarnate."

Sandy gave me an uneasy glance. "Yeah." Then, sucking in a deep breath, she said, "Let's get back to the party. You have B&B guests coming tomorrow and you'll want to be ready to open."

And tomorrow, any vampire that wants can walk into this house without asking. But I left my thoughts unsaid, and instead just nodded, pasting a smile on my face. My Prosperity spell had worked. In the past week we had booked every room for the rest of the year and into January.

"Come on, let's go drink and dance the night away."

THE BAND WAS taking a break from their set. I walked out to the back patio, freezing in the dark of the night, but unwilling to go find my coat. As I stared up at the stars cluttering the sky, Aegis joined me. He wrapped an arm around me and kissed the top of my head.

"Where did you and Sandy go?"

"Up to the attic. Well, one of the storage closets." I inhaled the sharp tang of snow and cold and wood smoke.

"You're wearing your weapons again, aren't you, Mad Maudlin?"

His voice was so soft I almost missed what he said, but then it seeped through and I slowly turned to face him.

"The blade and the stake, aren't they? Rumors say they're sterling silver, with a core of adamant."

Barely able to breathe, I forced out my words. "You know about them?"

"Of course I know. Don't forget, I'm far older than you and have walked the back paths of the world for centuries beyond centuries. I told you, I knew who you were the day after you bought this house. I did my homework. Before you told me about it, I knew you were Mad Maudlin, vampire hunter. One of the most successful in history."

"What else do you know?"

He laughed. "I know that you hunted down Dracula, that you traced his family and destroyed most of them. I know about the fires that haunt your dreams, and why you don't like to talk about the past. I know that it was Dracula who turned the love of your life." Aegis's eyes flared, crimson for a moment, then back to their sparkling depths.

I leaned against him. "You know all of my secrets. But I didn't tell you one. Essie knows who I am."

He tilted his head to the side for a moment, staring at me, his expression unreadable. After a moment he held out his hands. "And that's why you must wear your weapons, my love. Maddy, you and I bridge the gap. The bridge between the living and the dead can be a narrow one, but we manage it. I trust you."

I reached out, the fingers of my left hand wrapping around his. And in the core of my heart, I could feel the stirrings of doubt, but they fell silent as his lips neared mine. "I trust you, too, Aegis. And yes, we will manage this bridge."

And right then, in that moment, he leaned down and kissed me, and I left behind the guilt over loving him. As he wrapped his arms around me, the stars sparkled like diamonds and everything felt clean and new. And at that moment, Mad Maudlin returned and I welcomed her into my heart.

~End~

If you enjoyed this book, you might want to read Blood Music (Bewitching Bedlam, Novelette), the prequel to Bewitching Bedlam, for only $0.99.

The next Bewitching Bedlam book will be out in October 2017. Until then, I invite you to check out my Fury Unbound Series with Fury Rising and

Fury's Magic.
And stay tuned for my upcoming releases:
Novels:
March: Souljacker
(Lily Bound Series, book 1)
May: Moon Shimmers
(Otherworld Series, book 19)
June: Fury Awakened
(Fury Unbound Series, book 3)
September: Crow Song
(Whisper Hollow Series, book 3)
October: Maudlin's Mayhem
(Bewitching Bedlam Series, book 2)
October: A Bewitching Bedlam novelette
(To be titled)
November: A Bewitching Bedlam novelette
(To be titled)
December: Silent Night
(An Otherworld Novella)

Playlist

I often write to music and here's the playlist I used for this book.

Air: Napalm Love
Alice Cooper: Welcome to My Nightmare, Some Folks, Poison
Asteroids Galaxy Tour: Bad Fever, Sunshine Coolin', My Club, X, The Sun Ain't Shining No More
AWOLNATION: Sail
B-52's: Quiche Lorraine, Love Shack, Is That You Mo-Dean?
Beck: Qué Onda Guero, Cellphone's Dead, Nausea
The Black Angels: Always Maybe, Indigo Meadow, Don't Play With Guns
Blondie: One Way or Another, I Know But I Don't Know
Boom! Bap! Pow!: Suit
Broken Bells: The Ghost Inside
Butterfly: Crazy Town
Cake: The Distance
The Clash: Should I Stay or Should I Go
Cobra Verde: Play With Fire
Damh the Bard: The Cauldron Born, Obsession, Willow's Song, Gently Johnny, John Barleycorn, The Wicker Man
David Bowie: Fame, Let's Dance
Dead or Alive: You Spin Me 'Round

Elektrisk Gønner: Uknowhatiwant

Eurythmics: Sweet Dreams (Are Made of This)

Fatboy Slim: Praise You, Weapon of Choice

FC Kahuna: Hayling

Fergie: Fergalicious

Fluke: Absurd

Gary Numan: My World Storm, Are "Friends" Electric, Voix, My Shadow in Vain, Bridge? What Bridge?, War Songs, Outland, Praying to the Aliens, Soul Protection, I, Assassin,

George Benson: On Broadway

Gorillaz: Demon Days, Dare, Clint Eastwood, Hongkongaton, Feel Good Inc., Stylo, Fire Coming Out of the Monkey's Head

Hayzi Fantayzee: Shiny Shiny

Hella Good: No Doubt

Hollies: Long Cool Woman (In a Black Dress)

Justin Timberlake: SexyBack

Kills: Dead Road 7, Sour Cherry, You Don't Own The Road, Wait, Nail in My Coffin, U.R.A Fever

Kirsty McColl: In These Shoes?

Ladytron: Black Cat, Ghosts, I'm Not Scared

Lorde: Royals

Madonna: Beautiful Stranger, 4 Minutes

Men at Work: Down Under

Men Without Hats: Safety Dance

MIA: Bad Girls

People in Planes: Vampire

Puddle of Mudd: Psycho, Famous

Pumped Up Kicks: Foster the People

The Pussycat Dolls: Buttons, Don't Cha

Ruth Barrett: Faeries Love Song

Shriekback: Big Fun, Intoxication, Underwater Boys, Now These Days Are Gone, The King in the Tree, The Shining Path

Spiral Dance: Tarry Trousers, Boys of Bedlam, Rise Up

Steeleye Span: Blackleg Miner, The Fox

Stone Temple Pilots: Atlanta, Sour Girl

Talking Heads: Burning Down the House, I Zimbra, Life During Wartime, Moon Rocks

Tempest: Nottamun Town, Queen of Argyll, Black Jack Davey, Mad Tom of Bedlam

Thompson Twins: The Gap, Watching

Tuatha Dea: Irish Handfasting, Long Black Curl, Tuatha De Danaan

Wendy Rule: Let the Wind Blow, Dance of the Wild Faeries, Elemental Chant, The Circle Song

Zero 7: In the Waiting Line

Biography

New York Times, Publishers Weekly, and USA Today bestselling author Yasmine Galenorn writes urban fantasy and paranormal romance, and is the author of over fifty books, including the Otherworld Series, the Whisper Hollow Series, the Fury Unbound Series, the upcoming Bewitching Bedlam Series, and many more. She's also written nonfiction metaphysical books. She is the 2011 Career Achievement Award Winner in Urban Fantasy, given by RT Magazine.

Yasmine has been in the Craft since 1980, is a shamanic witch and High Priestess. She describes her life as a blend of teacups and tattoos. She lives in Kirkland, WA, with her husband Samwise and their cats. Yasmine can be reached via her web site at Galenorn.com.

Books by Yasmine Galenorn:

Fury Unbound Series:
Fury Rising
Fury's Magic
Fury Awakened (2017)

Bewitching Bedlam Series:
Blood Music (prequel novelette)
Bewitching Bedlam
Maudlin's Mayhem (2017)

Whisper Hollow Series (in order):
Autumn Thorns
Shadow Silence
Crow Song (2017)

Morrígan's Blade (2018)

Otherworld Series (in order):
Witchling
Changeling
Darkling
Dragon Wytch
Night Huntress
Demon Mistress
Bone Magic
Harvest Hunting
Blood Wyne
Courting Darkness
Shaded Vision
Shadow Rising
Haunted Moon
Autumn Whispers
Crimson Veil
Priestess Dreaming
Panther Prowling
Darkness Raging
Moon Shimmers (2017)
Harvest Song (2018)
Blood Bonds (2019)

Otherworld: E-Novellas:
The Shadow of Mist: Otherworld novella
Etched in Silver: Otherworld novella
Ice Shards: Otherworld novella
Flight From Hell: Otherworld--Fly By Night crossover novella
Earthbound

Otherworld: Short Collections:
Tales From Otherworld: Collection One
Men of Otherworld: Collection One
Men of Otherworld: Collection Two
Moon Swept: Otherworld Tales of First Love

Chintz 'n China Series:
Ghost of a Chance
Legend of the Jade Dragon
Murder Under a Mystic Moon
A Harvest of Bones
One Hex of a Wedding
Holiday Spirits

Lily Bound Series (in order):
Souljacker (2017)

Fly By Night Series (in order):
Flight from Death
Flight from Mayhem

Indigo Court Series (in order):
Night Myst
Night Veil
Night Seeker
Night Vision
Night's End

Indigo Court: Novellas:
Night Shivers

Bath and Body Series (under the name India Ink):
Scent to Her Grave
A Blush With Death
Glossed and Found

Anthologies:
Once Upon a Kiss (short story: Princess Charming)
Silver Belles (short story: The Longest Night)
Once Upon a Curse (short story: Bones)
Never After (Otherworld novella: The Shadow

of Mist)
Inked (Otherworld novella: Etched in Silver)
Hexed (Otherworld novella: Ice Shards)
Songs of Love & Death (short story: Man in the Mirror)
Songs of Love and Darkness (short story: Man in the Mirror)
Nyx in the House of Night (article: She is Goddess)
A Second Helping of Murder (recipe: Clam Chowder)

Magickal Nonfiction:

From Llewellyn Publications and Ten Speed Press:

Trancing the Witch's Wheel
Embracing the Moon
Dancing with the Sun
Tarot Journeys
Crafting the Body Divine
Sexual Ecstasy and the Divine
Totem Magic
Magical Meditations

Made in the USA
San Bernardino, CA
09 July 2018